Jon Bauer was born in Wimbledo[...] broadcast on national radio, performe[...] [...] [...] the stage, and published in the *Sleepers Almanac* and *The Bridport Prize*. *Rocks in the Belly* is his first novel.

Praise for *Rocks in the Belly*

'This is such a beautifully choreographed, sensitive and accessible novel, it's hard to believe it's Bauer's first ... his orchestration of grief and comedy, innocence and pessimism ... has emotional honesty that matches the best Helen Garner.' *Australian Literary Review*

'Anybody who reads this book and isn't instantly a fan probably wasn't paying close enough attention. *Rocks in the Belly* is both a masterpiece and a very challenging piece of writing ... With this beautiful novel, Bauer teaches us the meaning of "too little too late", with an ending that is sure to bring a tear to even the most stoic reader's eye.' *Australian Bookseller & Publisher* ★★★★★

'Jon Bauer tells his dark, psychological story obliquely and with dramatic precision ... what dazzles most is Bauer's eye for physical and emotional detail.' *Sydney Morning Herald*

'One of the most unsettling novels I have read in a while, with an emotional sharpness that hurts. Oh, and it's quite funny too.' *The Australian*

'*Rocks in the Belly*, a debut novel of considerable power, covers rare territory and culminates in scenes of tenderness and compassion that are never sentimental.' *Australian Book Review*

'A powerful book ... It is marked by candour, humour and sadness, and seethes with so much frustration that in parts it becomes difficult to read. However, its ultimate sentiment moves towards compassion.' *The Weekend Australian*

ROCKS IN
THE BELLY

JON BAUER

A complete catalogue record for this book can be obtained from the British Library on request

First published in 2010 by Scribe Publications Pty Ltd, Melbourne, Australia

First published in the UK in 2012 by Serpent's Tail,
an imprint of Profile Books Ltd
3A Exmouth House
Pine Street
London EC1R 0JH
website: www.serpentstail.com

ISBN 978 1 84668 845 4
eISBN 978 1 84765 811 1

Printed and bound in Great Britain by Clays, Bungay, Suffolk

10 9 8 7 6 5 4 3 2 1

FSC
www.fsc.org
MIX
Paper from
responsible sources
FSC® C018072

Carried, but never held.

I used to tell people I was a foster child. As a boy I'd tell every new stranger until it started burrowing into me as a sort of truth. A truth that's still here, keeping me from belonging.

I used to tell people I was a foster child even though I was the only one in our home who wasn't fostered. And now I'm supposedly a man, everything about me is still fostered — my country, the history I tell people.

I can't even bring myself to belong to my own childhood.

But I can still feel it, despite moving overseas, disavowing myself entirely of my past. It doesn't matter where you go, or what you do with your feelings, your truth lies in wait. My childhood haunting me in much the same way my fists haunt my hands.

Moving away hasn't allowed me to leave my parents behind either. I carry them in those remembered moments they inflict on you. Mum especially. Funny that of all those steeped-in memories, the one where she's most vivid is from a day of supreme greyness. The day we buried Robert. Everyone gathered round the television to watch that video of him.

Not the Robert who'd come up our path years before, hiding behind the social worker. Not that thoughtful, clever little Robert. *Special* little Robert. But the Robert we turned him into.

I remember the TV was turned up too loud, Robert full of gangly smiles towards the camera while they strapped him up. His played-back face looking right at me. Someone making a comment about how great he looks in his orange outfit, and Mum managed a smile too.

Then Robert's hair was fluttering on the screen, both him and the man behind him wearing goggles. Robert all tongue and teeth and movement, his trembling brain fidgeting him with excitement.

There is a rough edit.

His hair is really blowing and he's strapped to the man and screeching with a mix of fear and happiness. They shuffle him along on his bum, and from the movement of the camera you see Robert, the walls, Robert. Then, through the open door, the clouds. Great, billowing clouds in a vast sky. Robert of the Clouds, Dad always used to call him, or Robert McCloud. Our lounge bursting with people. All of them dressed in black, and carrying the colour as if it were heavy. Everyone crying over Robert's happiness coming at us from inside the TV. From back in time. Crying because that's all that was left of what he might have been.

The camera pans to Robert perched on the edge.

'1'

His tremors are still there, his eyes smiling. The man tells him to put his head back and Robert's exhilaration erupts as a giggling squeal.

'2'

He is totally still. I remember the whole room stopped too. Everyone who'd come to bury him held their breath.

I

I walk out of the train station and down the hill, dragging my suitcase along this familiar parade of shops. The whole time I've been overseas they've just stood here, in all weathers. People sitting inside them, waiting for a livelihood to trickle in. Everything here having remained painfully familiar and yet undergone the subtlest, almost imperceptible changes, as if the shops are oozing slowly, glacially down this hill.

A million years and they'll be collected into a melted pile at the bottom.

I look behind the sheltered bus stop and my graffiti is still here, the faded marker pen signalling change like lovers' initials engraved on a tree. The lovers having long since split up, just like I've lost touch with the me who used to wedge himself in among the litter and undergrowth back here, sniffing thinners from my blazer sleeve instead of going to school.

The bus comes and I stick out an arm.

I pay the driver, wondering if he was at the helm seven years ago when I rode this bus in the other direction, and whether coming back will unravel all the work I've done while overseas — striving for some kind of invincible.

I lift my baggage onto the rack and lurch down the bus as it takes off, an old woman staring at me from the front seat and two school kids stewing at the very back, out of school, feet up on seats — their own small version of invincible.

My home town passes outside the dirty windows, the glass vibrating the image as the bus accelerates, then refocusing it all as the clutch dips for the next gear. I fall into staring, feeling what being here does to the vibrations in me.

When we reach the top of Hawke Street Hill, I slowly stand, push the button for my stop.

There's that house of my childhood. I get off but the driver nods back behind him and I climb up again, blushing, retrieve my luggage.

The bus leaves me in a fumy quiet, my suitcase trundling along behind then throwing itself off its wheels, yanking my wrist over. I stop to right it and walk on, the houses quiet, just the sound of little plastic suitcase wheels.

I reach our gate but pause at the threshold. I recognise this moment I'm standing in. This is the moment before. This is the breath you take.

I look from the front door in its rotting frame, up to the clouds. I had my childhood under this bit of sky with its fairy-floss athletes, white rabbits and all the other bulbous shapes that floated by on invisible air streams. The Loch Ness monster came by once.

But most of our precipitation came with the foster children. Lost souls carried between these hedges to the aprons and hugs of my mother. Children with pasts I was supposed to pity them for.

I used to park my little bum on that front step there, trying to hit makeshift targets with stones while Dad stepped back, sipping from his mug of tea, a few privet leaves gracing his wayward hair. He never let me use the hedge-trimmer but he kept me in money for sweets and catapults if I lugged black bags full of trimmed hedge.

I automatically lift the gate to open it, like always. The hedges obscure the path now so I have to weave my way by, carrying my suitcase to silence my approach. I set it down at the door, iron out the red marks it has pressed into my palm.

After I've knocked there's a silence.

I go and look through the front window at the posh dining table we never used, the dust on it like the coating that settled over our lives after Robert. We had no use for the special occasion table then, only the beaten family one in the kitchen.

Now there's the sound of someone shuffling down the corridor. I adjust my posture, flatten my hair. The footsteps reach the other side of the door and I make myself still in front of the little security eyelet — my insides held. The eyelet darkens. I try for a smile but it comes out sad.

The door opens slowly like something out of a horror film. As if it should be Igor standing there and lightning going off, but it's a shiny day and not Igor although it does look like Frankenstein in a dress. Dad used to say that about ugly women. He said that about my Auntie Debbie especially. Auntie Deadly he called her.

'Hello, Mum.'

She looks like somebody impersonating my mother. Or Mum in disguise. Looking at me with the same blue eyes but her face bloated and unsure. She thinks she knows me but isn't certain — something drying at the corner of her mouth.

We stand here and I'm trying not to gasp at how inclement time has been to her — that or the illness, the reason I'm back here.

I close the gap between us, shutting out the trembling of the moment by moving in and hugging her, my hips held away from hers.

She smells of clothes that have been wet too long then dried, her body swollen but bird-like, frail. I stare out from the hug, looking at the hallway, every detail of it cut like a hill trail into my brain — the vase full of my grandfather's homemade walking sticks;

that ominous lump of mica rock; someone like me staring out from old photos on the wall — that uncomfortable face.

She breaks the hug and leans away, her hands on my upper arms to keep me at a close distance, her eyes scanning from one to the other of mine, drinking me in.

'Hello,' I say again, shrivelling. 'It's me.'

Her mouth opens, trying to form words but there are only sounds in the back of her throat and then a closing of the offending article and a shaking of her head. I've been warned about this.

She leads me down to the kitchen and the old familiar smells, her face turning back to me occasionally with the urge to say those perfunctory, greeting things — the cupboard in her head empty but still she goes back to it.

Then we're both in the kitchen, the overgrown back garden looking in at me through the windows, my suitcase at the door like a dog that wants to be let out.

'How's work?' she says, surprised at having got some words airborne. Then her back's to me as she second guesses herself about something as simple as making the tea.

Seven short years have turned her into one of the uncertain, the old. Now she has that way old people have of crossing the road or telling a story, all the time waiting to get it wrong. Saying Hong Kong instead of King Kong, or the other way round.

'Good. It's good, Mum — as work goes.'

She gives me a smile that's a frown again before she's turned fully away, and I'm gazing at the back of her head but remembering the way her brain looked on the light box a few weeks ago during that flying visit I made. When she was all propped up and unconscious, hospital tubes running through her. A clinician pointing his biro at her CT scans as if gesturing to a weather forecast. The single tone with which he spoke about my mother's life, up there in lights. The way he had of dealing out reality, like prison food. Her mind lit up except for that dark walnut growing in her brain. Right inside of who she is.

I wonder what part of her it's elbowing its way through now, while she waits for the kettle.

But I remember looking at that dark walnut on the CT scan and thinking it's me. That's me in there eating its way through her. If that growing darkness is a specific part of Mum, it's the me part. The son part. The disappointment. The one who did that thing all those years ago.

I'm the black walnut.

2

The government says that children under 13 can't sit in the front seat and anybody who sits in the front has to wear a seatbelt. Clunk-click. I don't have to wear one in the back which is sort of a consolation prize for not being in the front, but really I always want to be up in the business end.

Dad calls it that when he lets me ride shotgun. Usually only once we get round the corner from Mum and up the road a bit. I have to sit on the first aid kit cos the seat's too low.

Every time I'm climbing over he's always getting me to say when my birthday is and my answer is supposed to be today's date but thirteen years ago, as if it's my thirteenth birthday. And I'm supposed to look smug when I say it to the police officer if they catch us, then tell them we're off to celebrate at McDonald's.

Dad says it doesn't matter what you say as long as you have some facts in there with your lies. So if we get pulled over all I need to do under pressure is know today's date and I always know that because I have a calendar on my wall and a thermometer stuck on the outside of the window and I mark off the overnight lowest temperature every morning and check the water measurer on my window ledge for rain.

I like the weather and when I grow up I want to be a weatherman cos they're famous and get to tell the future and people will tune in and wear different things based on what I tell them. Plus by the time I'm a weatherman technology will be so amazing that weathermen will be able to ask the weather computer, which is called Nimbus, to predict when there's going to be a bomb or a war or a car crash.

We've got a new foster boy staying with us. Dad calls him Robert McCloud because he loves clouds. He's been here 4 days so far and is all sulky and soft and quiet, boring. He just sits outside in the garden a lot and looks at the clouds or reads in his room and doesn't do anything mysterious or suspicious so that I get really bored of spying on him, really fast.

'Come on, folks,' Mum says, leaning out the back door to the garden while I'm in the kitchen. 'I've got to pick some stuff up but I'll take you for a nice dinner after.' She has her foster kid voice on rather than her mum or wife voice.

Robert is 12 and so it might not be many days of the year until he's 13. Plus he could lie about his birthday and have had his real one recently with his bad parents and then get another birthday out of us good people who are helping him out of the kindness of our hearts. Mum says good people should have children but she has only had one, me.

We're running to the car like Hunchbacks of Notre Dame cos it's raining again. This is the first time Robert has ridden in our car, except the time we went to the video shop and Mum and Dad sat up front and tried to act normal.

'You have to go in the back too, Robert,' I say as we're running. Mum is covering her hair with a hand and running round the car. 'No, he doesn't,' she says. 'Jump in the front, Robert.'

I stop on the lawn and watch them. I'm keeping very still and instead of thinking about what Mum just said I'm wondering why everybody makes such a fuss about rain. It's only water. Robert looks back at me and frowns as he opens the door to the front. He gets in without needing the first aid kit and slams the door.

Mum starts the car but then she's standing half out of it again with smoke coming from the back and Robert's pink face is in the warm, water running down the car window so that he looks sadder.

Mum is getting very angry and is in a rush cos of the rainwater. I wonder how many millimetres have fallen in my collector.

Every raindrop has a small grain of dirt in it. Which might be what the fuss is about. God put dirt in rainwater because the clouds need to turn into rain but they need something to turn into rain on. Like the steam in the bathroom has to turn into raindrops on the mirror or the walls or the windows. Clouds use dirt in the air to make rain, which is why mums don't like it when their washing gets rained on.

'YOU GET IN THE CAR THIS INSTANT OR I'LL GIVE YOU SOMETHING TO THINK ABOUT, YOUNG MAN.'

'YOU HAVE TO BE THIRTEEN TO RIDE UP FRONT.'

I feel all little here in the middle of the lawn.

'1!'

'It's not FAIR.'

I'm feeling sheepish, like Dad says. So I'm on the lawn but suddenly I've got little hairy legs and my hair is curly wool.

Only I'd be lambish cos I'm not 13. Once you get to 13 your life properly starts and you can probably be sheepish then. I'd be lambish now.

'2!'

'IT'S AGAINST THE LAW!'

Rain makes people speak loudly. Must be the dirt.

Mum is marching towards me with her scary lip. She gets it when she's angry. Her mouth sort of goes down at one side and her teeth come out and chew at a bit of it. Like my friend Ralph's grandma after she had her stroke.

I run for the car but she's got me by my wrist, the rain making noise on the car roof and I can't hear what she's saying but she SAYS, IT, HARDER at the same time as her hand hits my bottom and legs.

I make a lot of screaming in pain noise so she doesn't hit me as many times as she might if I'm quiet.

The front car door opens and Robert is all dry and warm and pale. He shuts it very quietly behind him so as not to put my mum off her stroke. Then he gets in the back and shuts the door just as quietly. Mum is pulling me up by my wrist now and saying things right into my face and there's saliva on her lip and her hair is wet. She looks like a crazy woman and up this close I can see the black dots in her nose.

'You didn't get to 3,' I say but I'm trying my hardest not to cry. She shoves me into the car and slams the door almost before my legs are out the way. I'm practically on top of Robert. He moves over.

Now there is that horrible waiting moment when Robert and me are in the car on our own and Mum is marching round the back bumper and there's a raindrop on my nose and it has a single invisible grain of dirt in it.

Mum is talking half to me half to herself through the car roof and huffing round to her door and I've got the beetroots from Robert looking at me which might be why I leap forward and lock her door. Then I lock Robert's door before he can do anything. Then I lock all the other doors and sit back and I'm in the biggest kennel ever.

Mum goes quiet. There's just the rain and my breathing, the engine. I can't see her face, only her blouse and waterproof coat which is a bit open.

She doesn't do anything for a sizzly moment. Then she pulls on the door handle a lot and screams.

I think I giggle even though my heart is going like the crappers.

I smile at Robert but he doesn't think it's funny. I stop smiling and look at the car keys wobbling in the ignition from where Mum pulled on the door handle. The engine is running very quiet, sort of purring. The car really is going like a dream. I'm tinkering, Dad says when he has his head under the bonnet. Usually when Mum is vacuuming. I hand him his tools and we pretend we're operating on the car.

'Screwdriver.'

Surgeons don't have to say please or thank you.

Robert is fidgeting in the car with me and I'm worried he can hear my heart, or my spanked bottom cos it's like when a bell is still dinging just a tiny bit ages after it has been struck and you wouldn't know unless you got very close or touched the bell but then you kill the little tiny ringing. I like that.

I look at her tummy in the window and try not to cry. Then she says in a very different voice that I should open the door immediately.

'You should unlock it,' Robert says but doesn't look at me. He doesn't look at anyone much, he must have a bad secret.

'You have to be thirteen,' I say to him. 'HE HAS TO BE THIRTEEN.' Then I cross my arms in case they do as they're told. Robert leans up and puts his hand on the lock.

'No, Robert,' Mum says, peeking in. 'I want YOU to open the door.'

I slouch down and look at my shoes with their little bits of wet grass sticking to them. There's another raindrop on my nose or it might be a tear which means it will have salt in it not dirt. Like your body needs salt to make sadness.

Or maybe there's dirt in tears too along with the salt and that's why we cry, to get the dirt out. Which is why you normally feel better after you cry. Even if it is in front of Robert.

Mum's voice is all careful now like I'm a wild horse in a meadow and she's holding a head collar. I like hearing her use that voice, even though I'm scared. If I was a hero I'd drive the car away and never come back. Plus driving away isn't a bad idea because otherwise I'm going to be hungry in my bedroom for a very long time.

She says my full name cos I'm in trouble and people are always formal when there's trouble. Then she says the shortening like when I'm a good boy. I want to lock them both out in the rain, and Robert is trying to tell me something but I stick my fingers in my ears 'LA LA LA CUCUMBER SAUSAGE CUCUMBER SAUSAGE!'

His lips stop moving and I take my fingers out and Mum is saying 'Try to be quiet, Robert. I can handle this. Thank you for trying, you're a good boy.' She has that wobble in her voice like she gets when she talks about Grandma. I think I'm probably dead too once she gets hold of me.

'You won't be in trouble,' she says. Yeah right. 'Open the door and you won't be in trouble, you've already had a good spanking today.' She uses a mixture of her voices saying that. 'I'm sorry I lost my temper but it's really raining and — OH, HE WON'T RIDE IN THE FRONT TILL HE'S THIRTEEN, OK!'

'When's your birthday?'

'May the 14th,' Robert says then looks at me like he's wondering if that's an ok birthday by me.

'Taurus,' I say, thinking. 'Taurus people are strong and stubborn.'

Soon as I can think straight I'm going to work out exactly how far away it is until May 14th but it isn't that far off because this is February which means it won't be long before I'm going to have to be stuck all the way in the back while Robert gets to be up in the business end with my mum.

I take my salty tears away and climb over the back seat, curl up in the boot next to the first aid kit. I'm crying and it's raining and I'm balled up tight.

I hear the thunk of the lock and my tummy vanishes and leaves a hole behind.

The door opens and the engine stops and Robert is so quiet it's like he's in the kennel instead of me, which is what Dad calls it when

I'm in the doghouse. Sometimes my dad is in the kennel and he tuts at me and smiles. 'Your dad's in the kennel again.'

I'm not sure Mum has ever been in the kennel. She'd have to vacuum it first.

The boot opens and she tugs me by the same wrist she hurt earlier, dragging me along with my legs sort of running in the air and sort of on the ground. She hits me a few more times and her rings hurt my ear. I'm crying for a hundred squillion reasons, and I'm crying because I'm crying. Crying makes me sad like throwing up makes me want to throw up.

Meanwhile Mum's trying to get the house keys out and talking too fast to make sense and I hate everything and how unfair not being a grown-up is and that Robert is watching. I hate him most of all. And even more than that I hate his parents for being bad because if they were good like my mum then I wouldn't have to share her.

Mum always says I don't like the foster kids cos I'm an only child but I think it would be amazing to have real brothers and sisters. Sometimes I pretend I do. I think I'd like a brother until I'm 13 then I'd like him to turn into a girl so she can bring her friends home, and I'll like girls by then and have them as a harlem.

Dad says he wants a harlem. If he had one he might tinker with it when Mum is vacuuming.

Now I'm in my room and not allowed out until she says so and she tells me not to hold my breath.

I hold my breath and time myself anyway.

38 seconds. My lungs are still growing.

I make a note on my chart. Then I take off my clothes and put dry ones on and go and look at my rain collector on the window ledge. 34 mm. Which is quite a lot. I make a note on my chart. Then I imagine 34 mm spread out across the whole area of where the rain has fallen. Then I imagine it all across the weather map and the weatherman taking his arms and gathering up all the rain from the map and putting it in a big rain collector measurer on the official weather centre window ledge. I wonder how tall it would be to catch all that 34 mm spread out over that far. Imagine. That's why 34 mm of rain is a lot, when I think about it like that. Cos 34 mm may be the size of Robert's doodle, but take all the 34 mm fallen on the whole country and it would be an enormous doodle. It's scary how big the world is.

Then I try to picture how much dirt has fallen if there's been 34 mm of rain but it makes my brain itchy.

I'm still in my room when Dad comes home. He sneaks me a yoghurt (strawberry) and an apple (apple) for dinner. Plus he gives me a talking to but is actually kind. He says it's a bit rich to be stroppy about Robert being up in the business end considering he's legal in a few months and I'm closer to being a baby than legal and yet still get to ride up front.

He has a point, except for the baby thing. I ask him to tuck me in and stroke my forehead until I fall asleep.

He tucks me in and strokes my forehead which always calms me down but he's never done it all the way until I've fallen asleep, my dad. A little bit because he always gets bored, and a little bit because I have to try so hard to fall asleep fast before he gets bored that I never feel too sleepy. Plus he always ends up pretending to pick my nose as a joke and I always get exasperated or flabberghastlied and he just laughs and kisses me goodnight but I beg for one more minute and he gives me thirty seconds.

This is our routine ritual and doing it after what happened today makes me feel less bruised in my tummy.

'What time is Robert's bedtime?' I say as Dad is leaving but he tells me not to pay so much attention to Robert who is older than me. Then he says 'Comparisons bear no fruits,' which is one of his sayings that doesn't make sense but you can tell it means No.

'But does he have a set bedtime?'

He hushes me and comes back and strokes my forehead some more. He smells of boiled carrots and beer. Then he says, slowly, in time with each gentle head stroke he does, without picking my nose at all, he says, 'You. Are. My. Son.'

3

There is a short, happy period between waking up, and realising I'm in my childhood bed in my childhood home. My feet hanging over the end of the mattress gives it away.

I open my eyes and it's past eleven, another morning almost gone. No messages on my phone and my head still clogged with all the drink I plied myself with last night, sitting in the garden while the old lady snored on the couch.

Day 3 of my paused life.

I pad out into the hallway and her bedroom door is open. There's a little trepidation that she died in the night but her bed's empty.

I stay in the shower as long as possible. Then dry myself, dressing slowly in order to postpone downstairs and the woman I'm stuck on my childhood desert island with.

When I do eventually venture down the washing machine's going, its powder drawer still open with some undissolved powder in it, most of it, though, is on the floor. A pair of knickers on the tiles that look way too small for her now she's all blown up on medication and ice-cream.

The steroids that shrink her cancer also grow her appetite but to me it's like she needs to eat all the food she would have eaten if she weren't going to die so young. Sixty-two. They lived longer than that in the 1800s.

I wander into the kitchen, the freezer door open and a puddle in front of it on the floor. There's an empty ice-cream container on the counter and Mum standing by the sink, gazing out the window, her jaw working on something. She finishes chewing and puts her hand back into the sink, comes up with some titbits and tilts back her head, puts them in, some of it falling onto the floor via her shoulder.

I move a little closer. 'Mum, don't eat that stuff!'

She turns her head, her fingers out in front of her, all mucky. I clean them off with the tea towel then lift the little metal sieve that catches the gunk from the washing-up and show it to her. 'Don't eat this, Mum, it'll make you ill!'

She looks at me, swallows, makes a contented noise. I open the fridge — we *are* overdue for a shop. I rest my forehead on the door, my socks soaking up the defrosted freezer ice.

I slam both doors and she's rushing out the room, me in pursuit. 'Where's your tablets, Mum? Have you taken them?'

The washing machine is beginning its noisy spin cycle, hopping quickly from foot to foot. The same machine that was here when I left, its ancient motor whining, the sound bouncing off the floor and filling the house — Mum still walking away from me, raising a hand to dismiss my question.

I catch her up, halting her by the arm and she emits this enormous shriek.

'If you don't take your tablets you'll get *worse*.'

The washing machine's like an air-raid warning and the old lady is shouting out and crying, trying to unpeel my hand from where it has her arm. The cancer makes her hold nothing back, her emotions raw and unbridled, her mouth open, her tongue coloured by the washing-up gunk she ate.

I march off into the kitchen looking for the little white box of letters and doors with her tablets in — her days of the week drug regimen.

'Please take your tablets, Mum. It doesn't just impact on you. I'm here too.'

I'm the one with my life on hold.

She's making these strained grunting noises from the other room so I march back, hitting out at the ice-cream tub on my way and it flies at the freezer and makes a plastic thud, skids away along the floor into the table leg — oozes some melted vanilla goo on the lino. Another job.

When I get to her she's tugging on the washing-machine door even though it's still spinning, tugging at it and grunting and crying, wrenching at the handle.

'You can't open it while it's *going*.'

But the machine's coming in to land now, juddering faster and faster like a dropped penny settling onto a table. Mum sitting back on the floor, giving up, her head in her hands, deep breaths. She looks up at me with tears rolling down her face but she isn't actually crying, you couldn't call it crying. She wraps herself round my legs, her head on my thighs, holding on tight.

This is not what I've imagined all those times I've thought about coming home and confronting this woman. I've been picturing a confrontation with the woman she used to be. A woman who was just as disappointing but a hundred times as strong.

'Mum. *Please.*' I extricate myself from her and retreat back to the kitchen, looking for her drugs again and eventually find the box wedged under the tablecloth — the lump conspicuous in my sadness where it wasn't in my anger.

I open up today's day and there they are, the little steroid tablets that keep her from deteriorating. The only thing stopping the pressure in her skull from affecting her brain. Such as it is. That tumour turning up the heat all the time, growing, forcing itself into that finite space in her head. Pushing her out of her own life.

I get some water from the tap and chuck the plughole sieve away while I'm at it.

When I come back she's gone, the front door swinging on its hinges. I go out into the sunlight, still holding the tablet box and a glass of water, one of her shoes lying on the path. I get to the road and there she is hobbling away up the hill, one shoe on one shoe off. I call to her and she accelerates, doesn't look round.

I give chase, frustration and tiredness pulling me in two directions, making me talk to myself, the glass of water spilling over my hand until I empty it onto the verge — my socks still wet from the freezer water and now grimy from the pavement.

I easily catch her up and she isn't crying, just this lost and determined woman. I stand in front of her and she stops, waiting, breathless, not meeting my eyes.

Looking at her now I see how afraid she is. Not necessarily of me. She's just afraid. Everything softening in my centre, my hand that's holding the tablets dropping, rattling, down by my side because I can see Mum now, in among all that deterioration. There she is.

We're standing here and I'm looking at her, a breeze shuffling what there is of her hair.

Maybe she recognises the change in me too, or rediscovers who I am, because she turns and faces the way I'm facing and I hold out my elbow for her and she smiles, her wet eyelashes half black and half mousy-blonde from where she last had them tinted. We link arms and she drops her head gently onto my shoulder for a second and we make our way back down Hawke Street Hill together, towards our house and Dad's out-of-control hedges sticking up over the neighbour's fence.

'You have to take the tablets, Mum. Please?' She's looking down at her feet as she walks, confused suddenly at the distinction between her shoed and shoeless foot. She stops and looks up the road.

'Your shoe's in the garden, Mum. Don't worry, I'll get it for you.'

We turn in through the gate but she halts me when we get to her shoe sitting on the spot where Robert came undone. She gazes at it and sighs a ten-ton sigh, turning to me with that familiar look on her face. Her eyes flicking from one of mine to the other. Searching me.

'Let's get you inside,' I say trying to tug her away.

'No.' Her body stiffens against my tugging so I leave her there and walk in, conscious of my walk, conscious of those eyes looking at me as I go. Her discarded shoe marking the spot. Her face marking the question.

There was always that question.

4

'Elbows off the table. And we don't want to see what you're chewing, thank you.' Mum is a manners Nazi. Dad said so. She puts her knife and fork down while she chews. 'More meat, Robert? A piece of fruit after? Perhaps something sweet, eh?' She's got her best foster child voice on tonight, and her war paint. 'We can watch a video after, if you'd like?'

'Dumbo, Dumbo!'

'Robert's too grown up for Dumbo. Aren't you, Robert.'

After dinner she sends me upstairs early as if I've been bad, but I can play in my room and go to sleep when I like as if I've been good.

I think Dumbo is lonely. I wrote a poem at school once called Alonely Only Child. Miss Marshall said it was perfect, especially as I'd made up a brand new word. But when I showed Mum she got really funny and screwed it up and threw it in the bin. I was already in bed when Dad got home that night but next morning my poem was all creased up on the fridge under a magnet.

I don't want to go to bed and leave Robert with them but I'm being as good as possible so I decide not to argue. I creep past the big vase which is never full of flowers but always has my grandad's homemade walking sticks poking up.

Grandma died of cancer and Dad had to clean up all her blood in our bathroom when she collapsed dead in the night. He did it for Mum before he woke her up so she wouldn't have to see what came out.

They know Grandma was dead before she hit the ground cos she didn't use her arms to protect her face. And I know that because I spied a conversation Dad had once. He had to pick her teeth out of the blood.

Nobody knows but there's still a spot of Grandma's blood on the back of the loop the loop pipe behind the toilet. I look at that spot of dead Grandma's dying blood almost every time I pee or poo. Sometimes it makes my doodle go all strong, just from looking at it.

The foster children are normally really naughty but Robert is quiet and good which means I'm having to try extra hard. I run my toothbrush under the tap and put some toothpaste in my mouth, then get into my jimjams and climb inside my secret lion's den which is actually my sleeping bag but I go inside it head first. I like it in here and I've got my torch and my Transformer which turns from a green and blue monster to a blue and green robot. Only it looks more purple cos the sleeping bag is red inside. Like I was swallowed by a snake.

There are two all time amazing times in my life. Number 1 is the times when they've run out of foster children and it's just Mum and Dad and me. That's like Christmas and birthday and the roads closed, all packed into a big chocolatey ball. I like chocolate but it gets me in trouble, all energetic and electricity. That's when Dad calls me Nutella the Hun, which is funny only cos of how he says it, plus I can tell he loves me when he does. Nutella the Hun was a baddie from the olden days.

The foster kids spoil everything when they're here. Plus they make Mum and Dad work really hard and are almost never polite or grateful or love them back. I love Mum and Dad and I am grateful so I don't see why they won't just stop nasty people coming.

The last boy persuaded me to climb a tree then wouldn't help me down. He just left me. Mum had to wait for Dad to come home to get me down, which was TWO HOURS. I had to pee from the top branch.

That was Marcus. He belongs to the government now.

The second most amazing moment in my life was one time after I'd thrown up and Mum let me get into bed with her and Dad and they had the TV on and it was about dolphins and we all snuggled up together.

Together is my favourite word.

If Robert threw up I wonder if they'd let him in bed with them. It might be against the fostering rules hopefully. Except Mum says they're mainly silly, the fostering rules, and they can damn well send her to jail for properly caring for a child if they want to.

There's always a reason why a foster boy is here. Like sometimes the parent is in jail so we take the kid for a while. Or sometimes the mum or dad is ill, or they're arguing in court.

Some mums and dads are just better than other mums and dads. My mum says she's especially good which is why she gets to take in kids whose mum and dad are not so good, or just struggling but good deep down.

Normally Mum doesn't tell me what's wrong with the mum and dad until after the kid has gone, unless there's something I need to know. Like we had a boy once who loved to start fires and Mum had to buy an electric thing for lighting the stove and throw away all the matches.

Plus I'm never allowed to get the door, or leave it unlocked, or say my name or address when I answer the phone because one day a bad parent might find out where we are and come try to take their kid back.

We never have any foster girls. Ever. Probably because girls are treated better than boys, that's why. Or girls behave better. Or parents love girls more than boys. Or girls are only born to good parents.

I can hear Mum and Dad talking to Robert downstairs but I get into bed and play games with the moon. If I relax my eyes there are two moons and they're like a wolf is looking down at me.

I wonder if you get moon rainbows at night if it rains. I don't see why not but I've never seen one. I think moon rainbows would be made up of all the sad colours like black and midnight blue. Which means moon rainbows might exist but you just can't see them cos they're the same colour as night.

Only owls can see them.

This morning I wake up happy then remember Robert's here. Robert gives me the same feeling as a maths test or the dentist or Sunday night. That snaky tummy feeling. Plus I can hear them all downstairs together already like they never went to bed and had midnight feasts and played.

I check for overnight rain but there's just a tiny bit probably from dew so I don't mark it down. I do my hair nicely and dress up in my scratchiest clothes. I even clean my teeth. Then I'm scared to go down but scared to stay up and let them play happy families without me.

When I get downstairs Mum is dressed nice too and her hair is done. 'What you doing all dressed up, silly!' she says and laughs at me. Robert's at the kitchen table watching and Dad is out digging in the garden but not in his digging clothes.

Everyone is dressing up for Robert but Robert's wearing the same clothes every day cos he had to leave his home in a hurry.

Today is his 11th ever breakfast in our house and I ask Mum how many more breakfasts she thinks he'll have with us but she gives me one of those nothing answers and her laser beam look. Robert fidgets.

I eat as much as him maybe more plus finish his leftover orange juice even though I feel like a boa constrictor that just ate a boa constrictor that just ate a goat. Dad says that after most dinners.

Robert is 12 which is a lot older than I am. I want to be 12 but when I'm 12 he'll be, well, by then Robert will be …

17.

I'll never catch up.

The day he came Mum asked me to show him round while she spoke to the social workers. There was lots of paperwork to sign.

'Why don't you take Mic — I mean Robert on the grand tour?' she said. Then she got the serious beetroots. 'Sorry, Robert.'

Sometimes she accidentally calls me Michael too.

The social worker with the big boobs watched her and I quickly took my Alonely poem off the fridge and hid it in my pocket but later on Mum made me put it up again. 'You were most insistent about having that poem up, young man.'

After lunch she gives Robert and me a chocolate biscuit. Robert eats his bickie really quickly in the living room. He eats everything fast. I wait till he's finished and then go in and show him mine with only a little nibble out of it.

'So what,' he says. 'I enjoyed mine you haven't yet. Makes no diff.' He shrugs then looks round me at the TV. He's starting to get a bit brave.

I turn the TV off and run out the room and he calls me a little brat and gets up and turns it back on.

I put my biscuit on the oven where it's still warm, and wait until the chocolate is changing colour and getting melty. Then I go through to the freezer which is big and long like an enormous pirate's chest. I open it and go on tiptoe to put my biscuit inside on a box of chicken kievs.

'WHAT are you doing playing in the FREEZER!' Mum can creep up on you better than any spy. 'Are you stealing food, mister?'

'I was just putting my biscuit in.'

'Why?'

I shrug. Robert comes and stands behind her, wondering what the fuss is about.

'No more playing with the freezer, thank you.'

'Why!'

'BECAUSE. Besides, if you fell in you wouldn't be able to get out.'

I stare back at Robert for a second, really hard. 'I would. Easy.'

'It's a heavy lid and it can get quite sticky. Put the lid down, good boy.'

'I'd be able to get out. Men are strong, women are weak.'

'Is that right.' She picks me up and puts me in the freezer on top of the food and then the lid is slammed shut. It's very black and cold. I push on the lid then wriggle into a better space to push again and I push and it's not opening and my heart is all squishy like when the water hose kinks.

I do that to the hose sometimes when Dad's watering the garden. Then I always run and hide and he huffs and walks over and unkinks it, looking around in case it's me. And I'll sneak back after a minute and kink it again. Eventually I end up getting a good spraying.

I can hear my breathing all around me in the freezer, really loud and fast as if there are a hundred boys panicking in here with me. I need the toilet.

Mum's voice is all muffled. 'Come on, strong man! Are you trying to open it?' She's giggling a bit like Robert is tickling her.

I'm screaming and screaming and it finally goes all light and she picks me up and says 'See what happens to little boys who get too big for their boots. We'll have no more playing with the freezer thankyouverymuch.'

I've got chocolate and crumbs stuck to my school shirt and Robert is walking away and trying not to laugh. I dry my eyes and go upstairs and get into my lion's den. I feel heavy, like when I stay in the bath while it empties.

Eventually I get too hot and climb out my den, go over and look at my biceps in the mirror. I'm still growing.

A bit later Mum comes in and sits me down, stroking my hair away from my forehead. 'I'm sorry I did that but you do ask for it sometimes. You know we have a foster placement here, and what does that mean?'

'Best behaviour.'

'Xactly. More jealous than your father aren't you, little man.' She messes up my hair. 'Robert's very special and needs a lot of love at the moment. Don't make that face, it's not the end of the world. Other children have to share their mum and dad. They manage.'

She gives me a really tight hug and even lets me eat my lunch in my room but I hear them all talking and want to go down again. Sorry is supposed to be like abracadabra or hey presto but they are all just words. Real magic doesn't work like that.

I hide the green lunch bits under some paper in my bin then creep down to listen to them eating and talking.

They've lit a fire!

Mum and Dad are saying to Robert how I'm usually like this with new foster children and Robert shouldn't worry. She says I'm harmless and that I always settle down eventually.

I don't like them talking about me and nor does the snake in my tummy.

Plus Dad has lit a fire even though it isn't cold out, and I'm ALWAYS asking Dad to light a fire and he nearly always says not to be silly, that it's practically summer. Except he says this all year round and thinks he's funny but I just want us to be all snuggley together. The three of us.

Maybe Dad lit a fire to warm Robert's mood up.

The firelight makes the vase of walking sticks sparkly. I'm not allowed to touch them cos they're Mum's pride and joy even though she didn't make them, Grandad did.

Robert and Mum leave the table and go outside. I race upstairs and stand on my bed with my shoes on and watch them. I can hear Dad doing the dishes in the sink.

I'm down low spying on them from the corner of my window, Robert pointing at boring things in the sky, Mum looking at Robert a lot when he isn't looking, then smiling at him when he is. Or she's looking at the house, probably at Dad in the kitchen window, and making these stupid happy faces to him behind Robert's back.

Robert lies down on the grass and the sun is out and Mum lies sort of next to him and they look all colourful and sunny like they're a washing powder advert. Then she reaches out and finds Robert's hand in the grass and takes hold of it. And he LETS her.

I don't know what happens then cos my face is in my pillow and I'm shouting and scrunching the bed sheets in my fists.

By the time I look again they're gone and I can see the different coloured green space on the lawn their bodies made together.

I get a whiff of smoke smell coming out the chimney. I check the thermometer and it says 22 degrees outside.

I run downstairs with the snake big and thick in my tummy and I'm pacing by the fire. I take one of Grandad's walking sticks and try to snap it but it's too strong for me, like the freezer lid. I beat the couch with it instead, throw it down and I'm pacing and pacing while Mum and Robert and Dad are in the kitchen together and I want to go in but I'm too dizzy about everything. Then Mum says something and Robert is LAUGHING. His first laugh in the house ever.

Dad told me once that people who are in big terrible life and death situations can do amazing things, which might be why I can keep my hand in the fire for the longest time.

I walk into the kitchen with it after and Mum is running with me to the bath and I'm sort of miles away, my hand feeling super bright like it's the sun or something. She puts me in the tub in my clothes and Robert's white face is here and Dad sends him away but he doesn't move and my hand is all blistering and black like a monster's. The bath running with cold water and Mum making me put my hand under the surface, and shouting for Dad to get things from the freezer and I'm crying at what I've done.

Mum is crying too but in a sort of scared angry way and she's almost in the bath with me, my hand in the water and feeling so hot I think it might make the bath boiling.

Dad runs in with ice and bags of peas and chicken kievs, my favourite, and dumps them in the water, Mum screaming something at him and he really shouts back at her, tree roots showing up on his neck. But I can't really hear them. I can't hear the water thundering out the tap or the frozen peas coming out of the blurry bit where the plastic packet was pulled open, bright green dots bobbing up and down in the bath.

But Robert is crying. I'm pretty sure he's crying.

5

We're at the family table, me in the seat that was always mine, Mum in hers. Old habits. There's two empty chairs at the table with us, pushed right in out the way. And a certain type of silence.

Outside, the afternoon is slowly taking on an evening light, my jetlag making it seem out of the natural order, uneasy. We sit here though, neither of us knowing what to do with one another while we wait for the nurse. This being the hollow period then, like the ice age after the comet struck.

Day 4 of my paused life.

While sitting here my gaze is drawn reluctant but greedy to the operation scar on the side of her head, metal staples holding the flesh together. The hair she's lost. The family pictures taking over the walls — all that past. The dirty dishes sitting in the sink. The freezer door a little ajar again, a puddle of meltwater at its feet.

I put my elbows on the table, hands in my hair, stare down at the congealed out-of-date milk she put in my tea. And at all the familiar shapes and scratches on the surface of this old wooden table.

'Is the nurse usually this late, Mum?'

She offers a smiling shrug and I don't know if she can't compute the answer, or the question. I give her one of those polite, lipless smiles, both of us looking occasionally at the two empty chairs — even Mum seeming to feel a palpable sense of the way things used to be, before the comet. And yet she looks at me like I'm a stranger.

'Work?' Mum manages to say, the pronunciation a little like she's deaf — that numb-tongued sound.

'You already asked me that. Work's work. Can you remember what I do?'

She looks for the answer on my face and I have to look away, down at my lumpy tea, then back up at her but she's already fallen into staring.

Alfie II is curled up on the sunny windowsill — our female cat named after Alfie. When the first Alfie died Mum and Dad just went out and got another one and named it the same, even though he was a she. Now she's snoring loudly through the scab-like growth jutting out from her nose.

Even the cat has cancer.

'I'll give you a clue,' I say, managing to keep some softness in my voice, like I'm the parent.

'Prison!' she says.

'Very good. But can you remember my name?' Which plunges her back into that gap in her mind, as if I really am the bit they took out of her.

'Robert,' she says and smiles, then looks down at her hands like she doesn't recognise those either.

There's a knock at the door and we both jump. I wander away doing my hair.

I never used to be allowed to answer the door. Before the accident there were always visitors. Afterwards though it was mainly nurses, like this one. She does a double-take when she sees me.

The three of us are seated now, all offers of tea rejected. The nurse sitting in my dad's place at the table, a part of me wanting to bring her a chair from the dining room instead. Mum fidgeting, a persistent smile papered over her inability to partake in the simplest etiquette of Hello, fine thanks, how are you? She can only nod and stammer truncated fragments of words, then shake her head and smile as if it's really all just a simple mix-up. Laughable being preferable to terminal.

I reach out and take her hand in mine and she smiles. She's even forgotten she doesn't let me touch her. She turns my palm over to look at what's causing the roughness, then sits for a moment, confused by the scar.

She's not bad the nurse, early thirties, homely in the right places, South African accent, sun damage visible where her uniform opens towards the collar. Her breasts would be brilliant white contrasted with that dappled brown on her chest.

She asks me a little about myself and I watch Mum hang on my answers.

'I'd better get on,' Nursey says eventually, 'I'm running behind, as usual,' and she bends over to open her case. Big arse. Not just big though, nice and big.

'I'd best leave you two to it then,' I say, Mum having caught me gawking.

'No, stay. It'll be better if you know the things to watch for. *You don't mind if he stays, do you, Mary.*'

She unwraps a compact blood-pressure machine then stops midway through rolling up Mum's sleeve, gives a theatrical sigh. 'I *told* you now, didn't I,' she says, tugging the rings off Mum's fingers.

I hadn't noticed the rings — only half on, a load of swollen flesh backed up behind them. The nurse struggling to get them off and Mum shaking her head, earnest and sad, wanting to keep them on.

'I know these are important to you, Mary, but the steroids will make you swell up. You want us to have to cut these gorgeous rings off you, *do* you?' This stranger patronising what used to be my indomitable, all-powerful mother.

While the blood-pressure machine whirs, Mum is sat there looking at the ring marks left behind on her fingers, the nurse sneaking glances at me, or doing her hair, pulling at her uniform as if she's trying to get her body to feel like it fits her.

She shines a light in Mum's eyes, makes a note on a chart.

The sound of the Velcro rip disturbs me from a funk, Mum rubbing her arm and smiling at the nurse even though her head's down making a note and talking '… and if there's anything Mary hates it's taking her medication, don't you, Mare?'

The nurse ferrets around in her bag and comes back with a bound booklet, a picture of a car engine on the uppermost page. Mum's irrepressible smile slipping a little. She sits back in her chair, looking down at her hands.

'I know you hate this, Mary,' she says and stands the booklet up on the tabletop, 'but say the word for me, if you can.'

She lets Mum sit staring at it, my chair creaking into the fidgety silence. Alfie snoring on the windowsill next to that chunk of mica rock glistening now in the sunshine. Mum looking at the picture, her brow knitted, mouth open.

'Let her try the next one,' I say and Nursey looks at me, flips the page to the next image — a corkscrew. Mum blank of words, her body burning with the wanting to say it. Knowing it maybe. Her mouth like a fish out of water.

Whereas the nurse is in her element. She spends her days in the awkward quiet of illness, the way waiters and waitresses spend their day in that pause in conversation while they work the tables. Every job has its own brand of silence. Like the one just after shutdown at my work, as every inmate takes stock of another day of their incarcerated life.

Like the silence between deflated lovers.

'It's ok, Mary. Try this one.' And with every turn of the page the images become easier and easier until we're down now to the simplest cartoon shapes. This one of a cat and Mum shrieks excitedly, pointing at Alfie, then puts her hand over her mouth to stop the demeaning release.

'Alfie,' I say brightly, trying to encourage her.

'Oh, it's *Alfie* is it?' the nurse says. 'I wondered what he was called. *I asked you that, didn't I, Mary. Didn't I ask you that.*'

It seems that all questions to my mother are rhetorical now.

'He's a she,' I say, through my teeth.

'I thought so,' she says, unruffled. '*I said he looked like a she didn't I, Mary. I said that.*'

'She's not an idiot.'

'Excuse me?'

'Maybe you could stop talking to her in that voice.'

Again the nurse-face stays nailed on, the only leak being a slightly prolonged blink.

'Your mum and I have been going just fine here in the time it took you to show up.'

My chair groans as I push it quickly back and head outside, pacing the garden and thinking about cigarettes. I haven't smoked one in three years, haven't craved one this sincerely in months.

When the nurse finally comes out I wander right up to her at the gate, all smiles. 'Sorry but I didn't catch your name.'

'Vicky.'

'Vicky. Right. Sorry about that, in there. It's just a bit of a shock, Mum being ill and everything.' I tilt my head over and smile, watching what my proximity does to her.

'Of course. You're in unfamiliar territory. I understand. I haven't done this job without developing a thick skin. It's ok.' She wants to go but I'm in front of the gate and she doesn't seem so comfortable suddenly. She can't hide behind her nurse status now. Out here she's just a woman.

I take a loose hold of her arm and her face turns down and away a little, starting to blush.

'Vicky, I really appreciate what you're doing for my mum.' I'm close enough to smell her sweat. 'Maybe you should make us your last appointment of the day next time? That way you and I might spend some time afterwards, if you'd like?' And I give her that look.

'Well, I ...' She laughs a little laugh. I release her and she grabs for the gate. 'That's awfully ...' She's frowning at the latch now. 'But I've got a full ...'

I lean in even closer in the process of lifting the gate and opening it barely enough for her to slide through. 'Goodbye, Vicky!' I'm grinning for the first time in days, watching the unflappable nurse flapping away.

If I'm going to be stuck here, I'm going to need some entertainment.

I give my shoes a thorough wipe on the doormat, whistling a tune. Mum isn't in the house so I head through the kitchen and out into the back garden, the plum tree looking despondent as if nobody wants its fruit.

Over near the shed is one of her shoes, lying on its side. That errant, repeatedly shoeless left foot of hers a reminder that your right brain is responsible for the left side of your body — the tumour eating its way through the right side of her brain.

There she is, her right shoe on, a bruise spreading from a focal point on her left ankle. I shut my eyes to the idea of her stumbling out here confused and alone, the ankle rolling over and her hobbling away from the pain. That shoe left there on the lawn like a relic of who she used to be.

She's gazing up at the clouds, the light fading quickly around us. I watch her, half like she's an alien, half like she's a celebrity.

It's still so strange to see her again after all this time. Except she's so diminutive now, standing there smiling up at the sky, looking for shapes in the clouds.

The simplest, cleanest truths are uncertainties to her now. Her identity slipping from her like she's locked in a ship's cabin on high seas, her past sliding along polished tables and falling into pieces on the floor. Everything's moving for her and she's staggering about in there trying to hold on — straightening the memories hanging on one wall as they fall from another and smash. Almost familiar faces looking back at her from under broken glass.

I join her in exposing my throat to the house and looking up at the sky, and it's the sky off *The Simpsons*, with fleets of perfect-sized clouds making their way eastwards, where the weather goes. One of them looks like a pig with a quiff, leaping slowly over us. This was the family game after it was Robert's game.

I look to Mum to show her the pig but her face stops me. 'What is it?' I say, and she looks at me without recognition for a second then sniffs, wiping her eyes, glancing from me to the sky and then back again. 'Is it Robert?' I ask, and she breaks fully into tears.

I traipse the distance and hold her, looking over her shoulders as they rock up and down, the smell of her hair reminding me of spying between the balustrades, and of hot baths and tea.

'But you've forgotten so much.'

Not him though.

My eyes gaze out from the hug, staring at this familiar garden. This familiar heaviness. Familial. All of it reminding me of that part of myself I've worked so hard at leaving behind.

And it's frightening, because if it pushed that eight-year-old as far as it did, what am I capable of at twenty-eight.

6

I don't tell anyone at school and nobody knows except Mum and Dad, and Robert, but now I have to go to a psychologist. Dad says it's like a check-up and most boys and girls have one and really it's just like when the doctor holds your balls and tells you to cough, only it's your brain.

This is my first visit and Dad's taking me. Next week Mum will, so they both get a turn at mending me.

Robert says they might electrocute my head. I ask Mum and it ends up being the first time Robert's got in trouble. I like that.

I'm dressed up ready and my hair done and I've got my robot with me to stop me feeling anything. I go to Robert's room where he is without any food and he calls me a snitch and says I'm crazy.

'People with bad parents shouldn't throw stones, Robert.'

'Look at your bandaged hand, crazy boy. You look like a mad mummy.'

'WELL, YOU … YOUR MUMMY'S MAD.'

Dad's waiting in the car and Mum doesn't stop Robert and me fighting, just screams until he gets off me. I kick him and run out to Dad, my hand hurting and Mum coming after me with her scary lip.

She starts shouting at Dad who's just sitting in the car with the radio talking. From here it sounds like farting in the bath.

'We're living in a MADhouse.'

Dad comes over to talk to her but she just kisses me hard on the forehead and says 'Be good' then slams the door so we're both left on the step like Jehoover's Witnesses.

We reverse out of the drive with Dad's gearbox whining like it always does. It doesn't like going backwards. Robert has his head at my bedroom window to watch me leave. He isn't allowed in my room! I squish my face at him as we pull away and he sort of crosses his eyes and pretends he's getting electrocuted or having a fit.

Sarah Loe from school had a fit in assembly once and suddenly there was a mess and she was writhing about in her own puddle and Mr Jones held her head and moved everyone away. Mrs Halmer didn't notice and carried on playing the piano for ages. Mrs Hammer we call her. She's bad at piano but she's all we've got.

Dad stops around the corner and I'm already holding the first aid kit and grinning so hard my ears moved.

'Come on then, Sonny Jim.' Which isn't my name but I like the way his voice sounds when he says it. I clamber in and get to change gears and we sing along to the radio together and even though it's up too loud for me to hear the engine I can still change gear on time by watching Dad's knee on the clutch. I'm good. Lucky I didn't burn my gear changing hand.

Sometimes he pretends to push his knee as if he wants me to gear change but it's just a red herring trick, and even though we're on our way to the psychologist I still get the giggles every time.

My tongue pokes out when I'm concentrating. Dad calls me Three Lips Macavoy when that happens. I imagine Three Lips Macavoy can concentrate very hard and is a private detective. And plays a mean saxophone.

We park in the car park and I get the squishing snake in my

stomach but Mr Gale the psychologist turns out to seem quite nice and not scary.

Dad calls him Jaws afterwards, like the baddie out of The Spy Who Loved Me by James Bond.

Dad calls Mr Gale Jaws because he has braces on his teeth even though he's quite old. Dad says he must be vain, or maybe just a late developer and might still do a paper round too.

Dad goes in to talk to Jaws first and leaves me in the waiting room. I can hear them talking but not what they're saying.

When they come out Mr Gale says hello again and asks about my burnt hand. It has a big bandage on it and a plastic protective cover.

Jaws watches while Dad takes me into this big room with a desk and posh work stuff at one end and toys and things up the other. There's a white line stuck to the carpet to divide the room up into two halves, the toy end and the posh office end. Plus there's a big window of glass on one wall but you can't see through it to anywhere and it isn't a mirror properly either.

Jaws watches while Dad explains to me only to play with certain toys and not to cross the taped line on the floor between the play bit and the work office bit. Then they leave me all alone but I'm not to worry cos they're just next door.

I get scared on my own but pretend I'm a robot. Mostly I play with my monster robot and don't touch any of the psychologist toys because of all the crazy boys who must have touched them and Robert has been saying 'Stay away from me or I'll catch your crazy germs.' I'm not crazy I don't think but I don't want to catch crazy germs off the other boys who come.

It's hard playing with only one hand but I like how Mum has to sit with me every day and change the dressing plus she's a bit softer now as if the heat from my burn melted her.

They say I'll be scarred for life. Mum says she will too.

Eventually Dad comes in and plays with me but he's a bit funny and keeps looking at himself in the half mirror window.

Afterwards we get to go and he takes me for fish and chips and I'm all happy I didn't get my brain fried.

The chip shop is always steamed up inside and the counter smells of vinegar. Plus we normally get to pinch a chip just after the man has salt and vinegared them but before he wraps them up. And they're always so hot we chew them like a dog chews a marshmallow.

I like the fish and chip shop except being here today with all the hot surfaces makes me scared my hand will get burnt again. I'm always getting these really big daydreams about bad things happening and they're so real they make me jump.

When the food is all wrapped and paid for Dad takes it off the counter and it always leaves a mark and I stay behind to watch the hot mark fade because if I don't Mum and Dad will die.

Then I run to catch Dad up and he's pretending I've caught him with his face guzzling the package of food.

We eat the fish and chips in the car by the park. I eat slower than usual cos I can only use one hand. When Dad's finished his dinner he starts on mine and even holds my good hand so I can't stop him. I love it when we get the giggles.

From where we're parked I can see the chemical plant chimney lights winking through the steamed up car windows. You can always see birds flying around in the light at night, 'getting high on the chimney fumes,' Dad says. I'm scared of the fumes but Mum says it's just steam.

He lets me change gear in the front all the way home and I only crunch once but that's because he says Robert might be with us for quite a while and 'maybe you'd like to start trying to get used to that.'

He hits my hand off the gearstick because I try to put it in reverse instead of third and probably take a few teeth off the gearbox. Maybe it'll need braces now too. He shouts at me. I climb out the business end and lie in the back. I'm full of food but empty, my fingers up close over my face and they smell of salt and vinegar or bedwetting.

By the time we get home Dad has already forgiven me. He always forgives me really quickly and says that when it comes to me he's like a forgetful goldfish.

We get in the front door and there's the smell of food in the oven and the table laid nicely and Dad hides the scrunched up fish and chip paper behind his back and she's 'gone to all this trouble for nothing.'

Her and Dad go out and sit in the car and Mum's behind the wheel and Robert and me spy from the upstairs window and watch their mouths moving really fast like they're in a silent film.

It's already Tuesday and Mum's turn to take me to see Jaws. Her and Dad haven't spoken since last time I went. Dad says it's another Cold War.

Mum's late and has to quickly stop off and do a hundred things on the way. I wait in the car and my tummy is snakier than last week.

We're running later now and she gets us lost and expects me to find it from going last week but I'd been singing and changing gear plus Dad knows his way round town from the days when he was a boy and helped out the milkman in return for milk.

Whenever we go round town he can tell me what some of the buildings used to be or what was there before that building was there even. Or he'll pretend to look dreamy and say, 'I remember when all this was just fields.'

He especially likes saying that when we're way out of town and there are just fields.

Mum is from a big city up north but Dad's always lived here and says he always will. Mum makes a face when he's sentimental about where we live. She calls our town Snoresville.

It's raining and I'm sitting in the back and Mum won't look at me in the mirror but her face is stiffer. People always look more serious or sad when they think nobody's looking, but tougher when they think they're being looked at but are pretending they don't know. A spy knows these things.

Mum is talking and I'm watching the raindrops going horizontal on my window. The faster the car goes the faster and more backwards the raindrops go, except sometimes the wind blows and they sort of go flat and wriggle against the glass and don't move.

I'm sniffing the plastic cover over my bandaged scarred for life hand and Mum asks me why I think we're going to the psychologist. I used to have a plastic cover over my mattress too when I was young and bedwetted.

I shrug.

'Did Dad have a chat to you on the way to Mr Gale last week?'

'Not really.'

She goes quiet for a minute.

'He didn't say anything about me and Robert?'

'No.'

More quietness. Then she's going on about how Mr Gale is a special man who can help me because I upset them when I burnt myself like that, and that they can't have a son who hurts himself, not with all the pain already in the world. 'What would the world come to if little boys went round hurting themselves all the time?'

'Why doesn't Robert and his parents see a special man instead?'

She takes a deep breath. 'Robert isn't the one who burnt his hand,' then before I can say it she says 'I know, I know, it was an accident. But Robert needs our help, full stop. And that doesn't mean your dad and I don't love you to bits.' She changes gear quite hard and not very well. 'I'm looking forward to you finally getting used to foster boys being here. You happen to be in a good family which makes a difference to the world, rather than being a normal family that only thinks about itself. We aren't a normal family, Sonny Jim. Count yourself lucky you were born where you were.'

I don't like it when she calls me Sonny Jim. It's Dad's line. It sounds different in his mouth.

'Right?'

I nod. 'Right.' I hold my robot and look at the rain bouncing up off the road like really hot oil in the frying pan.

There are a lot of people running around the streets and I pretend I'm in a big truck and going through the puddles on purpose, sending enormous waves coming up and washing them all away and knocking the buildings down into rubble and the electricity in them sparking and catching fire and black smoke everywhere.

I wonder how much is in my rain collector.

There are lots of people out there and some of them have their coats sort of off but up over their heads to cover them from the rain, like when criminals leave court on TV and they don't want to be recognised.

We get to Mr Gale's place and I run ahead while Mum locks the car, a plastic bag over her hair from the rain. I push Mr Gale's door buzzer and there's just the sound of it buzzing, a bit like when the old men who play cards near the supermarket clear snot out of their noses. Mum always gags when they do that. She's scared of throwing up. I can make her freak out just by putting my fingers in and tickling the button in my throat. It's my secret weapon. Even if I only pretend to feel sick she starts being nicer to me.

We wait and Mum does her hair and I can feel the snake big and thick and hissy in me. Then the door clicks and Mum quickly says 'I love you' just before Jaws opens it and smiles with his metal and shakes my hand while he looks at Mum. His hand isn't warm and is quite small for a man hand. I don't like men with small hands.

'How's your burn?' he says. 'Healing nicely?'

He can probably read my mind like God and Grandma. I nod and try not to think anything he wouldn't like.

He asks me to wait in the waiting room and I can't stop looking at his braces when he talks. Sometimes my lips move when people speak to me, like our mouths are connected. I know that cos Dad gets the giggles at me and messes up my hair.

Jaws takes her away with an arm on the middle of her back and I sit with my robot in my lap. I shut my eyes and pretend I'm at home. Then I get to thinking Jaws is ripping into Mum with his metal teeth, tugging at her like she's one of those chewy bars that get all stringy and won't let go. Meanwhile she's sort of stroking his hair and loving being eaten.

I sit still and try not to think, like my robot. I need the toilet.

When they come back Mum is ok and there's no blood in Mr Gale's teeth but I still feel like I'm going to pee myself. Plus Mum has this face on and Mr Gale is watching behind her like he knows exactly what she's going to say and what is going to happen and I feel like that big social worker is next door ready to take me away. Mr Gale is eating me with his eyes.

'Where are you going, Mum?'

I'm sitting here feeling like Alice when she got shrunked. I get off my seat and fall for an hour before my feet hit the ground. I hang on tight to Mum.

She looks at Mr Gale and he nods. They have a secret about me. She holds me away a bit saying what I can and can't touch like last week but I'm just leaning into her and pushing my robot up against my bladder and I want her to take me to the toilet so we can get away from Jaws, just for a minute, so I can talk to her and have a hug. Just for a minute.

'I'll only be next door,' she says and her eyes are a bit wet because she's saying goodbye. I'm never going to see her again. I'm too bad, and now my hand is scarred for life she doesn't want me anymore. She wants Robert.

I hold on to her but she pushes me into the room and closes the door.

'Just for a few minutes,' she says from through the big tall wood with her voice wobbling. I try the handle but it's locked.

'Mum, my robot! MUM!' I let go of helping my doodle with all its wee so I can bang on the door. My robot is all alone out there and I'm in here with the python. It's getting thicker in me, like it's working out its body. Tensing it. Ready to come up out of my tummy and swallow me from inside. I turn and look at the toys up at this nice colourful end, then at all the stiff things in the posh working end.

I don't know how long it is before Mum and Jaws come rushing in shouting. I stop what I'm doing and run away into the wendy house. They can't get me in here. I shut my eyes so it's dark like the lion's den. I'm panting from doing those things and my trousers are all warm and smell like the fish and chip shop counter. Plus my scarred for life hand hurts from being used. I'm all curled up small in the wendy house and Mum's shouting. They're definitely going to send me away.

Now I'm in a towel from Jaws's bathroom. A big towel. Mum is out in the waiting room, steam coming out of her ears probably. She has my wet clothes but the wee is still on his desk, and all the torn pages and broken books. I love that. It's like with the spot of blood on the loop the loop at home. I love that too. Some things that maybe shouldn't be nice are nice. And some things that should be, aren't. I blame the snake.

Mr Gale has his hands like a newsreader but he's not at his desk. He seems to be thinking very hard like he needs a poo. His lips have disappeared.

'What d'you think we should do about the damage you've done to my office today?' he says.

'Are you going to send me to live with another family?'

His eyebrows go up which makes the skin on his forehead look like the sand after the sea has gone out. I wriggle in my seat.

He opens his mouth to speak and his braces have a tiny bit of lunch in them. 'Why do you think that would happen? What makes you think something like that?'

I shrug and look at his shoes. 'You have shiny shoes.'

'Yes,' he says, looking down at them as if he forgot all about his feet. 'One of my favourite jobs actually, I —'

'Maybe you could do that job instead of this one then?'

'What, shine shoes?' He laughs a bit then stops quickly like he wasn't really laughing in the first place. 'I don't think the pay would be as good. But I do feel very calm when I'm shining them. Is there anything that makes you feel calm?'

I shrug. Three Lips Macavoy would put the moves on him. 'My lion's den.'

'Where's your lion's den?'

'You get to it through my sleeping bag.'

He smiles. 'Tell me, how d'you think your dad is feeling at the moment, about having Robert stay?'

I can see the ceiling fan going round and round in his shiny shoes. He switched it on to get rid of the vinegar smell but pretended it was just because he was hot.

'I dunno. Dad likes it probably. But not as much as Mum.'

'Oh?'

I look at him.

'Your mum likes having Robert to stay, then?'

'Loves it.'

'How much out of ten?' he says, and his mouth stays open like my answer is a biscuit.

'More than nine.'

'More than nine?'

'Can I have my robot?'

'In a minute, you'll be going home soon. But why not ten, if it's more than nine, why not ten? What's missing from it being ten for your mum, having Robert staying with you?'

I sigh and look at the fan. If you make your eyes follow it you can actually sometimes see the blade instead of the blurry whirring. I like that.

'She loves it 9 point 9999567 out of ten.'

'That's very precise.' He licks his lips and fidgets, leans in closer. 'So what's that little bit missing? Is that the part of her that maybe suffers a bit too? Like you are?'

'Can I go now, please?' I'm thinking of things to do while I'm shut in my room for the next 300 years.

'Just a couple more minutes. This is important. You know you're here because Mum and Dad are worried about you? You're going through an awkward time. That's why you burnt your hand and did all this to my office. But you don't need to be struggling. It's not fair on a little boy to be struggling.'

I shrug.

'So why not ten out of ten? What's missing for your mum.'

I show him my bandage.

'You think that's the bit missing, that you hurt yourself? You *do*? Ok. Anything else?'

He's leaning in really, really close now with his mouth open again and some yellowy fur goo on his tongue and one of his eyes has something sort of clear yellow growing on the white bit, and there's still food in his braces. People look better from a distance.

'Nothing else? You don't think she finds it hard to foster boys *and* have a son *and* a husband, and do all of those things all at once?'

'It's Michael's fault.'

'Who's Michael?'

'I want to go now please, Mr Gale. I'm sorry about your office.'

He sighs and I can smell the tongue fur. He writes something on a pad of paper. 'I know you do. Thank you for apologising. It's ok. They're just things. But are you telling me you think the bit missing that makes it nine point, lots of numbers, not ten for your mum, d'you think deep down you might think that missing bit is you? That it's your fault? It isn't your fault, mind you. But I wonder if maybe you've decided it is your fault.'

'Why do you have metal on your teeth?'

'To make them prettier. Did you hear what I said?'

I nod but I'm thinking his teeth look much uglier than teeth without metal. He sighs and I panic maybe he can read my mind for real.

'And how do you feel about everything at home? Because that's important isn't it — how you feel?'

I shrug.

He licks his lips really fast. 'Do you know what I think?'

He asks a lot of silly questions. I shrug.

'I think a special little boy like you who's burnt his hand and done these things to my office is expressing something sad. I think little boys who do things like you've done are having lots of feelings which aren't their fault. They just need a bit more looking after. Feelings are hard. I don't think what you've done to my office is your fault. I think it's a bad thing to do, don't misunderstand me. I think what you've done is a little bit bad, but it certainly doesn't mean you're a bad boy. That's important to remember. Do you think you can remember that? Good. And do you know what else?'

I'm looking at his carpet. I shrug.

'I think it's very sad but children are sometimes the only ones brave enough to show the feelings that are really going on at home. Like a barometer. You know what one of those is? *Course you do*, clever kid like you. So you're very brave, you see? Not bad. *Look at me. You aren't bad.* You might do bad things sometimes, like all children, and grown-ups. But your mummy and daddy still love you very much.'

I nod but with my eyes still locked on to the same spot on the carpet, like my eyesight has been glued there and they're going to have to cut the piece out to get me home.

'No doubt they're fond of Robert,' he's saying, 'but they love you much more than they love him — what. What did that face mean?'

I shrug.

7

'Yes, it is,' I say, looking out the window at the weather Mum's pointed at. She's trying to spread her toast but the toast isn't toasted enough and her knife is tearing the bread.

'Here, take this one, it's already spread.'

She looks at me, her knife still going, spreading the butter on the mount of Venus on her palm, the part that's supposedly commensurate with your libido, your tenderness. She looks down at her buttered hand like someone did it to her, brings it up to her face and licks at it while the knife butters her hair.

I look at my own mount of Venus and the burn scar across it — push my chair away. She watches me go to the sink and wring out the dank rag. I come back and wipe the butter from her hand and she lets me, her face concerned. The butter is on the rag now and in between my fingers, and the rag stinks so much that our hands need cleaning.

Her face is impassive but there's a watchfulness in her eyes. She's still in there somewhere underneath all that dying. I can see it. Feel it. And it's this bit that I want to get at. To help. Even if it's also all that's left of the woman I blame.

'I need …' she says. 'We …' She stands up.

If that black walnut is in one easily recognisable part of her head it's the part that speaks. She's always missing the key word in a sentence, never the contextual. It isn't grammar she's lost, but the things in life. The important words, names of people she's supposed to have loved, the things she needs.

'The ...' Her mouth open, a finger pointing to the cupboard door. 'Need to ...' She stops, her body folding back into the chair and slumping those dejected few inches further. She shakes her tumour.

'Talk around it, Mum. If you can't find the one word just talk around it, like they said.' She's frowning at herself but pointing at the cloth. 'Clean? You want to clean the cupboard?'

If this were a game show, I just won the steak knives.

I look at the cupboard door and sigh. I don't want to spend the today part of my life cleaning a larder. Although, in the not-too-distant future I'll be emptying it alone. Selling up my childhood. Flying back to my safe little life. One ticket. One way.

'Ok, Mum.'

As I'm finishing the washing-up she comes back with a little toothpaste on her chin and a look on her face like she gave herself a pep-think in the bathroom and she's ready for action. She grins at me and opens today's day on her tablet box, a letter on it denoting each day of the week. I fill a glass for her and she makes a show of taking her medication.

'Ok,' she says. 'Clean!' And marches into the larder, starts coming out with cherries in syrup and glass jars of dried lentils; rusty-bottomed tins, her slippers shuffling across the floor, everything teetering in her grip. She sets them on the table and smiles at me, her eyes twinkling.

'What are we doing then, Mum?' She comes out with another armful of stuff. 'Do you have to put them down *there*?'

She looks at me but deposits them on the table and a can of something rolls off and lands on the floor, doesn't move, the resultant dent holding it still. She grins and vanishes back into the larder again, trying to sing a tune but the words won't come.

'Mum.' Deep breaths. 'If you don't tell me what you're doing I can't help, can I.'

She points at the buttery rag next to the dripping tap and I go get it.

'You want to clean the shelves?'

She shakes her head then disappears back in. I move closer and turn on the light, lean on the wall and fold my arms. She comes out with cereals in Tupperware, old biscuit tins.

I'm trying for nonchalance. Patience. I'm trying for What does it matter?

'You can't throw this stuff away yet. What are you going to eat every day, *ice-cream?*'

'No ...' She has a longer sentence but leaves it hanging in the air along with all her other unfinished sentences. Along with everything else unsaid. Whatever she was going to say next was left behind in a kidney dish in the operating theatre. Incinerated. That sentence might be soot now in the big chimney rising out of the hospital. Or in the air as dust — a thought that makes me think of a raindrop.

She pulls me over to the table where all the packets of flour and spices and tins and pulses are sitting.

I pick up a little herb jar of rosemary and look at it. 'Rosemary. What, you've got something against rosemary suddenly? You're throwing it out?'

I just won the car. She comes skittering back with an empty black bin liner.

She's worse today. The insistent unrelenting cancer growing and growing in that tiny space between her skull and brain. Like she's trapped in a prison cell with an inflating bouncy castle. The air compressor running all the time, more air coming in. Her body pressed up against the wall, her ribcage squashed so that she can't breathe properly. Can't talk properly. She's slowly being squeezed out of her own inner world, the steroids all she's got against the onslaught but the dosage can only go so high.

She's running out of runway in there and we're cleaning out the larder.

Deck chairs — Titanic.

'Best before ... wow!' I say, looking at the rosemary. 'This is *ancient!*'

I just won the holiday, Mum grinning at me. I pick up the cumin. 'Bugger me, Mum! You can't even make out the best-before date on this anymore.'

She's giggling but without making a sound, her hand covering part of her mouth, her cardigan off one shoulder.

'And these cherries went off *eight years ago*! They look like red raisins.'

She's hobbled by laughter and I'm starting to catch a little of it. I pick up the flour. 'Can flour *even go off?*' She has her legs together and her hands in the prayer position wedged between them like she needs the toilet but I think she's just laughing, her body shaking soundlessly, waiting for the verdict. 'Five years ago! *Five.* FLOUR! How can flour go off!'

I pick up the packet of falafel mix but I don't tell her the date, I'm just laughing. Really laughing, so that this must be some kind of release and she's letting it out but the tears are running too. She sort of skips into the larder, comes back with other things in her arms, spilling icing sugar on the floor as she goes. Meanwhile I'm going through the dates, announcing them like vintage wines or train times or gym comp. scores. Both of us laughing, a bubble of relief rising up now because perhaps there's still time for Mum and me.

'Are there antique-food dealers?' I say and a snort comes out from the larder.

I put the radio on and it's some ABBA half-hour, reminding me of sitting at the table, Mum cooking my lunch. The daytimes we had to ourselves while some belligerent foster boy was at school, Dad away at work totting up numbers for clients. Balancing the books.

She's humming tunefully along now, a few of the lyrics coming easily out of her for some reason, and me joining in tunelessly, under my breath.

We bag up the stuff, throwing out things that may have been on these shelves when Dad was here. Things which perhaps sat and looked at him as he went into the larder and did that Dad thing — standing with glazed-over eyes and calling out, 'Where, love? Where did you say you were hiding it?' And she'd go in and find it without looking, the way he'd looked for it without looking.

I'm laughing along with her but the sadness is coming behind it too because we're throwing away all that history — sending it out the house in a plain black bag. A thought that stops me, makes me look at Mum and her hive of activity. The way she's coming in and out the larder, laughing, smiling, singing, the table filling up with old, faded, out-of-date packaging. Mum stopping to try and make a comment but having to go away again.

It all comes to a black bag in the end.

A DJ starts chatting, a fake smile tainting his voice. I turn the radio down and Mum unloads more stuff, a wet patch at her crotch, which drops me that inch that sadness drops you.

I'm stood here wondering what the rest of the world is doing now. Cars spewing up and down roads and I feel like nobody out there is understanding or living like Mum and I are. That's how it feels to me anyway. It feels like right now, in this moment, only that fragile Mum-type lady and me are really with life. We're the only ones where life is fully hitting home. This being one of those moments when you can feel the record light flashing in the top left-hand corner of your life.

She shuffles out of the larder, holding porridge oats.

'Come 'ere,' I say and pull her to me, the porridge packet digging into us. I wrap my arms around her and we're there for a second but she laughs and pulls away, goes and sits in a chair and just like that, she's sad and quiet.

Just like that she's through laughing and out into sadness, changing quickly down through the emotional gears. Just the way Robert always did after his accident. The way he could be grinning but with his eyelashes still wet from crying.

Now she's sobbing, holding the porridge like a hot water bottle and I'm asking her what's up, even if my feet are planted on the spot rather than going to comfort her. Her face asking me how this happened. Her tears showing me that she sees it finally, what these best-before dates signify. That she's lost control. She's getting left behind. Running to keep up but life is moving on without her.

Everything is going to go on without her. Even I am going to have to go on without her.

'It's ok, we're setting it straight, Mum.' I turn to the table of things, wanting to meet her eyes but failing. 'Look,' I say, picking up a box of instant mash, 'this is only three months out of date, can't throw that out for at least a decade.'

There's a smile for a moment but it has tears running over it. She licks her lips and one of those tears goes inside her. Icing sugar and flour on her cardigan. Me standing here fidgeting in the mixture of messes on the floor.

She's not the only one pressed up against the wall by her illness.

The doorbell goes and I stumble away through the house, running a hand along the corridor walls. I peek through the security eyelet and it's Mandy, the social worker — older, but there she is. She was forever in and out of our house, the conduit between our family and the foster-care system. Plus there's a man behind her, about my age, maybe older, holding a big bunch of flowers.

I look down at my clothes, raising a hand to brush the antique food off but it's a lost cause. I open the door and they bustle in with their happy rhetoric.

'Hello, how are you, this is Marcus. You remember Marcus!'

I remember Marcus. I spent two hours up a tree because of Marcus. Angry Marcus who liked to put pins facing up out of my bedroom carpet.

'How's your mum?' she says, all earnest and serious.

I lead them through the house rather than stand here being looked at. 'We're just clearing out the larder, actually. Most of the food's from the Jurassic era.'

'Oh well, you can still eat that for years yet!' Mandy says and Marcus adds some quip but I don't catch it.

Mum's still in the chair clutching the porridge when we come in, her eyes lost to something out the window, far away.

'I'll leave you guys to catch up,' I tell them, unable to watch Mum fail to navigate the clear discrepancy between what she was and what she's capable of now. These people knew her when she was that strong, forthright woman. Now look at her, whittled down to almost nothing. Threadbare.

I shut the front door behind me and march up the hill, hell-bent on cigarettes. Enough is enough, this isn't the time for martyrdom. Even the condemned get their smokes and their phone call.

The cloud is low but intermittent, the sun peeking through, the light changing every few seconds and the temperature making me lament the absence of a coat. Just a t-shirt with flour all over it. I look like a cocaine addict who sneezed.

Coming back out of the shop I put the change in my pocket and a cigarette in my mouth, take out a match. But now I'm finally about to give in, my mouth full of expectant saliva, I don't need it so badly. So much of temptation is about the giving in rather than the actual pay-off once you've weakened. We just like to weaken.

By the time I get back, Mandy and Marcus are shutting the door, grave expressions on their faces that are quickly discarded when they see me, the cigarette still in my mouth, still unlit.

'Forget your lighter?' Marcus says, all smiles.

'Must have left it up a tree,' I say then turn to Mandy, sensing Marcus dropping his face for a moment.

'Tell me,' Mandy says, 'what have the doctors said? What treatment's Mary having?'

'She's had all the treatment, I'm afraid. Now it's just —'

'The poor love. Just *awful.*' She sucks air in over her teeth. 'Listen, I'll stop by again. In the meantime you take care of *both* of you.' And she's tottering up the garden, the overgrown hedges forcing her from the path. She can't get away fast enough.

I ignore Marcus' retreating face and go and stand on the doorstep, the light going out now as the clouds win the tussle — Marcus shutting the gate behind him then giving me a last needy look like I'm his long-lost brother rather than a kid in a foster home he terrorised.

So many people have kids they can't cope with. Kids who then get deposited in other people's families. Sometimes it's not the parents' fault. Sometimes life is too much. But sometimes it's not like that. Like Robert's parents, the worst of all cuckoos, the way they left their offspring to be raised in the nest of another. And we know what happens to the offspring whose nest a cuckoo chick ends up in.

I put the cigarette back in my mouth, reconnecting with a grim, old friend, a match in my hand ready. It's amazing what a context can do, the way it can invite you effortlessly back into old feelings — old personas. This old anger and resentment, this old smoking habit. I look at the match, me stood on the doorstep between what I have to face indoors and the rain threatening out here. A car going up the hill with its lights on already. Daytime darkness.

There's bad weather coming. I can feel it. Rain forecast and nothing but old habits for company.

8

I thought I'd be in the biggest kennel but Mum and Dad went and steamed up the car for hours and the next day I got my own TV instead of having to go and see Mr Jaws Gale ever again.

My OWN telly. In my room! Robert doesn't have a TV and he isn't allowed in my bedroom under any circumstances, unless I let him which would be nice if I did. Dad said so.

'Your home is broken, Robert, which is why you're here and why you don't have a TV in your room. Once your home is fixed you might have a TV in your room too.'

Sometimes I sit and watch it even when I'd rather be outside or downstairs or something, just because it's nice to have one and nice that Robert doesn't.

I hear him when I'm in my room, my TV on but the sound down and me listening to the bubbling of their voices coming up. Robert is all little when I'm around but I hear a whole lot of him when I'm not. Plus Mum and Dad always sound happy when he's chatty as if it means they're special. Like it's their fault he's talking.

I got the TV though.

He gets good marks at his new school now since he's been borrowing my parents. Mum says his grades are going up and

I should let him help me out, that he won't be here forever and I should take advantage of his brain while I can. She always says that to me. 'He won't be here forever.' Sometimes that makes me feel better for a little bit. Except it already feels like forever.

Plus Robert is always good, not like the usual foster boys. His only weakness is he eats too fast. Dad hates the food competition, he says. But he told me once that actually Robert eats like that because he never used to know where his next meal was coming from.

They don't tell him off about his manners either, they just let him pig out. Meanwhile I get told off all the time. 'Elbows off the table. Don't post it. Chew properly. Cut don't tear.'

They say Robert just has to get it out of his system but when I try that line it never works.

The only thing Robert gets kind of in trouble for is that Mum and Dad keep finding things hidden in his room. Food normally but also yucky things like rubbish, banana skins, empty crisp packets, and lots of Mum's cotton wool that she uses to take off her make-up with. Even her perfume and dirty clothes. Knickers!

A lot of Mum's things but mainly food. Mum checks his room every few days and if he hasn't hidden anything he gets a prize. I don't hide things and I don't get a prize, except sometimes, sometimes she gives me a prize too. She does.

Robert stayed late at school for something today so I'm on my own in the back of the car on the way to get him, turning my robot into a monster and wondering what's coming because I had to wait in class today while Mum and Miss Marshall had a chat without me. Which means about me.

Mum says my name in that sort of way which sounds like something's coming. I look out the window then quickly start turning my monster back. Robots don't feel anything. Like Roberts maybe.

'Yes,' I say to her while I'm looking at a man who's hitting his dog beside the traffic lights and the dog can't hit back. It's just squishing itself closer to the pavement and sort of licking the front of its lips really slowly and crouching down.

'Miss Marshall had a word with me at school today, Sonny Jim.'

A robot doesn't feel anything and is superhuman but monsters have feelings, like King Kong who fell in love with a woman even though she was too small for him.

'When's your birthday?' she says.

I stop changing the Transformer for a moment because my scarred for life hand is sore. I only just had the bandages off and the doctor said it all depends on how the scar responds to my hand growing. Plus I thought this chat was going to be about what I did to Simon during English.

I answer her and keep holding the robot, flipping its legs round. From green and blue to blue and green. Nearly there, I go faster. I used to time myself changing from the robot to the monster and my record is 42 seconds but that was when I had the flu and I was only just 7. I'm slower now though probably, with my hurting hand.

'And where was I when you were being born, hmm?'

I sit the robot in my lap and hold on to him. My burn is singing a stinging hot chilli song.

'Can you sit up?' she says. 'In fact move to the other seat so I can see you.'

I do what she says a little bit so she can probably only see the top of my school cap which I pull down. She reaches round and touches my knee, then comes back to change gear. Not a bad gear change, for a woman.

'Where was Mummy when you were being born?'

'In hospital.'

'The same hospital as you were born in?'

She's gone doolally. I nod.

'Yes. So you came out of me?'

'Yeeessss.'

'And Daddy was who got me pregnant?'

I giggle and she looks round and grins at me. When she turns back her face goes stiff.

'So why did you say you were fostered today, in class?'

I shrug then smile at my robot, a bit of the beetroots making my face feel like my hand.

'Robert's fostered, lovey. He was born to different people and we —'

'I know.'

'We've got him only until his parents can straighten everything out in their lives. Some people struggle more than —'

'I know I know I know I KNOW.'

I'm breathing fast and the snake is thick inside.

'Alright, alright. So you can't be a foster kid unless something happens to Mummy and Daddy and you have to go live with other people but you know we've made arrangements for if that happens. Not that it's likely at all.'

I think I'd rather go live with the real Jaws than be brung up by Auntie Deadly. When she hugs me my face gets wedged into her enormous fun bags. Dad is a big fan of fun bags but he says Auntie Deadly would have to lift her frock to show off hers.

She's old now and actually my mum's auntie. My great aunt. Only she's not great, she's crap.

She had a big fall once and Dad says she probably just tripped over her tits.

Mum's ones are quite small but that doesn't matter, we're all the same underneath. Except me. She's talking about foster parenting again and how it's our duty to play a part in the whole world and not just our bit of world and I've heard it heard it heard it heard it and me and my robot are looking out the window and forgetting to speak instead of nod so that she always makes us repeat our nodding in words. The robot is answering for me. I'm not here.

'But can you see how it would hurt our feelings then to have you say that in class? Can you see how I'd be worried about you thinking that?' Then she says 'I love you, you know, silly head.' But only to stop me embarrassing her at school again.

We're late for Robert cos of me which I don't mind. Whenever we get to his school I always try and be the first one to spot him before he sees us and before Mum sees him, which is pretty easy cos he doesn't have a school uniform and everyone else does. This is his new school while he's with us and Social Services haven't coughed up the money for uniform yet. Mum hates that part, the getting money out of them. Meanwhile Robert just wears a white shirt and trousers until they buy him a uniform. We can't even get him a haircut without permission.

Today I see Robert first. He's not sitting in one of his usual spots reading, but standing with his arms round himself and shivering.

'Robert's all wet, Mum.'

When he sees us he leans down and picks up his bag and walks slowly over.

'What's happened to the poor love?' she says and unbuckles herself, puts on the handbrake and opens the door all at the same time. She rushes over and I watch their faces and mouths like it's a film on TV somewhere where the sound's turned down. Like the fish and chip shop. Or my TV.

Robert doesn't say hardly anything and his hair looks blacker and all stuck to him, same as his trousers and shirt. You can see his nipples!

Mum takes his bag and goes to put a hand on his shoulder but he throws his arms around her.

'You're getting her wet, Robert! ROBERT!' They can't hear me with the windows up.

They come over together and he gets in and just gives me a look, doesn't say hello. Normally he says a little hello. Tiny. And Mum always says 'Say hello to Robert then' before I can get a word out.

She gets in and keeps looking in the mirror at him while she puts her belt on and the car in gear. The indicator is going and she noses out into traffic and I'm watching Robert looking out at the streets.

Sometimes when we pass something dark I see his reflection in the window for a second, like a sad ghost hovering along the road with us, just outside the car.

'Please tell me why you're wet, Robert?' She says it in her extra special Robert voice. Peanut butter and honey. He's looking down at his trousers, his hands in bad fists.

'Why are you wet, Robert?' I say. 'Did you fall in the pool? It hasn't been raining since Tuesday. Nine millimetres.'

He shakes his head without looking at anyone. 'It's nothing.' We pass a dark parked car and the ghost is crying.

'They been picking on you again?' Mum says and the car slows down a bit as if it's waiting for the answer too.

He wipes his eyes with his wet sleeve.

'Let's just get you home shall we, poppet? Anything you want for tea tonight. Anything at all. Ice-cream soup if you want, eh!?' And she's leaning in closer to the rear-view mirror to smile at him into it even though that takes her further away from him. She's got wet in her eyes.

'How come he gets to choose dinner just cos he cried!'

'Shut it, mister, or you'll be having no dinner at all. Robert's had a bad day.'

He wipes his eyes again with his wet sleeve.

'Use my sleeve, Robert, it's dry.' And I hold out my arm to him but he just gives me a wet smile and turns back to sniff at the sad ghost.

9

I bag up the hedge I've trimmed. There's still some left to cut but it can wait till later. There's only so much hedge you can cut. Only so much Dad you can bag up ready to burn on an evening fire — smoke hovering in the cooling air, splitting sunlight into rays.

While Mum is upstairs assembling some clashing clothing ensemble, I seek out where she's hidden her plastic tablet container. Finding it, eventually, slipped beside the microwave along with the old takeaway menus — Dad having circled things she'd have called out to him on some Sunday night while she bathed Robert or struggled him to bed. Me out stewing in my adolescent funk.

I open today's door and there's the tablets unswallowed so I'm marching towards the stairs with them but stop myself. Why take them? And why get your hair cut, which is point a) of today's exciting agenda. Why not just lay yourself down to die. It's amazing that any of us go on with our lives when you consider the odds.

She comes down looking remotely presentable in a floral dress and blue cardigan, her stomach muscles forgotten, her outfit straining to hold her girth.

Of course she's going on in the face of death. Just like she went on fostering in the face of what it was doing to me.

I lock up and we get into her faded orange Volvo, back it out of the faded blue garage, ready to take her off on her highly important errands when actually we should be picking out gravestones, choosing hymns and saying everything we need to say.

But I'm not saying those things. I'm sitting in her car now, parked and waiting up the way from the beauty place while she's in there de-Frankensteining herself.

The dashboard clock buzzes gently, the second hand sweeping continuously around the face. I remember when that was something to marvel at — not ticking but sweeping.

I get out of the car and pace up and down, smoke a cigarette, kick a tyre. Hands in pockets. Hands out of pockets. Scuffing bits of gravel under my shoes. Pissed off that I'm smoking again, as if it's some sign of the other old weaknesses I'm losing the fight against.

I get back into the car — this being the model after the one I locked her out of. There's Robert's ballpoint scribble on the roof interior. This being the car they used to strap him into after what happened. Strapping him in and taking him to swimming or physiotherapy. To the doctor's. Not that measured, thoughtful Robert, but broken Robert.

A couple of old women come out of the beauty parlour with this look of sadness and sympathy on their faces and I know it's about Mum. They're doddering up the pavement towards me, obviously talking to one another about the gravity of what was inside the beauty parlour, a sort of forced sympathy on their faces. They aren't good people but people *being* good people. There's no such thing as a good or bad person, there are just people who do good or bad things. And we can swap, like that.

I sneer at them as they get close with their shaking heads and faces of solemnity. They're only thinking of themselves. There's no such thing as genuine sympathy. There's only empathy. Only with a seed of ourselves can we feel for somebody else. Just watch what a man does when he sees another man kicked in the balls.

Is that sympathy?

Working in prisons finished off whatever faith I had left. Seeing what happens to a person and their supposed goodness when they have their backs to the wall, even the low-security inmates. But mostly it's about what happens to the prison guards. Even the good, kindly men who joined us. How succinctly power corrupts. You don't know who anyone is until you've seen them with power or powerlessness.

I get out the car and slam the door, give the geriatrics a menacing grin and they accelerate quickly away, linking arms and looking back to see what I'll do.

'Morning, *ladies*.'

Suddenly they're not so slow on their feet. I stare at them all the way, even after they've stopped looking back.

Another cigarette.

A few years after Robert's accident I was in town and saw him out with The Sunshiners, the organisation that took him every other Saturday, shoe-horning some religion in along with their compassion.

Those Saturdays were supposed to be a respite for us but the house always felt sad and brittle without him. All of us feeling guilty for being relieved of the burden, but uncertain somehow about what to do with ourselves in his absence. Like it was a guilty pleasure. That's what living with Robert was, his absence like the ringing in your ears after a rock concert. The way he had of being there even more when he wasn't.

I was probably about fourteen that day, walking in town with a freshly purchased album in my hands. I saw The Sunshiners on the other side of the road. There was Robert out and about in a wheelchair, surrounded by his retarded friends, all of them filling the street with their happy madness. I stood and watched from a distance, feeling like I was seeing Robert in a different light, perhaps how others saw him. And I was savouring the sensation of that somehow, because he didn't look tragic or wronged for once. He looked happy.

Then this bloke left their side of the road and crossed over, our eyes meeting in some implicit acknowledgement of the gaggle of kids. 'Where's a shotgun when you need one,' he said and grinned at me as if we shared an opinion.

I look down at my cigarette. I've always thought back to that bloke and his comment, wishing I'd stood up for Robert rather than turning the comment against myself.

I had to watch Robert go through puberty in that state, stubble on his face — our little volcano of humanity, so distorted and yet all the more human for that somehow. All the emotion and life in him still, but shuffled into an incomprehensible jumble.

Jumbled up as he was, he could still touch you like no person has ever touched me. Always such candour in the way he reached out to stroke your face, his eyes full of tears. The same candour Mum expresses her emotions with now, so that you can't help but be swept along with them.

I shuffle away from the car and come back and lift my foot, rest it on the side mirror, pushing it on the cabled joint that allows the mirror to absorb an impact instead of smashing. I adjust my balance and move the mirror to its full extent, then try for a little further. The cable creaks. I push a little harder, daring myself.

I let it go and it snaps back.

I lean against the car, feeling the fender bowing a little behind me. This car will have to be sold once she's gone. Everything from the day-to-day is going to have to go.

I stub out the cigarette, fold my arms. All the talismans of my childhood will have to be sold up and gone and I don't know what lies beyond that. Because if your home and your family are taken away from you, what tethers you to life then?

Robert had to face that at thirteen.

A train's coming, the familiar sound of scratching steel. Now I can see it, carrying a smattering of passengers and a ton of graffiti. It thunders across the metal bridge, little brown stains where the rainwater rusts the rivets, the sun coming from behind a cloud and blinding everything, the beauty shop standing out with its two pink awnings down over the windows like made-up eyelids. The train heading away again and suburban silence swallowing its sound.

Here she comes, helped out of the shop by a bleached blonde who's looking up and down the street until she sees me, then relaxes and waves. I don't wave but I do traipse a little closer to Mum as she approaches the road, stopping to turn and wave goodbye to the blonde who takes her hand quickly from where it's been hovering, concerned at her mouth, probably wondering if this is the last time.

Mum has a side road to cross before she can continue up the hill to where I'm parked. She stumbles a bit down the kerb, then lifts herself upright as if dignity is to be found in the higher climes. Especially now that what hair she has is tinted, cut and blow-dried. She seems fluffed up in herself too, more plentiful. A wry smile on her face, all of her emanating this self-satisfied aura. Feeling like she just struck a blow against the monster gorging on her.

I relax my hands, little red crescents left behind on my palms. She looks tiny out there in the middle of the road and yet she's that shape of my childhood.

I move to her door and unlock it. Here comes my mum, soft and fragile now in her illness. I stand straighter too, the door open and ready for her like I'm a private in the army. Here comes the general. Standing up even to cancer — a car hurrying towards the junction she's crossing. I leave the open door and head down there, looking from the oncoming car to my beaming mum — a porcelain woman surrounded by metal and tarmac.

The approaching car brakes reluctantly for Mum and she stops to take it in, confused. The car halting just shy of her and hooting a sharp impatient blast that sends her stumbling over, another train clacking across the bridge and I'm marching down the hill, our car door still open behind me.

Now I'm jogging.

Running.

Mum on her hands and knees in the road, her handbag spilling contents, a scrunched tissue rolling away in the breeze, the receipt from the beauty parlour still in her hand, her red face looking up, a hand out towards me. The road sharp on her bare knees. I'm sprinting, my vision narrowed to the door handle on the guilty car still sat there shining in the road, its engine growling. My head full of breathing. I leap over Mum, the car driver's hand locking the door but realising his window is down, his face whitening and I'm shouting as incomprehensibly as Mum, down there on the tarmac. The driver crunching the gears towards reverse, the engine revving and I'm running with the reversing car now, pulling at his door, roaring, running full speed until he is too fast and away, my hands going to my pockets for coins to throw at him then boom.

I catch up with him and the parked car he's backed into, the blonde coming out the parlour and screaming something, the driver covering his face because I lunge in through the window and he's so pathetic now I've punctured his safe little car-world. The feel of my knuckles on his face. That sound bone makes. That thunk. The feel of the python. The driver falling into the passenger seat, lying over the handbrake and all caught up in his seatbelt, his hands covering his face, music coming from his stereo, rosary beads swinging from the rear-view mirror. My top half in through his window like a lion at a safari park. My swinging arm going through the rosary and splitting it, the rear-view mirror coming unstuck from the windscreen and clattering on the gearstick. I'm flinging the beads at him and shouting, picking them off the seat and trying to stuff them into his fucking mouth. He bites down on me, wet and painful. I hold his face and his biting mouth, bang his head back into the other door, blood on his face and I'm pummelling him again — bad punches, my elbow glancing the interior ceiling of the car, taking the power out of the swing. I fire another towards his face but it strikes him on the ear and he's rummaging at his seatbelt button, the engine stalled, his console beeping, he's screaming.

Something in me adjusts. Just like that, I've run out of rage. Burnt off my stockpiled fuel. His keys swinging back and forth in the ignition, I turn them and the music and beeping stop too. Silence. Both of us panting, right in close in this proximal space. I yank his keys out with shaking hands, something metal tinkling onto the floor. He's whimpering now, all messed-up hair and terror in his eyes, his face scuffed and red like he just came out of a scrum or a headlock.

Silence reverberates in the air now after all that noise, all that violence. There's no train clattering across the bridge, only this frail beseeching from Mum, standing there looking at me through the windscreen, my body still half in this car. All the pampering and make-up running down her face. She stumbles a little closer and lets out a sob, a hand outstretched, the blonde from the parlour running back into her shop the way people rush for a ringing phone.

The driver is right here with me, leaning away. Breathing. His body tense, hands up, his jacket hanging in the back. I'm holding his keys. I can smell his cologne. All of it such an unwanted intimacy. My anger having thrust me in here and then abandoned me, leaving me with the proximity and the aftermath. The passion gone but the intimacy still there. Like after sex.

I'm withering as I back out, everything trembling and I can't believe it's me that created that look on his face. I've seen that look before.

Mum's whimpering doubles in volume as my head clears the car and I'm out in the open again, breathing hard. All the pleading in her sounds but none of the sense. Just a gentle cooing, her hand out, the other hovering near her mouth and all that ruined make-up. Her handbag dangling from her elbow.

My knee starts knocking inside my trousers, the sunlight coming at me. I look at his car keys in the palm of my hand, the main key broken off halfway, blood snaking around my fingers and dripping on the road. I scuff it with my foot and it smears over the white line.

I bend to look in at him, and with an icy calm that surprises me, my heart disturbing the timbre of my voice, 'You couldn't wait a few seconds for a dying woman to cross the road? You've really got somewhere *that* important to be? Well, fuck you, mate. Fuck you.' But it comes out more like thank you. My knee really juddering now. Mum on pause, the driver leant away, everyone waiting for what I'll do.

I don't know what to do so I throw his keys into a garden and his energy changes now he senses I'm going to leave him.

I'm relieved to walk away too, conscious of my gait because I know he's watching. The blonde from the parlour back outside and staring too. A woman in the shop window gawping from under the pink eyelids, silver foils in her hair and a back-to-front gown on. My ears ringing, like after Robert's accident.

I walk slowly up to Mum and take her arm, hushing her words but she pulls away from me and screams, stationary and defiant in the middle of the road. A car stopping behind the crashed car. Everyone's looking at me and what I did. Everybody watching as Mum's face breaks into proper tears — as she lashes out at me but loses a little of her balance and lets me steady her, then pushes me away again. Everyone looking at the man who made her cry.

'Come on, Mum. Please.' But I can only say it to some part of her forehead rather than look her in the eye, because she's looking at me like she's sure now. Finally she knows.

'If we don't go I'm going to be in deep trouble. *Mum*.'

The driver opens his car door and stands, most of his body still in the car. 'Did you see that! You're *all* witnesses! He *attacked* me. You all saw it! Don't move, *buddy*. Call the police someone!'

'It's ok, mister, I called them. You alright?' The blonde.

I look at her and she scuttles into the shop, her face joining the other one steaming up the window.

'Mum, we *have* to go.' I say it quietly. 'Who's going to look after you if they lock me up, hey? You'll be all alone.'

She's crying harder but she lets me lead her away, a train coming, scratching the tracks then clacking over the bridge. My body can barely walk I'm shaking so much, conscious of their stares striking my back, our car up there with its door open.

'You go home with *Mummy*, mate. Go on! We've got your number plate, don't you worry about that!'

Once the old lady's in the car I hustle round the back bumper and hop in. The car starts and we cruise slowly away with everything seeming muffled now in here, after the violence. Everything with a wash of blue over it like bruising. My knuckles bleeding and sore around the steering wheel. The cut bloody from where he bit me. Autopilot kicking in and one eye on the rear-view mirror but nobody's there — not the man, not the police. Not yet.

After a while Mum says, 'You.' She's looking at me, her lips stammering, summoning up a word, as if willing it, tugging at it.

Then it erupts. 'Robert.' And she gives a mad little laugh at what she's done to my face with that word.

'Not a good time, Mum.'

'Robert Robert ROBERT!' She brings her face in close to me, saying it and *saying* it. I correct our position on the road, an oncoming car flashing its lights at me. 'ROBERT!' And she hits the side of my head with the tips of her fingers, the beauty receipt still in her hand.

'*Don't*, Mum. I'm *warning* you.'

'You!'

The blood is sticking my hands to the steering wheel. I try to focus on my breathing or my feet, something to ground me while the bruising spreads through my body, leeching under the skin, branching out all over me, creeping over the collar of my t-shirt and on up my neck — blues and greens and purple darkness infiltrating out from my centre so that everyone will be able to tell. A purple and green monster. Cars moving everywhere, too many, changing lanes — a white van close up behind us and I think it's the police, unmarked. People using mobile phones in the street, talking about me. Heads following our slow progress along the road. This madwoman wedged in here with me, squealing. Make-up all over her face.

This is the bruising I went overseas to avoid.

'Robert.' And she pushes my head again, her hands flailing at me, tugging my hair.

'*Get off!* STOPPIT!'

She's knocked the rear-view mirror and it's showing me my face. I straighten it, the road reappearing.

'Don't push me, Mum.' But the shake in my voice betrays me. She grabs the handle and opens the door to get out, the sound of the rushing road, the tyres and the street coming in at us. I lean over and yank the door shut but it catches her ankle in the gap, her head throwing back and emitting such an enormous wail like a hole wrenched in her, letting out a bit of her soul.

I release the door in order to right our position on the road, slowing down, Mum clutching her already repeatedly sprained ankle, the door swinging right out into a parked car and slamming back so hard, window glass erupting over us.

Now we're both crying, my foot going down on the accelerator, the engine lifting, more and more street noise and wind coming in through the broken window.

I swerve into a side street and take a series of lefts and rights. The white van gone now and Mum covered in perfect little glass squares, sobbing and unpicking them from herself. Reaching occasionally down to nurse her ankle. More bruising.

'I'm sorry, Mum. I'M SORRY OK! *Please* stop crying.' She isn't listening, her belly moving in and out under her clothes. 'You're messing up your nice hairdo, eh Mum? Please?'

I turn down another street towards home, slowing down, breathing through the tears, wiping them away on my forearm because my hands hurt from punching.

'Robert,' she says in an aching lament.

That's it. I pull over, the wheels squealing to a stop, her face going forward, no seatbelt to restrain her, her hands coming out to the dashboard, still holding that receipt. I yank up the handbrake.

'Put your seatbelt on and shut up!'

She doesn't look at me, just flails hysterically for the door handle. I slap her hands away from it, holding on to her wrists, her mouth arcing open at my *grip*.

She stops crying, just like that. Something in her reconfiguring itself. I let go of her and she wipes her face. A long breath coming out of her.

I take a similar breath. 'You have to calm down.' I reach out to unpick some of the glass from her clothes but she shoves my hand away.

'No.' Tears threatening again but she sucks them back. 'NO!' She roars it out, right up close to me. Her face that angry shape.

I feel my teeth nibbling at my own bottom lip, that anger coming up, both of us mirroring the same angry face to one another.

'We're going home and we're going to talk about this. And you're going to *shut up* about Robert. He shouldn't have been using them anyway.'

I sit here beside her, hands on the wheel, engine running, my gaze looking straight ahead, staring into the distance and wondering, if I drove fast enough towards those houses at the end, whether the flux capacitor would kick in and we could both go back in time. Or just smash into the shops and stop time altogether.

Anything but the present.

10

Robert wants to go out to dinner for his birthday. Then his parents are going to come and have an access visit for the first time since he invaded our house. They have to have a social worker with them though cos they can't be trusted.

It's me and Robert at breakfast. I eat slower than him so he's already washing up his bowl and putting away the breakfast things. I've got my eye on him.

'Why aren't we going ice-skating, Robert?' He shrugs and puts the sugar away. 'Still need the sugar.'

He comes back with it but he's looking up at the ceiling like I'm tiring him out. 'I just changed my mind, I suppose,' he says, 'about the ice-skating.' He shrugs again, standing there holding on to the back of Mum's chair and waiting to see if I'm going to say anything else. He swallows. 'You don't want to go out for dinner?'

'Boorrring!'

'It'll be fun.'

After he's said this he gets ants in his pants. I think birthdays make him nervous, maybe because he did lie about when his birthdate is so him and his folks could get some free presents out of us good people.

'Then your real parents are going to pick you up, Robot?'

He stops fidgeting. I put a bucketload of sugar on my Krispies. I like it when you get to the bottom and there's just the milk left and it's crunchy with the sugar sort of half dissolving inside it. You don't even really need the Krispies.

'Try and smile a lot when you see your parents, Robot. And you might maybe want to think about being less nerdy or something. Then they'll like you more and want you back. There's a good lad.' I feel like Three Lips Macavoy. Like I could put the moves on him. Meanwhile Robert looks like he's trying to push out a sideways poo.

'You looking forward to seeing your bad parents, Robot?'

'Don't call me that!'

'What, Robot? What?'

He has white fists on instead of hands now. Plus his face is red. Red and white Robot. White and red monster. He's standing there like the chemical plant, steam coming out of him.

'It's your birthday, Robot, you should be happy.'

'I'd be happier if you were dead, crazy brain.'

'Telling Mum you said that.'

'She won't believe you she always believes me.'

'SHE DOESN'T LOVE YOU SHE LOVES ME. NOBODY LOVES YOU!'

Feelings haunt you like you've got ghosts. Feelings are supposed to belong to you but they don't and I've gone and said it too loud and Mum comes in behind me and tugs me from my sugar milk and her finger is right up close to my face and I can't hear what she's saying cos I'm concentrating on not crying, which means thinking about my feet and wiggling my toes like Dad taught me.

Robot is watching, this look on his face.

'Say sorry to Robert!'

I look at his shoes. The front of them are pointing in towards each other like they're having a chat.

'1'

'He says things too!'

Robert puts on a wounded innocent face.

'2'

I say it.

'So he can hear it!'

'Sorry.' Robot.

'That's better. Now upstairs with you.'

I walk away, Mum right behind me and Robert smirking at the table, clearing my sugary milk away.

She follows me all the way upstairs and I'm waiting for the spanking but she stops outside my room, me inside, the temperature gauge on my window looking at me.

'No more nasty comments to Robert, he doesn't deserve it. He's here as long as he needs us, just like you are. Get used to it.'

'He says things too, only QUIETER!'

'I'll have a word with him as well.'

She shuts the door and I don't know what to do with the snake inside wanting me to do horrible things to my room. To Robert. And today's his 13th birthday so he'll probably ride in the front on the way to some boring prawn cocktail elbows off the table evening, rather than ice-skating and burgers! And I bet his parents aren't better or off the stuff.

I bet I'll be stuck with Robert until I'm 99.

I creep back down to hear what Mum might be saying about me. Alfie is curled up in front of the empty fire as if he's waiting for it to be lit. He doesn't know we don't ever light it anymore. The vase of walking sticks is guarding it now.

Robert's reading his homework out to her. A project on clouds. Snore. When I have to do a project it'll be on spies or private detectives or blood. I listen to a bit of it and Mum is encouraging him with mhmms and yes's and very goods.

If Mum is the top dog at home then Alfie is bottom dog, even though he's a cat. He normally keeps away from me but he's asleep so isn't expecting it when I pick him up and carry him up the stairs.

Cats always land on their feet. This is their amazing fact. All animals have one. Like fleas can leap loads of times longer than their bodies and dogs have antiseptic tongues. All animals have one superpower. Flies can walk on the ceiling. Elephants can remember. Bears can hug. Rabbits can stare.

There are twelve stairs on the staircase but I usually test Alfie's superpower from the sixth one. I just dangle him in thin air, do a countdown like at Cape Canaveral, then let him go. He always manages to land on his feet.

Today is Robert's birthday and there were flowers on the table this morning for him. Plus Mum's been shopping for presents. That's why she was late to get me from school yesterday.

Alfie made it from the ninth step yesterday but today's his big day, like Robert. I carry him right up to the twelfth step and squeeze him between the railings, dangle him out above the ground. I like how his claws hang on to my arms and hurt. Then I turn him so his back is facing the ground to make it more impressive. Plus I decide to throw him down rather than just drop him.

He makes a really big THUD. His superpower worked but he walks away a bit wobbly cos he used up one of his lives.

I run down and catch him again, stroke him cos I love him. I like how warm and fat he feels. Sometimes he sleeps on my bed if I make him, and stroking him always makes my heart feel softer.

Mum comes in and asks me what I'm doing out of my room and am I ready for school and I say yes even though my bag isn't packed and I have swimming today (drowning). I pretend to kick her once her back's turned.

She goes out to the kitchen and says something happy to Robert and he has his voice on too and I don't recognise him saying such long sentences as he does to Mum. He doesn't need to breathe when he's talking to her.

I bury my face in Alfie's fur but he smells a bit bad and his body is all stiff like my insides. I carry him into the bathroom and lock the door.

'You smell, Alfie. You need a shower.' I put him down in the shower and it's still a bit wet from earlier. I close the glass door, Alfie trying not to walk on the water in there. Cats hate water. It's their Kryptonite.

I turn on the hot tap but the water comes out cold at first and gets my arm wet. Hate that. I shut the door again and watch through the glass. Cats must REALLY not like water.

Before the hot comes there has to be exactly as much cold water come through as the length of pipe between the shower and the water heater. I love things like that. The way the world never forgets to do what it does. Like a bike doesn't forget to rust or a ball to fall. Meanwhile Alfie is running on the wet shower floor and it makes me feel sad but better too. And anyway, he's a cat and can land on his feet.

Now the water is starting to steam and Alfie is getting very wet, making quiet little noises and looking up at me but I'm holding the door shut, misting up the window a bit on my side. Except the inside is steaming up too now but higher, not down where Alfie is. Heat rises.

Wow. Cats hate hate HATE water. I flush the toilet so Mum doesn't worry about the noise. She'll be glad he's getting a wash. She likes things clean.

The toilet is filling up again, hissing. Alfie looks funny with all his fur flatted down and making a fuss about the heat. He even looks skinny now he's washed. All little. His ears flattened too and his tail.

Mum calls me so I reach in and nearly burn my hand off from shutting off the tap. I look at my scarred for life hand with the water on it, the layers of sort of melted skin there. I hate it and like it, my scarred for life hand.

I dry it off with a towel. Meanwhile Alfie is panting like a dog and still trying to get his feet out of the hot water. There's steam coming off him.

He meows at me, a really big beggy meow.

'You're clean now, Alfie, you dirty little boy. Nobody loves you do they, little boy. Why don't you go play with the traffic or something.'

He shakes all the water off and I didn't think cats could do that, only dogs and beavers and tigers. I open the shower door for him and carry him to the front door and put him outside so he can dry in peace. Then I go wash all his fur off the shower tiles so Mum won't worry.

I'm whistling while I pack my bag. I learnt to whistle last Christmas. Soon I'll be able to raise one eyebrow like Dad can. I've been practising in the mirror. Three Lips Macavoy would be able to whistle and raise one eyebrow during a fight.

I feel a bit better now. And a bit worse too. Like I've got elevators passing each other in opposite directions in my chest.

I come downstairs and Mum is mixing a cake for Robert's birthday. She looks at me like she's measuring me. I keep my face very still. Robert stops reading to her, shuts his school project and gets up from the table.

'Why you stopping, Robert?' she says and he shrugs and looks at me, goes upstairs. Mum is mixing her love cake. I waggle my fingers to doom it so that it'll collapse in the oven or burn or choke Robert.

School time and we go out to the car but Mum has to take a picture of Robert first because he's wearing a proper uniform, not the shirt and trousers he's been having to go to school in. The uniform is one of his birthday presents from us so he won't get picked on anymore. Mum says he'd be in an old people's home by the time Social Services came up with the money.

Then she gives me the camera and asks me to take a picture of her and Robert. They stand in front of Dad's hedges and put their arms round each other, Robert looking up at Mum like she's heaven.

I chop their heads off and they won't find out until the film's developed. Dad gets it done cheap cos one of the clients he juggles the books for is a film developing shop.

Now Mum asks Robert to take a picture of her and me and while he gets to grips with the camera she puts her arm round me and looks right into my face with her softest eyes and says 'You'll be the death of me, Sonny Jim. But only cos I love you so much.' She turns to Robert. 'Take the picture then, starey pants!'

Robert is putting Mum's camera in his school bag after but I don't say anything cos she's trying to catch Alfie to find out what's wrong and I'm holding my breath.

Robert gets in the front seat. He has his eye on me while he's doing it, and biting his lip. Mum walks up to me and says 'Here, put this in your lunch box, special treat today.' Three chocolate biscuits wrapped up in plastic with a note in. 'Eat them in the car if you want,' she says.

Three Lips Macavoy can't be bought.

In the car I'm looking out the window or playing with the robot and don't look at Robert up in the business end, except once when I can't help but peek and the back of his head is just over the seat. The seatbelt is quite high up near his neck which means he should really be sitting on the first aid kit. I don't say anything and don't look again, except one more time while I'm daydreaming about an accident where we crash and the seatbelt cuts his head off.

It's only a little accident but Robert has no head and his bad parents are crying at the funeral and it's all their fault. Serves them right.

We drive past a lost dog sign stuck to a wooden power pole. You never see found animal signs. I worry about all the lost animals. Our town has so many bits of paper stuck to lampposts and walls and they're all for bands playing and lost dogs and garage sales. And people just come along and put their car boot sale on top of other people's lost dogs. It's so sad. Sometimes I wonder if maybe right at the bottom of all that paper would be an advert for a lost dinosaur.

The snake is fat inside me all day at school then it's Dad who's come to collect me.

'Why aren't you at work, Dad?'

'You don't like your dad collecting you?' He's holding the first aid kit and the front door open like a chauffeur, especially cos he's in his work suit.

'Doesn't Mum want to pick me up anymore?'

'Don't be daft. Hop in.'

I run up to the door and hope everybody is seeing me with my dad and getting in the front seat.

When we get home Robert has a split lip and tissue paper sticking out his nose. Plus his brand new uniform is ripped at the shoulder and the pocket and Mum is looking like she has a storm cloud instead of hair.

Now the whole car is full of storm clouds because we're all on our way to the restaurant, Mum's perfume arguing with Dad's aftershave and Robert not sitting in the front cos he got into a fight.

Yesss!

'Did you win the fight, Robert?'

'Shoosh about that, thank you,' Dad says, then looks at Mum. She has her head on her hand and her face up close to the window, watching Snoresville go by.

'Will Robert get in trouble with school, Dad?'

'What you going to have for dinner do you think, kiddo?' he says, and it's prawn cocktail probably, then chicken kiev. Dad knows this.

He'll have steak but whitebait to start. Mum usually has a glass of wine while we eat first course, and then something for main course that's never really the same thing each time. She normally leaves a bit of food and Dad tucks in and I call him Alfie cos Alfie is a fat cat. Except he didn't eat his dinner today for the first time ever. Maybe cos we fed him sooner than usual.

It feels funny going out for dinner so early. This should be homework time. Plus everyone is all serious even though this is supposed to be a birthday. I like that Robert is in the kennel, it makes tonight almost as good as ice-skating. Right up until I spill my prawn cocktail and the sauce goes all over the plate. I eat some of it off and Mum isn't at me about my manners tonight. Robert would usually have eaten all his by now but he's barely nibbled. Maybe cos of his parents coming.

When the waitress takes my plate her thumb goes into my cocktail sauce and I am totally puked out that she's touched my leftovers. She might touch my next plate after her thumb's gone in someone else's leftovers. Which means we have other people's dribble and uneaten food on our dinners and plates and I've probably eaten everyone's leftover germs in my prawn cocktail, especially since I spilt it on the plate she held with her dirty thumb.

Maybe AIDS came from waitress thumbs. AIDS is the latest craze and sometimes I think I've got it even though Dad says it's just for queens.

I watch when the waitress picks up Dad's and she misses the grease and lemon juice on his plate, like it's luck what you get in your dinner.

I hope nobody in the restaurant has been eating broccoli.

Robert is sulking. Mum and Dad start off trying to cheer him up, then leave him be. There's a bag of his presents and cards in the back of the car and it looks bigger than a bag of presents should be for someone who isn't even their son.

I left my car door unlocked specially. Tonight would be the perfect night for our car to be stolen.

Dad lets me have a sip of beer then rubs his hands together when the filthy thumb on the waitress puts his bit of cow down with the blood running out of it cos when she asked how he likes his steak he said 'I want it so that it's still mooing.'

She asks him if it's bloody enough and Dad is being all interested with her and chatty like she's from Baywatch. Meanwhile Mum is looking the waitress up and down as if she's from Mars.

When the waitress goes away for the rest of the food I ask Dad if she's from Sweden. Mum looks away and sips her wine. Dad says Sweden is where pretty was invented.

Kiev is in Russia. The best thing about chicken kiev is when it gets to me with all the garlic butter still in it. Sometimes it leaks out though and if it's at home Mum usually lets me swap with hers. Then you get to dig your knife into the kiev, really slowly, so that there's this splurt like you killed it and it has butter and herbs for blood.

When the waitress brings my kiev out Mum looks at me and my plate and says 'Oh dear.'

This is the worst day of my life.

Robert hasn't hardly touched his lasagne and Mum isn't really eating her risotto. I bet Alfie wishes he was here. If Dad can't eat all the leftovers he'll probably ask for a doggy bag but we all know it's a kitty bag really. Although quite often we get home and it ends up being a Daddy bag.

After main course they bring out the cake Mum cooked for Robert, lots of candles lit and they dim the lights so everyone else at other tables stops eating. The cake isn't burnt at all and Mum and Dad and some of the other people, even the waitress, sing Happy Birthday. Robert looks down at his lap, smiling like he just did a good secret thing. I move my lips but don't sing.

I make a wish really hard just as Robert shuts his eyes and blows out the candles. If you wish hard enough you can steal a birthday wish off the birthday person. I make a wish that Robert dies.

'What did you wish for, Robert?' I say.

'If he tells you then it won't come true will it, silly,' Dad says.

Mum is looking at Robert with her head to the side, her face all lit up like candlelight.

Robert only gets boring books for his birthday. And a geometry set and pencil case. The books are about clouds and the sky, and Mum and Dad sort of cuddle closer together as they watch him open them, as if the gifts are for them. He doesn't rip the paper he unpicks the sticky tape!

'Those are quite boring presents,' I say, but nobody notices.

Robert gets down and goes and kisses Dad on the cheek and then kisses Mum and gives her a long enormous hug and I don't know where to look so I take my balled up napkin from my lap and try to flatten it out. I always do that to napkins. It looks like a paper rock.

'I suppose your real parents will give you presents,' I say.

Mum doesn't like me saying real parents but I just get a look cos we're in public and she doesn't want to put out the fireworks.

'Hurry up and eat your cake, Robert McCloud,' Dad says. 'Your parents will be here in a minute! Are you *excited*?'

Robert smiles a small smile and sticks his head down over his cake, gives it a nudge with his fork. Then he looks up at Mum but she's staring off into space. She's sad. Dad looks at her too then sits forward and starts cutting some more cake. 'Your folks should have some of this birthday cake, Rob. Otherwise I'll end up eating it all and we can't have that now can we.'

We've finished eating and everyone's drinks are empty but we're still stuck here waiting. I'm bored but excited to see Robert's parents. They're late. Maybe cos they've been buying him presents.

The waitress is back and she asks Mum if she's Mary. I don't like hearing Mum's real name. Mum is Mum. The waitress says there's a phone call for her and points over to the bar with a bar maid holding a phone and watching. Bra maid, Dad calls them.

Mum stands up and drops her uncreased napkin in her chair, then straightens her clothes out like she's off to make a speech. She gives Dad a look and Dad passes it on to Robert and Robert gives it to his half-eaten cake.

Meanwhile the waitress sticks her thumb in cream as she takes all our plates away. Robert doesn't know where to look, Mum is on the phone, and we're just sitting here like somebody important farted and we're waiting for the smell to go away.

Dad opens the book on clouds and turns it round to show us a big picture of lots of heavy angry clouds with some gaps in and God rays coming down. He turns it back and leans in close to the page. 'Bloody hell. Guess what those lovely rays of light are called.' He closes the book but keeps his finger trapped on the page.

'Crepuscular,' Robert says without looking up from the crumbs on his bit of tablecloth.

'Spot on, kiddo.' Dad looks at the book again. 'Would you get a load of that. Pretty rays and they call them something pus-ridden like crepuscular.'

Mum hangs up quite loudly and says something to the bra maid who takes down a glass and tugs the cork out of a wine bottle. Mum is coming over and her lips have gone gone gone. We all watch. Dad with his finger still trapped in the book.

She picks up her napkin and stays standing while she folds it and puts it on the table. She never screws hers up like I do. She sits down and the waitress brings over a big glass of white, the outside of it all moist like the mirror after a shower.

'You're driving,' Mum says to Dad and he looks at his beer and sinks a bit, pushes it away. She stares at the top of Robert's head. 'Your parents had to cancel, Robert. I'm sorry.'

He doesn't do anything for a bit then wipes his face with a napkin and there's blood on it.

'Ooh, your nose has started bleeding again, Robert!' I say.

He gets up and Dad puts a hand on Mum to stop her going to him, Robert saying that he needs the toilet. His napkin up to his face, all neat and not scrunched.

He goes across the carpet really slowly, his spare arm not swinging. We just sit here, Mum halfway through her wine already and Dad looking at her like she might need an ambulance.

The car is very quiet on the way home and Dad drives slowly. The radio is on but down so low it might as well be off.

When I get to bed I can hear mumbles coming from Robert's room cos Mum's tucking him in. I slip out of bed and go listen and Robert says 'You're my *best* friend' to her, and she's all 'Oh, that's so lovely, Robert. But what about someone your own age? Who's your best friend of your own age?'

'You when you were younger.'

I go back to bed really slowly like I'm walking on the bottom of the ocean.

I think Ralph is my best friend. Except Simon is Ralph's best friend and Ralph is Simon's best friend. And I don't know what the rules are, whether you're allowed to be best friends with somebody that's somebody else's best friend.

Plus it's one of those nights when the moon isn't out and maybe I'm sad because I start crying about Mum and Dad dying. I've been doing that a lot since Robert came and I haven't told anyone in case it makes it come true. I don't want Mum and Dad to die.

II

I'm on a stool, slumped against the bar as if the alcohol is weighing me down. I always sit at the bar if I'm alone. Which I usually am, initially.

The nurse was due to come this afternoon but I cancelled, considering the state of Mum. And me. I could do with some nursing now though.

I'm in one of these places that doesn't know what it is. Some sort of bijou restaurant slash wine bar slash I don't know. A place that hasn't the guts to be any one thing so it tries to be everything. Which is why I can tell exactly who the owner is and who the staff are, just by looking at the facial expressions and the serving style.

There's mirrors everywhere to make the room look bigger, so I can see the reverse of me in that alternate dimension, sitting at that other bar over there — scabs forming on his knuckles, a band-aid over a bite.

I order another drink and the bar maid gives me a face like she isn't sure if she should. Nevertheless, she puts a fresh drink down on a new coaster and I sit here as if in the eye of a storm. All around me people are living normal lives, couples showing each other their fillings as they throw their heads back and laugh together. The laugh

exceeding the joke. How couples lubricate one another's lives —
making the other seem more attractive, more interesting, funnier.
Until they leave.

The bar itself is a long, low, polished table that creates an
insubstantial barrier between the bar staff and me. Friends share
beers, froth lacing the inside of their glass. Others look into the
glint of their mobile screen, their thumbs chasing people out of the
bushes. I watch all of this, a stranger, people avoiding my gaze but
staring when they think I can't tell.

Two women come in and take a seat at the other end of the bar.
A man comes to the bar at my left, and in looking like I make room
for him I move closer to the two women.

One of them is showing the other what look like holiday snaps.
She still has her tan. I imagine the one looking at the pictures is
bored.

The bar maid realises the music stopped a while ago and puts it
back on, the owner giving her a frown so she turns it down a little —
up again when he turns back to a wallet looking at a menu.

People raise their voices over the music which, like their
conversations, is as light and insipid as cordial diluted into an almost
nothingness. But they speak it louder, the music forcing mouths
closer to the other's ear so that lips are moving beside hair and
earrings. As if the whole place is whispering about me. Like they
know.

I burp some beery CO_2 into the glass, slouched on my bar stool
and looking over at those women like they're the last cake on the
plate. The opposite of the way the old lady looked at me today.
A thought that makes me put my beer down too hard and faces turn
my way.

Look at that man on his own.

I shrink a little as if Mum is screaming at me now — standing over
there among all those people at tables and just wailing. Pointing.

Everyone staring and she's there, crying and balding and screaming and pointing. At me. Here at the bar.

It's this familiar pain that always leads me to a familiar consolation. It's only women that comfort me. I seduce more and more of them until they've caressed and sighed me innocent. Each acceptance, the grace of their acknowledgement, like the glistening embrace of validation. Of forgiveness.

So I'm sitting here in this bar bistro restaurant reaching out to the women in the room. Noting each caught glance my way. Noting more each moment in which they aren't looking at me. Sat here playing peek-a-boo with people who don't know we're playing.

The women to my right are locked in on one another but the one with her back to me is giving me the corner of her eye from time to time. She has a slender back, a red sweater clinging to her, a large leather belt wrapped around over it — not holding anything up but a belt all the same. She'll be naked under that sweater, barring the bra I can see. I like the way it cuts into her flesh. I imagine unhitching her and her ribcage expanding. The skin red beneath the bra, a little sweat where the under-wire is, her breasts dropping that unique distance and I'm cupping them but my grip is around my beer and I'm staring.

I look down and my hand is really squeezing and I can still see my old lady's ankle in the car door, her head thrown back. She was quiet as I bandaged it for her when we got home. As if she'd already forgotten how it happened. I fed her a nice meal, then escaped as soon as she was asleep on the couch.

The sweater girl has a corduroy skirt on and stockings. I'm using my teeth to eat away at the crotch of them, eating at her tights until they start to give, and she's not looking at those photos but at the top of my head — a mixture of fear and consternation and excitement on her face. Flushed with desire and this piquant thrill at my unpredictability — the way I'm showing her I know what I'm doing. My hands touching her without trace of shaking or doubt or holding back. Her mouth trundling out lame words for me to stop. Her fingers sliding among the hair on the back of my head.

And yet I'd still be alone. With each sexual encounter I'm usually standing somewhere in my childhood. Just me and the empty corridors of the past. That habit sex has of vanishing me. Of making me haunt my own childhood — standing deserted in memories of loneliness. Aloneliness.

I swig my beer again, order another. Sweater Girl looking out of the corner of her eye, and her friend frowns for a moment.

Sex is always like that for me, the way it brings back images of childhood. As if the thread of a muscle or ligament tears fractionally from the exertion, and gives off where I was the moment it first formed — every cell in me like a time capsule full of the past. So that I might be having sex, but in my head I'm standing by the garden shed, or the wicker washing basket I used to hide in outside Mum and Dad's room, until they found out and moved it into the bathroom.

Or I'll be standing on that spot where Robert changed.

Sweater Girl's friend asks her if she's alright and gets an enthusiastic nod. She probably took most of those pictures in order to come home and show them. As evidence. Most people can't enjoy a holiday because they're always standing outside themselves wondering what sort of holiday they're having and how it would look to those at home and how to capture it so that it looks like they had *the* experience. They don't take the pictures for themselves, to remember, they take them to show. Doesn't sound like much of a holiday.

The friend heads for the toilet and Sweater Girl swivels to face her drink, gives me a look. I slide my stool a little closer and lift my glass to her, give her a smile. She smiles back, looks down, her elbow on the low bar, her other hand playing with the twirls of black hair spiralling out from under her ponytail, her neck smooth, pure, the hair curling.

In this moment she looks like Perfect.

She fidgets and her corduroy skirt rises up a little and there's a tiny ladder in her stocking. I'd tear them there.

'Holiday snaps?' I say and she blushes, leaning closer to me because she hasn't heard over the music, and I have to wilfully relax my hand around the beer glass.

'Holiday snaps?' I say again and point at the pictures sitting near a puddle of something on the bar.

'Oh. Yes,' she says, touching the photos. 'The Gambia. Looks nice.'

I raise my eyebrows, sip my beer. 'Impressive. Stay with me for a drink if you like, once the intrepid explorer goes home.' I say it as if I'm not connected to her answer at all.

She leans closer, blushing again, and I watch her bum inch to the edge of her seat. She hasn't heard what I've said again, her friend weaving her way back between the tables.

'I said, once you two have finished catching up, you might like to share a beer with me.'

'Both of us?' she says, probably looking for clarification it isn't her friend I'm interested in. Her friend who's standing behind her now. Not sitting down but watching the interaction like she's in a wedding dress and there's nobody waiting at the altar.

I know who Sweater Girl is. She's the person who sits listening to others, resenting them for taking up all the airtime and yet not daring to broadcast herself. She thinks she's boring and so is great at remembering facts about everyone she meets. She probably already knows what beer I drink. She's a master at detail so that when she sees someone for the second time, in that desert that is a social function — dry, unforgiving, endless, lonely — she can say, 'Oh, how did your x, y, z go?' Or, 'Did you manage to make it to blah

blah on time?' And she's the type that puts a little light touch on you at that moment, to emphasise her sheer niceness. She is nice. She gives head. She doesn't like all the attention in bed. She's used to selfish lovers. She's been with a string of those weak men who feel threatened. Men who like women that don't say much. She falls for men who take. Not men like me who need vindication, who need to give back too.

Sweater Girl has selfish lovers and so her orgasm face would probably be one of surprise.

My beer arrives and I let the bar maid flirt with me a little, watch what it does to SG. How she waits, forcing her friend to wait too — nausea rising in me from all the alcohol.

The problem though is that after that orgasm, life will shrink everything again as I succumb to my view of myself as second best. At best. Right now I'm going through life like one of those fluorescent bulbs that can't jump start itself. I'm only blinking towards lighting up. Everyone is, aren't they? You need another to spark across the gap, someone to meet you halfway so you can rest in the glow awhile.

But for a brief spell after we've gorged on each other, our bodies lying there humming, I'll get to feel as if a chiropractor has just clicked my brain back into the right shape and maybe for the rest of the night it will sit in its white bone throne in my head and look down on its kingdom, and feel glad. Me and Sweater Girl will both be there, holding hands, our chests expanded. And for a brief moment I'll experience that elusive wholeness.

Sweater Girl says 'Maybe' to me over the music, then turns her blushing to her friend. Her friend who is not used to Sweater Girl being the focus. Her friend who is with her *because* Sweater Girl is second place.

Not to me she isn't. To me she looks like a temptress out of one of those 1950s films. The way they always first appear on screen in that soft focus, as if viewed through the beginning of tears.

And I'm sitting here like a bell that's just been struck. If the other people would shut up for a second they'd hear that almost inaudible resonance coming off me. Sweater Girl having left me ringing with the promise of escape. Togetherness. Because she *will* stay late with me after her The Gambia friend has waited as long as possible to leave. The Gambia enhancing her own total insignificance by staying, *because* of her very outrage and refusal to be insignificant beside Sweater Girl. But The Gambia is surplus.

And you know what's most beautiful about this situation? That Sweater Girl, my woman, is going to turn on her friend in a minute. At this chance of glory she'll turn on The Gambia and accentuate every ounce of her new insignificance. Drying up all attention, stopping all feigned interest so that her non-friend will leave totally shrunken. Probably feeling betrayed almost. Cheated out of the usual hierarchy of attention.

I go to order another beer to celebrate on SG's behalf but the bar maid looks at the fresh one still sweating here in front of me.

I am the drunk bell, ringing at the bar. Because Sweater Girl and me will leave together and for tonight at least, I'll feel loveable.

12

Dad's gearbox wakes me up like usual but I don't get out of bed straight away. I'm thinking about last week when Robert's parents forgot him. I'm not allowed to talk about it and Mum's been nicer to him than before, even though she found out he's been hoarding again. Weirder stuff than EVER.

I go downstairs. Mum's normally up by now but only Robert is. He's polishing our shoes.

'What do you think happened to your parents last week then, Robot?'

He looks at me. 'Your mum says I don't have to talk about it.'

'Your mum says I don't have to talk about it.'

'Shut up, crazy brain,' he says and chucks one of my shoes across the room and starts walking out.

'YOU SH-ut up, Robert.' He always remembers to be quiet when he's nasty.

Once I'm dressed I eat some Krispies. I know Krispies are his favourite but he pretends to Mum that he likes vegetables and fruit and prefers water to lemonade.

He comes back in. 'Where's your mum?'

He always calls her that. Except once he called her Mum and

everyone got the beetroots.

I shrug.

'I'll go see,' he says. 'It's not like her not to be up yet.'

Like he's the expert.

I put more sugar on my breakfast and listen to him moving through the house, then thundering down the stairs. He comes in all pale.

'She won't wake up!' He picks up the phone and dials emergency.

You get in big trouble for that. I know.

'Maybe she's tired, Robot.'

'She could be DYING!'

'Alright shouty pants,' I say to him, but my heart's going. He's crying a bit.

'Ambulance please. Yes.'

I move my sugary milk away. Even looking at it makes me want to throw up. I push back my chair and it makes a big farty noise.

'Pardon?' Robert says into the phone, wiping his eyes. 'I don't know,' he says. Then he turns to me 'Quick, they want us to check she's breathing!'

Being inside an ambulance should be exciting. Robert is holding Mum's hand but she isn't holding his. The ambulance man is taking her temperature and the tubes and oxygen things and packets of needles all wobble with the road movement. The driver plays the sirens for little bursts sometimes, probably when we go through junctions. This means Mum might not be dying otherwise the sirens would be on all the time. Or they would be off because she's dead.

'Best phone your dad,' the ambulance man said to Robert as they were putting her on the stretcher at home, and I just watched while Robert got to be the son.

I'm the fostered one now.

When we get to hospital Dad is already there and his face all red and puffy around his neck but he has the best hug for me.

He hugs Robert too. Then we hold hands by Mum's bed but she's under this plastic thing like Michael Jackson because she might have a very tricky disease that makes your brain swell.

Dad cries. A lot. I tell him it'll be ok and try to make him laugh.

When Auntie Deadly turns up she makes a fuss. I'm supposed to go to her house but Robert isn't allowed anywhere without Social Services' permission and Dad hasn't got through to them yet. Which means Robert might get to stay with Dad and Mum at the hospital while I have to go home with Deadly.

Now I'm crying and Dad is kissing me all over my face and his stubble tickles but I don't laugh. Life's so unfair. Auntie Deadly starts taking me away and telling me to be a big boy for once and Dad gives her a serve and I can see Mum frowning under her tent thing, even with her eyes shut she's frowning.

In the end Dad gives Auntie D the keys and tells her to take Robert and me to our own house.

I hate leaving Mum and Dad, and most of all I don't want Dad to catch the illness cos then I'll lose them both and have to live with Auntie Deadly.

It's against the rules for Robert to be alone with Auntie D without her being checked out but Dad just hugs me when I tell him. Maybe they'll take Robert away.

When we get home I go straight upstairs into my lion's den cos I'm stuck at home with my two greatest enemies.

Dad phones later and I pick up the one upstairs to listen, my hand over the talking bit. He says Mum does have the meninsomething and Auntie Deadly says 'Yipee, now we've all got it,' and Dad tells her to keep us in and not to say anything if the social worker rings, and we'll need hospital appointments too. No school. Then he says 'Watch the little one, he's still playing up about Robert but go easy on him.'

It's been two days and Dad's at the hospital all the time and

Robert in his room. He won't eat. Today we had to go back in and a doctor explained to us about these enormous tablets we have to take just in case. Plus the symptoms to watch out for like a rash and not being able to get your chin onto your chest. I practise this a lot since he told me. It's impossible to get your chin on your chest without making a stupid face.

Auntie Deadly says we aren't to watch TV during the day, and last night she cooked us soup that was so homemade my spoon wouldn't sink into it. Plus I wasn't allowed to leave the table till I'd eaten it all. I was sat there for hours. She had to keep reheating it, and after every mouthful I was like Alfie when he gets fur balls.

Auntie Debbie says food is mostly about nutrition but Dad says food is mostly about eating things that hug your stomach.

Yesterday she gave us BEETROOT SANDWICHES. Even Robert admitted he didn't like beetroot. He still ate his, meanwhile I was stuffing it down my undies and just eating the purpley stained bread. I offered to smuggle some of Robot's beetroot but he was too much of a good boy.

Then I just shuffled to the toilet and flushed it all away. Simple. Three Lips Macavoy can't be poisoned.

Today Auntie D was by the washing machine though and called me over. She looked a bit like beetroot herself and asked me if everything was 'you know, alright downstairs?'

Next time I'm wearing my black ones.

13

The music has stopped now but I've not stopped drinking. The bar staff are gathered at the far end, relaxing in the quiet after the rush. Their own drinks loiter about them now that the owner has gone. They're chatting but watching the postures of the few remaining customers and their drinks, monitoring home time.

Most importantly, The Gambia just left the building and Sweater Girl is looking down at her drink, lonely now, exposed by her waiting.

Here she comes, wandering uncertainly over, carrying her stool with her. She puts it down.

'Hello,' she says, all upbeat, then turns away for her bag, giving her face time to drain.

'This is nice,' I say once she's sat. I give her a smile. She does her hair, looks at me, perhaps dipping her senses into her middle, measuring what I do to her insides. I order us drinks and there's a silence while we wait for them to arrive, as if we can't start until they do.

I put it on my tab, hushing her lacklustre rummaging for her purse.

'How was your Gambia lecture then?' I say and she raises her eyes heavenwards and smiles.

Our first in-joke.

'Anyone would think she went for a year, not a short break,' she says.

'So it's true then, The Gambia does give you the shits.'

I smile again, introducing myself. Not my real name. I hate my real name.

'Patricia,' she says. 'Good to meet you too' — her hand coming out for a handshake but this time I don't need to use one of my stock excuses to avoid the shake, I can just show her my cut knuckles and the plaster on my hand.

'Had a fight with the hedge this morning,' I say. 'It'd been left too long. It was *enormous.*'

She laughs more than the comment warrants, touching my arm as she does so.

Mostly women have cool hands. Bad circulation. Especially if they're on the pill, which I sincerely hope she is.

Patricia, not a bad name, although I wouldn't shorten it for love nor money.

'Is that a hint of an accent I can hear in your voice?' she says.

'Not you as well. I live in Canada. Moved there about six years ago — I hate that I'm losing my accent.'

'Wow, Canada.' But I see something sink in her. Perhaps she's disappointed that I don't live here.

'Yeah, I like it.' Liar. 'Civilised. Lots of space.'

'You don't miss your family? Is it a permanent thing?'

'For me,' I say, the elevator in my centre dropping at this ritualised conversation we're having, 'I just feel like I learn more about myself being away from where I grew up.'

She swallows some drink. 'I've spent time overseas too. Asia mostly.' She looks down at her hand on the glass of white, her eyes half focused. 'It was different for me though. I was just running.

Travel meant no ties, you know? No family, no old friends. A new past if I wanted. I went with that friend who just left,' and she wrinkles her nose at me, a sort of a smile. 'We used to play this stupid game, making up names and jobs to tell each new person we met. What was I ...' Her hand is out counting things off. 'I was a dolphin trainer, that was a good one; a prosthetic-toe maker. Oh and my great-great-grandfather invented the question mark.'

We laugh together at that for a second but it soon dries up, both of us staring into our drinks.

'But in the end, travel's often just distraction, isn't it,' she says, breaking the void. 'Kind of cheating. Not that I'm saying this applies to you at all. *Living* overseas, that's different. But when you travel you just come back to the same problems, plus debts.'

I go to slug some drink but it's empty. She looks at whatever's happening to my face and says an anyway — forces her voice, posture and face to brighten but it soon goes out again. It's not just me she's depressing.

'I live overseas because I feel good there, Patricia. I like my life in Canada — my career in the prison service.' I signal the bar maid. 'I don't necessarily need to drill beneath that, you know? But if I did, I'd probably dig up what you just said, in a nutshell.'

I don't like lying to her but what choice do I have. My truth isn't the type you'd want to take home and screw.

The bar girl arrives and I drain all flirtation out of myself — flirting with Patricia by not showing any interest in this attractive bar maid.

'Another?' I say to Patrish who's in some sort of inner funk, lost for a moment. She comes to and nods and the girl shuffles off with her bed floating in a shrinking cloud above her head.

The drinks arrive and I let Patricia pay, the bar maid putting the change on the bar rather than in her outstretched hand, then walking back to her sulking spot at the far end. I reckon I've got about ten minutes before we get chucked out and it's all over. Home alone.

I sit forward, my hand landing on Patricia's knee and moving a little in the landing, gliding up the corduroy grooves. And I'm sitting here drunk, my groin thumping at the risk I've just taken by reaching out and touching her.

I could resist the utter stupidity of relying on a stranger to validate me, but I choose to go with my foolish simplicity. You can't escape your blueprint, push a lever and you get a sweet. And however simple, a sweet is still a sweet. However enslaved — no lever, no sweet. Life's too hard to not be pushing those levers. Why feel guilty for the simplicity of our design. I'll deal with the guilt and discomfort afterwards. Right now I feel alive, I can tell by the hammering in my chest and the lump in my lap. Patricia looking down at my cut hand sitting there on her leg, me glaring at the top of her head. The bar staff waiting too probably — their conversation naturally pausing. We're all wondering what she'll do.

She's taking her bloody time.

'Prison, huh?' she says then moves an unsteady hand for her drink, does her hair, smiling. 'Not as good as dolphin trainer. It's not a bad one though.'

'Ha, ha,' I say. 'It's not exotic spending your time in a place bad people get sent to as a punishment.'

'I would've believed you if you'd pretended you were a model instead,' she says, making herself laugh, her gaze darting down to my lips.

Bingo. I'm always amazed at how different I must look to other people versus what I see when I look in the mirror. No matter how often I get this reaction I'm always surprised by it, like finding money you didn't know you had.

'Did you go to school round here?' she says.

'I did,' I say, experiencing myself through a kind of haze — all that alcohol and now endorphins in my bloodstream.

'Which one?'

'Ah, I went to lots. Bit of a rebel.' She's trying to rank me based on what school I went to and I don't like it.

'Wilson's?'

'For a bit, yes. Why?'

She shrugs. 'What you doing back, just a visit?'

Her fingertip runs along the back of my hand, tracing a circle around the cuts on my knuckles, then she takes a hold of my hand and turns it over, her body jolting just a little at the faded patch of damaged skin on my palm like a layer of wax that's melted then cooled. She looks up at me, then down again, a finger tracing the outline. She decides not to ask about it, just waits a polite amount of time before delicately depositing my hand back on my own leg, smiling. I console my scar with the beer glass — swallow a large thump of amber.

'I'm here because my mum's dying.' I like hitting her with that after she's just rejected my hand.

'Oh,' she says. 'God, sorry.'

'It's ok. It wasn't meant to be a conversation stopper.' I feel like me and Patsy here are rumbling along the hard shoulder of the interaction highway.

'Why, what's she ...'

'Cancer.' I tap myself on the forehead. 'Brain.'

'Oh, that's awful.' No shit. 'How are you coping?' she says. And on the 'you' she touches my arm.

I told you she was one of those. But it's just her way of getting through the world, nothing deeper than that. Push a lever.

'I don't know what I'd do if ...'

'Don't say that,' I tell her, touching her leg again, higher up, using my good hand this time. 'Everyone says how d'you cope, or I wouldn't cope. But what would you do, curl up and die? If I was my mum I'd want to curl up and die. If I was *her* I wouldn't cope.'

Her eyes moisten and mine do too, the bastards.

'I'm sorry,' she says, looking down again and taking my hand. I don't want her sympathy but I leave my hand in hers. Whatever works for her. Anything but get left sitting in the sadness. Not today, thank you.

'What about you — what do you do?'

'I *told* you,' she says, 'dol —'

'Dolphin trainer. Yeah yeah. Come on.'

But it's now, while I'm trying to get us off the interaction hard shoulder that the bar maid comes over and says it's time for us to be shuffling along.

'Oh,' Patricia says, straightening. She looks at me and I'm thinking of what to say but the bar maid is still standing here watching. I turn to her and say thank you — i.e. bugger off. Which she does, then shares a joke with the others and I look back and Patricia is holding a pen and rifling for a piece of paper.

No you don't. 'Why don't we go somewhere else for a drink, Patricia?'

She looks up from the innards of her bag and for a moment we're stuck here while she's doing this incredibly complex equation, probably involving things to do with her body image today and when she last showered and tomorrow's plans and my looks and her stage in her cycle, plus all the crap in her subconscious and the bits of hers that mine taps into — that unseen wavelength which runs between people, how patterns happen.

While that equation scribbles itself across the blackboard in her head I lean quickly towards her ear and tell her that I would really like to spend the night with her, not for sex, just because I think she's lovely. That I want to make a huge fuss of her body. My words blowing across her ear, and I can smell what it's like to be in close to her and I like it.

I lean back and, I don't know, maybe she sees the need I'm trying to hide. Maybe she sees the desperate part of me that's subtly *madly* pressing that lever, because she rummages for paper again and says, pausing to touch me, that she would love that too but she's going to have to take a raincheck.

What the FUCK is a *raincheck*! If you could stab a word.

Meanwhile she's writing her number and I'm sat here glaring at the top of her head and the bar maid has the box for credit cards left behind the bar, and she's *grinning* at me.

Sweater Girl hands her number over, clicking the button on her pen to retract the ballpoint while I'm doing my best to smile like it's no biggie. Like I don't want to run out of here so fast that I'll leave the feeling part of me behind.

'Thanks.'

Where's the comfort in a piece of paper? You can't hug a phone number.

'Cuthbertson or Teichmann. Or Wilkinson?' the bar maid says, reading out the names on the last three credit cards left — Patricia looking at me, waiting to hear my surname.

While they're swiping my credit card I sit here looking at Patricia's knees.

'Give me a call,' she says, 'I'd really like that,' and she leans in for my cheek but I turn and get her lips, giving the kiss everything I've got.

I pull away and she looks down to hide her beetroot face — puts her pen in her bag and I hate it all, the sweet smell of stale beer coming off the bar, the people putting their coats on to go home together. I hate the bar staff and Mum and Robert — Robert's parents.

'I might just do that, Patricia.'

I take the paper from her hand and stumble away, then come back and sign the bill. The bar maid giving me a look.

I take my card from her, hug Patricia for a second, long enough for her to stop me if she's changed her mind.

Then I'm out the door and as soon as I'm far enough away I am running but I don't outrun anything, all that happens is the alcohol in my stomach stops me, threatening to come out. I lean over for a few breaths then jog away from the disappointment, anger lighting up inside me.

At least there's power in anger.

By the time I'm a few streets away I'm incandescent with it. I go over to a shop window and look at my reflection, trying to see what Patricia saw, whether I got away with saving some face back there.

It's a photographer's shop window, pictures of smug grins and overly made-up women staring out from gilt frames.

I look at her number then screw it up and chuck it on the ground, stamping on it over and over. Pick it up again, straighten it out — wipe it down, put it in my pocket.

I peer in at the photographer's place. *Don Vincenzo's* it says above the big shop window. He's probably just called Mark or Gary. His pathetic little suburban studio with these posed shots of weddings and families. A failed photographer.

Like the day we all went to one of those studios and Robert came and the photographer guy made me feel tiny by using a puppet on me to get a smile. I was eight and he used a puppet on me in front of Robert and all I could think was What is Robert doing in our family shot? The photographer with a puppet in my face but treating Robert like an adult.

I search the ground for something, anything, my hand settling on an empty bottle of beer in the gutter. I step back with it then let the bottle fly and the photographer's window stops reflecting me but striates into sparkly lines and shapes and spider webs glinting orange with the streetlight — broken bottle fragments tinkling onto the pavement, the window hanging on.

I pick up the intact bottleneck and wander up to an untarnished bit of window, some blonde smiling at me from a big picture. My eyes adjust and there's my reflection. I bring the sharp bottleneck up near my face, touch it against the skin just under my eye, daring myself. Thinking back to those bar staff laughing at Patricia rejecting me.

I push and feel the sharpest shard puncture my skin and it brings that release. I pull it out, watch a tiny tear of blood ooze.

I bet this photographer has real images hidden away somewhere — proper art of his that means everything to him. He has this enormous shop window but all he can summon the courage to commit to are these cheesy images of bland everyday people. Trying for extraordinary but it's all just extra ordinary. Which must be why he can't call himself by his real Gary or Paul name. He has to be Don Vincenzo to make up for the real him he's afraid to be.

I pace up and down the shop front like a bear in a zoo. At the corner is a chunk of brick, a corresponding gap in the masonry. I toss the brick up and catch it, wandering out away from the window, into the road — weighing the rock fragment in my hand.

Then there's that blissful release of anger, the window making an enormous noise — I cover my face, the shattering and tinkling taking an eternity to subside.

A laugh escapes me but I'm squirming at all the noise I've made in the night, a little urgent sound starting up from an alarm console on the wall.

I lurch into the shop, this photographer to blame for everything, my shoes crunching on all the broken glass, the beeping alarm eating me. I rip the blonde off her stand and stamp through her face. Then start gathering up as many pictures as I can, lifting them from easels and off the walls. I'm laughing, stuffing the useless booty up my top and holding others under my arms, collecting as many of them as I can and singing a drunk song, the alarm's warning tone changing pitch suddenly. I can smell the fragrance he has in here, this pot-pourri photographer coward.

The alarm starts wailing and I want to cover my ears, staggering out through the window again with my swag of fake happy families — losing my footing on the glass. The bottle fragments out here too with my fingerprints on them and a strobing blue light spinning around the neighbourhood from the alarm box.

I'm running away with my arms wrapped around childhoods and families and couples. I'm running but giggling, the alarm quietening the further away I get, the anger subsiding in me now. A picture slipping to the concrete and I rush back for it, crouching to gather it up like my arms are full of washing and I've dropped a sock.

I can hear a siren somewhere but can't run anymore. I take the back streets until I reach our hill, crossing over at the point where the pavement drops down. The way I did all those years ago with Robert in the garden. Mum was sick then too, but she was on the mend. She was on her way home from hospital. That time she'd live. Not like now.

I go in through our gate, stumbling a little and the hedge catches me, tickling my face. I make it indoors, pictures slipping lower in my arms, making me hunch over, nursing them up the corridor and into the lounge.

I drop them and turn on the light, my back leant now against the wall, alcohol and exercise overwhelming me for a second. No sign of Mum, just crumbs on the couch. The stolen pictures looking out of place in our ordinary lounge. The faces larger than life and made-up and airbrushed, sitting in front of that pointless, oily background. Fake happy faces and fake happy families.

I take out my phone, rifling through my wallet for the nurse's card, sweat seeping quickly out of me. I dial and a recorded message tells me that if this number is unavailable to call an alternative number. Her South African accent reads it out and I can see the woman. I ache at the thought of her, then there's the beep.

'Hey, hi. I just, nothing urgent really ... Probably shouldn't be calling even ...' I'm walking through the house in search of alcohol as I talk, the light already on in the kitchen '... bad because it's an emergency number and all but this *is* sort of an emergency, of sorts and —' I stop though because all over the family table are pictures of Robert. Robert in the garden; Robert gazing at the sky; Robert at the photographer's studio, his clothes matching mine; Robert looking up from a book. And that broken Robert in his orange jumpsuit on that day of all days, long after what happened to him. The day we sent him up.

I hang up the phone, standing here looking at them all facing me. It wasn't some nostalgia of hers that got those pictures out. She's Miss Forgetful unless it suits her. No, this is no accident. She obviously wants to play.

I can play.

14

Dad has come home from his virgil at the hospital today. It's the first time he's been home since Mum got ill. He's all spiky and smelly and tired but says Mum's going to be right as rain and out of the woods. And that it's a good job she's such a wuss otherwise they might not have found out about the illness so soon. If she were tougher she'd be dead.

Nothing happens in my stomach when he tells us Mum's ok. Robert cries and goes up to his room and shuts the door. Auntie Deadly is wiping her hands on a tea towel and she shakes her head and says, 'That boy.'

She always calls him that.

Now that Dad is back Auntie D can go. Mum might even be home in a few days and Dad's with us mostly and sort of brighter himself. Plus he's a good cook and doesn't make me eat soups my spoon won't sink into.

I feel a bit sick though. I want Mum to live but I don't want those feelings to come back that happen to me when her and Robert are around.

Plus we can go see her today once Dad's had a power nap and a shower. He shouts upstairs to Robert that we're going to see

Mum and Robert starts woohooing and banging and crashing then thundering down.

I hate hospitals. They smell and are full of sick and stains and germs. Plus people with needles sitting in their veins, the blood going by. They put that sharp metal right in there, inside you, and you're supposed to just lie there with it rusting.

When we pull into the car park it's full and the hospital has a chimney poking up and I can't stop staring at it.

Dad sends us ahead while he tries to park the effing car. Robert and me are walking the corridors on our way to her ward.

'Slow down, Robert, she's not dying.'

He looks like it's Christmas Eve.

Her ward is called Nightingale and we follow the signs and I almost want to hold Robert's hand but I concentrate on turning my shoes on the lino so it makes that squeak. Probably cos a hospital is squeaky clean.

I try not to breathe too much so I don't catch things.

We get to the ward and there's Mum looking butter colour. Somebody in a bed next to her is under the covers with teeth in a glass beside her, and at the end of the ward is a TV up high out of reach and showing a golf ball in the air. You see the golfer looking at it flying, his hand saluting his forehead, his club still over his shoulder. Then he bends down and picks up something and the ball is still in the air sort of ahead of the picture then a bit behind then right in it and the clouds are rushing by and when the ball lands it barely bounces or moves. The crowd claps and the golfer tries not to look pleased.

Mum says Hi Hello Hey and kisses Robert's forehead a lot and holds out a hand to me and there's a clear plastic line running from it and a needle in her and she's holding it out to me. I stand still and turn my shoe and it squeaks. I feel like I'm inflatable and somebody's letting my air out.

'I'm not catching anymore,' she says.

I nod and smile at her. My body wants me to breathe. Meanwhile Robert is staring, giving her that look he gives her.

'You ok?' she says to me. 'You're quite pale yourself.'

She feels my forehead and gazes down at the floor cos that helps her measure my temperature better. I wipe her germs off with my sleeve after.

Even though it's the afternoon Mum looks like she does when she's just got up. I think she probably smells the way Dad does when he's just got up too. He smells a lot of sleep in the mornings, sort of a brown muddy smell. I try not to hug him till he's had a shower.

'What about you, Sonny Jim?' she says.

I shrug. I don't like being nice to her in front of Robert. I take some quick breaths through my nose then hold on again.

'Have you missed Mum? Did I give you a bit of a scare, getting ill like this? What's up with you, you look like you're pushing out a poo!'

Robert laughs his pants off then sits on her bed and she looks at him a second but her searchlights are on me again and a lady is crying behind some curtains next to us. Mum shrugs about it and whispers 'What can you do. I preferred it when I was catching and got to have my own room. Can't remember such peace and quiet. Except your dad snoring in the chair next to me.'

Robert's playing with the hand of hers that's got the line coming out, looking at her palm like he loves it.

'Don't keep squeaking your shoe on the lino, love,' she says. 'It's going right through me.'

'Can I go and watch the TV?'

'Golf? You want to watch golf rather than visit your mum? I haven't seen you in ages. Mum's been *very ill*.'

I shrug and get the beetroots.

'Go on then,' she says. 'Go on, if you must. You'll keep me company won't you, Robert.'

He hugs her, almost yanking out the needle. Maybe he'll snap it off inside her and it'll rush along the bloodstream and stab her in the heart. If he hurts her he's dead.

I go over to the TV meanwhile trying not to notice the beds with all these women looking like they're rubber puppets without a hand inside them. One of them is smiling at me and waving me over. I hold my breath harder and concentrate on the telly which is looking at a golf man looking at a ball and the hole. There's a man next to him with golf clubs, holding an umbrella over the golfer like he's the king of somewhere.

Robert is talking very fast and moving his arms and sitting on her bed with his shoes on the ground and his socks showing and Mum's mouth is smiling and moving a tiny bit while he talks.

Dad comes in and there are noisy kisses all round, he looks for me and waves me closer as if it's picnic time. He sits next to Mum on the bed and they all look like an advert for something you should want.

Then the golfer misses the hole. He misses it. The hole is empty and the ball is nearby and I don't know why but it makes me sort of sad. Like the golf hole is unhappy. Then the scary old lady whispers 'Hey, sonny' and waves me over to her again. I stay very still looking up at the TV, my neck really having to bend and the angle makes the tears get hidden in my hair.

Mum is coming home soon and I'm getting scareder and scareder. Feelings are nasty. I wipe my eyes without anyone seeing me, then breathe out some of the wobbles.

'Hey, Mr Ballesteros, come here!' Dad says.

I go slowly over and while they're chatting I'm thinking about how many people might be dying in the world right now. How many are taking a poo. Or sneezing out germs. How many animals are dying right now? Animals have to die alone. Nobody holds an animal's hand.

There are so many people in the world that someone is probably dying in this hospital right now or being burnt after they're dead.

All hospitals have a chimney and the smoke that comes out is made of people.

Dad says to me 'Whaddya think, eh? Sound like a good idea?'

I nod, even though I don't know.

The world's so big that thinking about it makes my brain itch.

Dad and Robert are on the bed with Mum, Dad talking about giving her a bed bath and she's pushing him away and I'm holding on to the metal railing at the end, her germy chart hanging off it and they're all bubbling words at each other even though we're all going to die.

Then Mum looks at my face and says 'Oh!' like I'm the cutest thing in the world. 'Come 'ere,' she says, all gooey and her eyes wet too, and Robert has to get out the way cos she tugs me in close. And she smells of her, even though she might die any minute.

I hate Robert seeing me cry.

Dad says Robert's ok to go back to school but maybe I had best take a bit more time.

Yesss!

He rings school up and what with the risk of everyone catching men in tights disease they like the idea of me staying away. Which means me and Dad are kings of the castle. Except I'm worried because at first I got the runs from all those big antibiotics I had to take, but now I've stopped taking them I haven't done one for days.

When I tell Dad he chases my bum round the house with the plunger.

Today we're trimming the hedges. He pays me extra pocket money if I lug black bags of hedge. I like working with Dad, except he won't let me have a go on the hedge-trimmer. It's his pride and joy and not safe for kids cos of how sharp it is and in case you cut the electric cord which is orange to make it idiot proof.

'There are no orange hedges, if the cord was green we'd get rid of a load more idiots from the world.'

Sometimes he lets me hand the hedge-trimmer up to him once he's gone up the ladder and forgotten it. I have to use two hands. And sometimes he passes it to me so he can come down the ladder. It's a good ladder but the ground's uneven so Dad doesn't ever let me go up it except about three steps when he's nearby.

We're having fun until Robert comes home and breaks up the party. He's old enough to get the bus on his own now. He goes indoors then comes out and reads his book about clouds and occasionally points some out to us. He shows us a lot of hedge shaped clouds today. Plus there's a great one that looks like a foot.

There's been 33 mm of rain since Mum got ill.

After a while Dad stops the hedges with part of them still not cut. I want him to carry on but he says dinner's more important and Mum probably won't notice the hedges anyway. Better to clean the kitchen. I help him pack up and Robert starts to join in.

'It's my job, Robert. DAD!'

'Let him earn his crust, Robert, good lad.'

Tonight we're going ice-skating even though Mum is still in hospital. I feel guilty about this for about 3 seconds.

Robert is crap at skating. So is Dad but that's just hilarious. I like ice-skating except I can't do it or think about it without imagining falling over and having someone skate over my fingers and cut them off. Some things are never the same once you know something bad about them.

Robert slips over on the ice and bumps his chin. I can see it hurts but he lies there smiling. I go over and for a second I want to skate over his hands. I want to. Some things you want even though you shouldn't. Some things you don't and you should.

It's chicken kiev for dinner afterwards and none of them have leaked their garlic butter and we watch Dumbo and I get to stay up as late as Robert even though Mum's back tomorrow. Dad and Robert are happy.

Nearly bedtime and Dad is whistling downstairs, the radio bubbling boring stuff while he's cleaning the kitchen. I get out of bed and go into my sleeping bag. Mum coming home tomorrow is kind of exciting but it also feels like Sunday night and maths tests and cod liver oil and leeks and the dentist. I bet Robert's awake too, tidying his room or practising being lovely.

Mum's coming home tomorrow and everyone's happy except me. I think I must be bad.

15

It's been weeks since I woke to an alarm but I set one last night so I'd be up to catch Mum's reaction. I shower and dress as fast and quietly as possible, my head feeling last night's drink, my stomach reminding me of the window I broke and of getting ruffled in front of Patricia. Still, I got her number.

I stand and look at the pictures of Robert, still sprawled across the table, then march up the road to the bakery. So much for her forgetfulness. Plus the attack she launched against me yesterday in the car.

I get home and there's no sign of her so I'm standing in the lounge admiring my work. I have to admit, it's good. It's really good.

I chuck the danishes in the oven and lay the table around the pictures of Robert, setting Mum up where she can best see my reply.

I hear her then, shuffling around upstairs in that zombie way of hers. I take the pastries out and put them on a plate, cooling the tips of my fingers in my mouth, a few buttery flakes for my troubles. I pour fresh orange juice, step back and look at it all — move the fruit bowl closer to her place at the table. She stumbles up there and something clatters. I go to the foot of the stairs. 'You alright?'

There's a sound like yes from upstairs. It's a weary sound though, maybe some tears behind it.

In the kitchen I grab the cereal, put milk in a jug, carry it all out to the table and set up the bowls and plates — the morning sun streaming a bright trapezoid onto the carpet, everything quiet in the street.

I perch on the arm of a chair and gaze at all those pictures of strangers up on the walls instead of us. Professional, sickly shots that are full of made-up faces and forced smiles.

I love the way a picture betrays the fault lines. Even with the professionalism, you can still see the subtle tussles to upstage the others in front of the camera — parents posing with their kids but the mother holding both of them, the dad sort of leaning in from the side. All smiles though. The positions people assume in that photographic moment tell you a lot. Or the pictures we choose to put up — the place we normally adopt in a group photo, whether we tend to seize the foreground or head for the shadows.

I walk into the kitchen and switch on the kettle. I'm whistling one of the tunes from the bar last night. As the water starts its low grumble I'm straightening out the piece of paper with Patricia's number on it, looking at the handwriting as if I'm looking at her — a corner of my angry footprint over the paper.

The kettle clicks off and I pour, the old lady creaking the upstairs landing. I dump the kettle and head out to greet her. She's up on the twelfth step, her gut peeking out, clammy skin showing where her shirt has ridden up. It takes her a moment to recognise my face. I put a smile on.

She drops a foot to the next step, her jowls wobbling, her chest almost buxom with the weight she's gained, her hand holding the banister I used to spy from. Then her other foot drops gingerly down, the bandaged ankle looking massive, my first-aid skills only just clinging on. In her spare hand is the plastic tablet container with most of the little doors hanging open, just a few tablets rattling inside. I only refilled it yesterday.

She limps down the stairs in this frail cancerous opera but I'm not buying it anymore. I know the real her is still in there.

I lift a fist near my mouth, mimicking a microphone: 'Ladeees and *gentle*men, I give yooooou *Mum!*' I provide a quick round of applause and she smiles under a frown. 'As you can see, Mum is modelling a *delightful* ensemble today ...' She's still coming one step at a time, sort of frowning at me but also unsurprised by my patter, as if this is what we do every day of the week.

'Yes, Ls and Gs, your EXCLUSIVE first look at "Summer Chaos" by Cancer Klein. Taken from his killer European show "Terminal".' More applause. 'This is the very essence of clashing, ladies and gentlemen. Note the juxtaposition of different shades of red. The men's work shirt, so working girl, and yet the cashmere cardy says, "I may be dying, but I'm casual!"

'And *what* about those off-white tracksuit pants inviting the eye down, past the belly (special thanks to our sponsors at MilkMaid Ice-Cream). This is turning fashion back to front, Ls and Gs, and frequently inside out too.'

She's reached the last step and I'm giving her another enthusiastic round of applause that she greets with a warm smile, her tongue playing around her teeth.

My heart's going as I race ahead of her to the table, other people's family portraits staring at me all the way, the pictures of our real family sitting out in that leaky shed. These new pictures not fitting the darker squares left behind where the paintwork has been protected from the bleaching sun.

I show her to the best spot at the table, watching for any sign of her noticing. I kiss her elegantly on the cheek and she smells of toothpaste, a bit of the bandage hanging off her ankle now.

'Sleep?' she says smiling sweetly and lowering herself into sitting, her half-bald little head and her twinkly eyes. She gazes down at the cutlery as if they're babbling nonsense to her.

'Danish, Mum?' I offer the plate, one hand behind my back. She looks at them, shakes her head. I fill her bowl with Krispies and pour the milk, sprinkle a bucket of sugar on top. She gazes up at me, her face almost free of wrinkles thanks to all the water retention and fat under her skin — smooth as a swollen knee.

'Sleep well?' she says, her voice going up into singsong at the end.

'Yes,' I say, looking at her for a moment. 'You've taken your tablets.'

Nursey said the things she's lost could pop back briefly at any time. Or not. Mum smiles, waiting for me to do something that'll remind her how we're supposed to be behaving. I sit and pour myself Krispies and milk, take up my spoon amid the snap crackle popping.

Still holding the days of the week medication box, she follows what I do and looks down at her own cutlery, back at my spoon, selects hers, looks at mine again. I take a spoonful and she copies me. Chewing with her mouth open, milk on her chin.

'I see you got the pictures of Robert out then, Mum.' Calm, conversational. Cool.

A blank gaze so I point my spoon at the photographs laid out at the end of the table. She looks at Robert, then down at her cereal again, her face held. I shake my head at her even though she isn't looking, I lean over, rifling through the pictures for the one of Robert sitting at the table where she's sitting, a tea towel tucked into his collar to protect his clothes, a plastic mat on the floor under his chair and a strap to keep him in his seat. I toss the image closer to her and it lands almost the right way round, my heart thumping at me, my guts thickening into that fat, terrifying flexing.

I point at the image, looking her in the eye, trying to keep my demeanour smoothed out and even. 'You've ended up just like him, Mum.' I smile and she smiles too, confused — has another go at a spoonful but gets only half of one, her forefinger wet in the milk. She chews absentmindedly like a cow working the cud, but she's looking at the professional photographs on the wall now, everything standing up on my body like static.

She's gazing at the one of the family posing all in a line, their backs to one another, the dad in front of the mum, the children all concertinaing behind.

Now the one of the little brunette boy in yellow dungarees, his brother beside him with glasses already, he's only seven or eight. His little hand on his brother's shoulder, uncertainty on his face. You can almost hear the orders being barked from the sidelines.

Why do we have to smile in photos anyway, as if we're always happy. What's so bad about having portraits of real life on our walls.

The old lady's mouth is open, staring at the strangers, her spoon and the tip of her forefinger in the milk. I'm watching every twitch on her face but chewing my food slowly, my body configured at the table the way she always bullied me to be — upright and proper. I'm watching her but looking like I'm not. The Krispies reminding me of Robert after his accident, everything in him crackling and snapping. Memories of all those dinners we sat down to afterwards once he was allowed home. Robert screaming at this dinner table. Robert wanting to be released from the big chair he was strapped into. Wanting his bib off. Mum trying to hold her nerve and me sitting here, quietly eating, my manners not under scrutiny anymore. More invisible than ever but appeased somehow. Or parked upstairs with a tray and my telly up loud enough to hide Robert's bedlam. Mum red around the neck with that stress rash clawing its way up her — turning even more towards Robert now that he needed her absolutely. Just what she'd always wanted, some pit of need to throw herself into. That and the little pack of valium in the bathroom.

Then a bigger pack ... Mum floating around the house.

A noise is floating in her throat now, her hand outstretched pointing the spoon at the pictures, milk dripping into the fruit bowl in the middle of the table, a wrinkly apple sitting in it.

'What is it, Mum? What's up? And try and get your elbow off the table. You know better than that.'

She doesn't look at me she just swallows, her eyes staring at all the portraits, her brow creased. She turns round behind her, the chair creaking — more strangers staring at her. Some of them aren't even the same ethnicity as us. She swivels back, her chest rising and falling. She pushes the spoon into the air towards them then half stands, unsteady. 'Who?' she says.

I take a spoonful of cereal and chew, loving the noise filling my head. I swallow. 'You're talking a bit today aren't you, Mum. Must be one of your good days.' Another spoonful, post it in, my face locked still, the box of tablets rattling a little in Mum's hand from the strain of holding herself half up out the chair. It's not valium she's taking anymore but there's still a gliding emptiness on her face.

Not right now though, she isn't gliding now.

'*Please,*' she says, ready to cry.

'Have you overdosed? Let me see your medication.' I put my spoon down, chewing with my mouth shut, mopping my lips with a paper napkin — reach out for the tablet box but she refuses so I stand and head into the kitchen, come back with a tea towel just like the one on Robert in the picture. I tuck it into her.

'There,' I say in my best foster-child voice, 'isn't that nice, Mum, eh? Who's a mucky pup *now* then?'

I turn the picture of Robert wearing the tea towel so that it's the right way up for her, but she's still frozen, looking round at the walls, searching her memory, a noise building in her throat. There she is in that little ship's cabin on those high seas in her head, trying to keep her memories straight on the walls. Look at them falling and smashing on the floor.

I don't like seeing her pain, but there's another part of me that needs the sound I can hear building in her throat.

'WHO?' she says, her bottom lip milky and wobbling, her spoon clattering back to the bowl but her fingers stay hovering in the air with the white on them, her face breaking its shape, tears running down, me biting mine back, breathing away the emotion.

'What is it, Mum?' I say suddenly, as if I've just caught on. As if this moment is very, very serious. I turn from her to the strangers staring at us from the walls — then back to her with her face begging me, all broken open and cut in half.

I make my own face aghast. 'What, Mum, you don't know who these people are?' I lean forward, slowly shake my head. 'You've *forgotten* them? Oh, Mum, you *poor* thing.'

Her eyes fill up with what's on my face, her crying slowing for a second, her breathing. A little white tablet falling from an ajar door in the tablet box and landing on the table, her eyes darting down at it, then back up to me, killing me but I'm not stopping, no way.

She goes for the dropped tablet, her fingers struggling to get purchase until it sticks to the wetness on them and she puts it clumsily into her mouth like a giant eating a person. She winces at the bitter taste, her hand going for her orange juice but I lunge, take it far away from her, gather mine up too, and the milk jug.

I put all the liquids on the sideboard, turn to her again, her tongue chalky, her hand up near her mouth, eyes wide. Now she looks as if she really doesn't know who I am.

'You don't know *your own family*.' And I shake my head, letting her see my tears, as if her forgetting is why I'm crying. Her chest going in and out with such violence that I think she'll die. But all I want is to hear that despair, my teeth biting down on my own lip.

'Why did you do it, Mum? Why didn't you care what was

happening to *me*?' I can feel the red dot fading on my chest now, from where I just jabbed it with my finger. Mum giving me that same pathetic, stuttering despair, plus a noise that's building, growing, heading for a big boom.

I want that fucking noise.

I'm standing now, fists holding my weight forward on the table, the breakfast things wobbling with my shaking. 'Look at you now though.'

I race round the table, my chair falling over behind me, and I'm picking up the picture of Robert in the same chair, the same state. I stuff it right in close to her face. 'Karma! It's *karma*, Mum. And you were screaming at ME yesterday.'

I grab the one of me at the photographer's all those years ago. 'I was eight! *Look* at him. What, wasn't he good enough? Wasn't he *broken enough* for you?'

I drop the picture in her Krispies and take a step back, sobbing, Mum looking up at my face and breathing in a long breath, and then …

Push a lever, get a sweet.

Eventually her lungs empty of scream and she stops, the air rushing back in. She looks down at her front, the tea towel still tucked into her collar — the strangers on the wall. Another scream gushes out of her and my body lifts into goose pimples even though her sounds are also tearing me up the middle.

She turns to me after that scream, Alfie sneaking quickly by, escaping out through the cat flap, Mum's face altering as she lunges for all the pictures of Robert, collapsing on top of him, sobbing and sobbing, clawing him to her, the tablecloth slipping, almost sending her off onto the floor, her bowl of Krispies tumbling over, spilling onto her. She gathers all the Roberts up in her arms and her sobs are muted now by her face right up against the table, the pictures creasing.

'Mum, I'm sorry!' I try to stand her up but she shoves me away and the doorbell rings like it's the end of a boxing match.

I freeze, the old lady still snivelling over Robert on the table. 'Shoosh, Mum!'

I take a step closer to the window, wiping at my eyes, Mum whimpering still, bent over the table, her belly hanging out of her shirt, milk and Krispies all over her.

I straighten my clothes, my hair. I feel a sort of calm now, standing here in the semi-silence, listening, my chest going up and down.

'Shh! I think someone's at the door.'

She shuts up too, stopping to listen, the whole house seeming to hum with all that's just happened in it. Grandma bleeding to death in the toilet. Dad and Mum drifting further and further apart until his heart went on him one morning while he was lying on the couch watching breakfast TV, heckling the weatherwoman about her tits as she gestured to the clouds in the north — black diagonal lines under them. Rain predicted. Mum coming in with an armful of washing and Dad sprawled out white as a cloud. No more weather for him.

The predicted downpour came the day we put him in the ground. The way it did when we'd put Robert there all those years before.

A policewoman appears at the front window and peeks in, her hands cupped against the light.

I jump, then manage to wave at her. 'Just a minute.'

She walks away saying something to someone beyond the window.

'*The police* are here.' My voice cracks and I flutter into the kitchen like a trapped blackbird. '*Now* look what you've done, Mum!' I come back out and want to wail at all these stolen pictures staring at me from the walls.

Put the cuffs on, I'm stuffed.

On the way to the door I stop in the hallway, straighten my hair, take a breath. Even if she says something they won't listen to some dying old lady. Surely.

I'm the innocent one.

I wipe my eyes again then brush off some of the Krispies and head down the hall.

'*Someone* at the *door*, Mum! Who could it be, eh?' The police looking like distorted sharks through the front door's peephole. Two of them.

I open up, the light striking me in the face. 'Good morning, officers, what can I do for you?' but my fluttering voice betrays me.

I try to think they're just a man and a woman in uniform but they don't look like a man and woman, they look like a policeman and a policewoman, both of them scanning me with their police eyes.

The policewoman turns down her radio while the policeman introduces himself but I'm thinking more than I'm listening so I only catch 'Senior Constable' something and a 'Williamson'. The policewoman smiles. She must be Williamson.

'Can we come in for a moment?' she says.

'Of course.' I drop my voice, 'But I have to warn you my mother has cancer,' as if it's contagious. A pause for them to do their face changes and mumbles. 'Terminal. In the brain. Really advanced. She's very confused.' I thin out my lips and nod solemnly, inviting them to quite understand. 'She finds it hard to talk … And doesn't make any sense when she does, I'm afraid, poor thing. Gibberish.'

'Well, we won't keep you any longer than necessary,' he says and I step back and let them in, the stampeding inside me becoming unbearable as they pause to wipe their feet and pass me by — the smell of cheap perfume, cologne, the muttering from their radios, all of it jamming my frequencies.

I shut the door to the hedges and follow the police-people into the house. Just keep your cool.

We congregate in the lounge, the policewoman staring at me while the other officer says a 'Hello there' to my mum, loud and patronising. 'No, don't get up, love,' he says. 'Nothing for you to worry about.'

Love.

'Would you like some tea, coffee? Krispies?' I say, a little high-pitched and smiling — Mum's hands up around her chest, wrists facing each other as if from an angry jumping-up dog. Like the police are all the bad news she's had over the years. This house has stood so much bad news.

The officers wave away my empty offers of tea, filling up the room with their uniforms, Williamson showing me her bum as she turns to look at the pictures — wandering around the lounge in her comfortable shoes, Mum watching her face as if she might have come to explain who's in these pictures.

I keep an eye on Mum, willing the words to stay inside her. She picks up the tea towel and starts kneading it, her face awash with new tears running down the tight swelling of her cheeks — Robert still strewn all over the table, Krispies and milk all over her, the floor. The tablecloth adrift. There may as well be my dead dad on the couch and Robert outside fitting in the garden. Grandma's blood inch deep all over the carpet.

While I'm looking at Williamson staring at the stolen portraits, Senior what's-his-face is watching me. I can feel his eyes, like he's framed and stolen too.

'It's ok, Mum, these officers have just popped by, nothing's the matter I don't think. There's not really anyone else left to die is there!' I look at her, trying for a smile but she's sobbing again. 'What have you come about, officers?' I say over the old lady's noise. 'As you can see it's not a good time.'

My leg starts up thumping then inside my trousers. *Whose* body *is it.*

Williamson is coming closer, Senior what's-his-face levelling his gaze at me. 'We have a report about a —'

Mum grabs Williamson, mumbling something to her, tugging on her uniform but glancing occasionally over at me. Limping heavily, she leads the reluctant officer to the pictures and all I can do is stare at the conspicuous mismatch between the portraits and the dusty, darker squares on the paintwork.

'Come on, Mum,' I say, the officers paying attention to her, waiting for some sense to come but I'm taking her by the hand that's still holding the tablet box. She wrenches free, shouts that deaf shout — a nothing word but it lights the touch paper of panic in me and it burns brightly, blinding.

'You've got some very diverse portraits up here, not all family are they?' Senior what's-his-face says.

'Ha, yes. Does look funny, doesn't it. Been rearranging them today, actually. Something to do, you know, while ...' I gesture at Mum then put my most stoic face on. 'Mum and Dad were foster carers for years. We've lost count of the boys, haven't we, Mum. Saving the world. Those are of the foster boys. And girls. Girls too. Plus their families, now they're grown up. Quite a dynasty. Marcus there, and Patricia look, that one. Patricia. You remember Patricia, Mum.'

She turns to the officers, shaking her head, stuttering unintelligible things. The bandage unravelling further behind her. My knee keeping up its *hammering*, the police giving one another a look.

I step to the constable, mainly to stop my leg shaking. 'Perhaps we should go outside, that would be better, wouldn't it,' the words coming out of me in that constricted rollercoaster voice — the G-force of anxiety.

I don't wait for a yes, I just move through the room a little and Williamson has her hands on Mum's upper arms, restraining her in a way, comforting her in another. The senior constable glances at Williamson and they pass one of those secret, partner looks.

'That might be better,' he says.

Williamson goes to release Mum but she drags her over to one of the portraits on the other wall, three children in it, the eldest holding a baby like it's too heavy. My mum pointing at it, then looking at Williamson for the answer.

'What is it, love?' she says in her patronising, policewoman voice.

'Just go outside, officers. *Please*. I'll be right behind you. Poor thing is so confused, aren't ya, Mum.' And I've got hold of her while she's hitting at me, trying to get away. I keep gripping on while the police leave, trying to keep my teeth from biting down on my lip in that angry shape.

The front door clicks and I march her out through the kitchen and into the back garden.

'*Listen!*' I'm facing her, an arm holding each shoulder, my lip in that shape but her eyes roll right up into her head and everything stops, her whole body, a puddle of bubbly saliva sitting in the bottom of her open mouth, her eyes just the whites.

'Mum!'

She starts to vibrate, her teeth locking together but catching a snippet of her lips. High voltage passing through her body.

Then just as suddenly her eyes come down and she draws in this long, hurricane inhalation.

'What the *hell* was that! Jeez, Mum, you scared me.' And I'm wondering what new part of her the cancer just forced its way into, kicking in another door. Looting who she is. Her eyes all unfocused, then settling and she's with me, her mouth still flooded with saliva.

'You ok? Look, stay out here, just for a sec. Sit down actually.' I fold her onto the grass. 'Look at the clouds or something. You're confused again today. You know you're not well, don't you?'

She nods, slumped on the grass with her arms wrapped round her.

'It'll all come back, Mum. You'll recognise those faces again tomorrow, I promise.' If I'm not in prison.

Her face brightens at that, searching me for confirmation. I nod gravely, looking her in the eye.

I kneel down then and take her hand, around the medication box she's still clinging to, my thumb stroking the skin, loving her hand — her grip cool and far away but wrapped inside mine. Both of us squinting out here in the fresh brightness of the outdoors, the plum tree all forlorn at the end of the lawn. I wrap my arms around her but she doesn't really respond, her body stiff, arms by her side. I imagine her eyes open and staring and bored over my shoulder. Mine are tightly shut though, her smell reminding me of hot baths and tea. Of Robert. And Dad. Dad especially, the loss of him coming at me now like a locomotive ache. Mum not hugging me back.

I leave her marooned in the garden brightness, barefoot and unravelled on the grass I'm always meaning to mow. It seems to take her over. I head indoors, steadying myself a moment, holding on to the kitchen surface with all the cut marks on it from where people haven't used a chopping board, just making a quick cut of something, a hunk of cheese to tide you over before dinner.

I tease a picture of Robert up out of the Krispies on the floor and it's him in a hospital bed a few years after the accident but it reminds me of that actual day, his real parents coming down the hospital corridor, their faces taut.

I could tell at age eight they belonged to Robert. The look of the mum, the look on their faces, as if they didn't fit into the everyday arena of society — even a hospital. They belonged on the fringes, shadow people living on the periphery. Apology written on their faces underneath the bitterness. The sweet smell of alcohol on them.

I stayed out in the disinfected hospital corridor, swallowed-up and tiny in a chair while they shuffled into intensive care. That quiet pause before the hysteria, the sound of breaking glass and shouting. Me holding my breath in the corridor and only eight and knowing that I was bad, bad, bad. Feeling like I was a stick of rock and what'd happened was written right through the middle of me. That red writing. It's still there, written up the centre of me.

I look at the pictures of strangers hanging on our lounge wall, wanting to go and take them down and throw them over the fence but the policewoman is at the window again. I smile at her, head into the hall, stop to wipe my face then traipse out to them, my eyes struggling to readjust to the front-garden light.

'This is obviously a difficult time,' he's saying and she's smiling a little, trying to show they come in peace. 'My mum went through a similar illness,' he says. 'But you understand we have to do our job and, so if you can just tell me —'

'The pictures.'

His eyebrows go up.

'Sorry.' I shake my head, reddening. Idiot! Robert on the concrete behind me, one of his legs bent awkwardly underneath him. The sound of the hedge-trimmer. 'From the speed camera,' I say, as if it's obvious what I meant, my hand reaching for Patricia's phone number in my pocket. 'I've got a speeding habit.'

They look at one another again. 'We're here about reports of a vehicle licensed to this address, registration number ...' he's reading it out and I'm glad the Volvo is in the garage, missing window and dented door and all. 'That would be your mother's vehicle, sir?'

I nod.

'And has it been out of your possession at any stage in the last twenty-four hours, borrowed maybe?'

'No. What's happened?'

'I assume your mother is no longer driving.'

I give him a look.

'If you'd just tell us what happened yesterday,' Williamson says, saving me from Mr Agatha Christie here.

'Yesterday?' I say, and my hand can't help but run itself shakily through my hair, Robert's blood up the sides of the officer's black, comfortable shoes. My knee hammering. 'Well, I took my mother to the beauty place and then —'

'Which beauty place would that be, please?' He has his pad and pen. I tell him and he makes a note, then lets the hand with the pad drop. 'I'm guessing you know what this is about. We've received allegations of someone meeting your description assaulting another driver. We have the gentleman's statement and that of witnesses. Were you involved in an argument outside the beauty parlour?'

Williamson is walking over to inspect the garage, looking in through the window. She's wearing tights under that skirt.

'I regret it, officer, I really do. I was waiting for my mother and ...' I sigh. 'She was crossing the road all dolled up and happy. It was lovely to see.' I take out my cigarettes but I'm regretting showing him how unsteady I am. I smile again, Williamson coming back from her inspection even though they probably did that before they came in. I know their tricks. Six weeks' training and they think they're something.

I turn back to the senior constable and the little scab of blood on his chin, thin as a snowflake where he cut himself shaving. He's got one of those chins with a bum line running down it.

'Mum was crossing the road and that guy came along in his car and, my mother really doesn't have long and I'm looking after her on my own, a nurse comes to check up on her once a week is all and she didn't even turn up this week. That guy in his flashy car can't wait a few seconds for Mum to limp across the road.' I take a drag and blow it straight out then look at the cigarette, the taste making me judder. 'She's not as quick as she used to be. This guy hoots at her. Not a toot, a blast. His bonnet almost up against her. She falls over because of it. I think he hit her. Not hard.' They give each other a look. 'She could have broken something, or run out into the main road. He could've seen from looking at her she was ill. You can tell, can't you?' Another drag, nods all round. 'I'm not proud of myself but I saw red, I really did. He's not hurt, is he?'

'He is actually. Pretty scratched up and bruised. Shaken. His key was broken off in the ignition.'

'Is that right?' I drop my cigarette and hide my face in stubbing it out.

'That *is* right. Plus there's the car he reversed into to consider. The damage to the driver's own car. The expenses mount up. Why did you leave the scene when there'd been an accident?'

'Why did I leave the scene?' Thinking time, thinking time. 'I'm not duty-bound to remain at an accident I wasn't a driver in, am I? Plus I suppose I wanted to get Mum home. She was very upset by the man and —'

'And by your actions, I would imagine?' the policewoman says.

'I expect she was, yes. I was upset too, as it happens. Didn't sleep a wink last night. What can I say. He frightened a dying lady. Driving without due care and attention. Stop sign. She was crossing the road. I'm happy to apologise to the driver. I regret it totally.'

'It's not really about apologies, it's about assault.'

There's Robert, fitting on the ground. There he is with the sky in his eyes.

The policeman-man looks at Williamson again and she says, 'The driver hasn't pressed charges at this stage. He's aware of your mum's poor health. It's up to us.'

Yesss!

I nod at her, really look at her for a moment, then down at my feet.

'We can still press charges though, even if the driver doesn't,' the constable says.

I'm feeling better by the second. Exponentially. Relief is probably the best of all emotions. That's all happiness is anyway, isn't it? Relief from sadness.

'I see.'

Now the police-people are waiting to see how that affects me when it sinks in. I try to hold on to my look of regret, hide my delight. They want to watch me realise they have power. But they're just public servants. And yet most of them spend their whole careers trying to believe otherwise. That's why they hate witnessing official documents; why they hate the beat; why they hate people asking for directions, picture opportunities. But they *are* just public servants. I should get them to mow the lawn.

'I understand,' I say, looking down like I'm nine years old and in the headmaster's office of whichever school I was in at that time. I went to a lot of different schools after Robert's accident. We went to church a lot too after Robert, Mum and me. Dad didn't do much after Robert, except wallow and eat. Digging his grave with his teeth.

'But considering the circumstances, we're not going to do that this time,' he says, hungry for my gratitude. 'I've decided to caution you.' And his voice and posture change as if with the weight of upholding the law. He goes into that formal spiel in which he cautions me and points out all the small print and how if there's another offence this one can be brought into consideration along with the new one.

He gets through it then says, 'Do you understand?'

'I do. Thank you. You've been more than fair.'

He nods, satisfied, goes to his car and Williamson paces away a little, turning up her radio again and cocking an ear into it, eyeing me occasionally. I give her my best grin.

Senior bum-face comes back with a pad from which he tears a printed piece of paper and it's the caution speech he gave me and numbers to call for advice and to appeal, and headings like *What if I think I have been treated unfairly?*

I take it but I'm not quite here anymore because I'm just relieved, and all I want to do is eat and smoke and — all the things you do when you've been scared. I'll ring Patricia soon as I get a second.

'There's a chance the driver will press civil charges to get his money back.' And he shrugs. 'But on a personal note, I do wish you all the best for you and your mother.' He looks me in the eye when he says it and it's the first time his face has really lost its police-officer mask. Williamson is softening too. Suddenly they're people rather than police-people, as if a formal ceremony has just happened and now we can all relax.

They say their goodbyes and make their way past the hedges.

'These are getting big ideas, aren't they,' he says, pointing to them. Doing his 'and finally' bit like it's the end of the nightly news.

'Yes,' I say, my hands ready to gesture to Williamson as soon as her partner isn't looking. 'You want to cut them for me, officer?'

He smiles and turns to unlock the car, Williamson's head looking at me over the roof. I make the phone sign at my ear then the writing sign, my eyebrows up, questioning. A grin spreads over my face but she's confused for a moment, then the penny drops and she looks round at her colleague who's getting in the car, oblivious.

It'd be pretty big to get the phone number of an on-duty officer — bed her while she's still in uniform.

I've had so many of these moments, waiting for the stamp of approval, but in my mind she's already half out of her uniform, her back arched. I want to kiss the long arm of the law.

He's in the car and she's slowly opening her door, those black letters on the roof of the car, for helicopters I guess. Or so birds know which cars to crap on.

She shakes her head at me, but I think she wants to, which is probably enough – her radio talking and she cocks her head at it, then she's in the car too, her colleague glancing at me, this strange look on his cut, bum face.

They leave me here between the hedges, my hand coming up to wave as the powerful engine takes hold.

Then that silence after they've gone, a breeze rustling the garden. A little more emptiness waking up in my insides. I look up at the sky, our patch of sky, the clouds looking like fancy French loaves.

I walk in and shut the door, my eyes cauterised of colour after the glare, the house dim and stagnant — dank with heaviness. I look at those photos of strangers, Alfie on the table licking up the milk, her cancerous nose making greedy pig sounds.

I take out Patricia's number and flatten it on the little table by the phone, wipe my hands on my trousers and pick up the receiver. I dial, my heart thumping when I look at the stolen pictures on the wall, remembering the way Williamson stared and stared at them while she was here.

I might get her back to my place, after all.

People have voicemail voices just like they have telephone-number-reciting voices. I listen to Patricia's, all the effort she's put in, the number of takes she must have gone through before she was satisfied. I leave a message, which I don't usually do. I give her my number, ask her to call.

It was a good message. Calm. Kind. Self-possessed, under the circumstances.

I walk through the lounge and give Alfie a stroke, leaving her to her free lunch. In the back garden the plum tree has its summer look — that waspy hairdo. More of the insects busying themselves with the fallen fruit rotting on the ground.

As a boy I loved to chuck the plums with wasps still inside, watching for whether the insect would survive the impact against the shed wall. Sometimes the wasp would fly woozily out of the wreckage, sometimes it would be scrabbling among the sticky goo, dying slowly — Dad telling me off for the stains on the shed. I can still almost see them.

Mum isn't in the garden but there are her odd socks and discarded bandage on the grass, sticking up like worms' tails. I sit down heavily.

There she is, there's the old lady. 'What you doing, Mum? I can see you.' Her face moves from the dirty windows, into the shadows. 'Why are you hiding in the shed?'

I lie back on the grass, my lower spine giving me that long, breathtaking pull as it lets go.

Since I last looked, some unseen wind has shuffled the clouds out of all that uniformity. They're elongated now, some of them billowing up into the air, hundreds of feet tall. Those are the storm clouds — cumulonimbus. The high wispy ones are cirrus. There are names for different types of clouds the way Eskimos have names for snow. I turn my neck and strain to see the shed, Mum's eyes on me.

'Come outside, Mum.' I point upwards at a cloud, as if I've seen something in it. 'Look!' and she leans forward but bumps the window with her face, pulls away again, a smudge left in the dust and cobwebs on the glass. I can still faintly see her in there, comforting her forehead.

I get up, waiting for the stars to leave my eyes, then head through the sunlight and into the shed. She's at the back now, her arms wrapped around some of the real pictures of our family.

'Well done, Mother. You recognise *those* people?'

She nods slowly, backing away into gardening tools at the rear of the shed.

'Are you planning to stay in here all day?'

'No.'

She sees the electric shock that simple utterance gives my face.

'No.' She says it again, pressing the button again, shocking me again. She looks just as surprised the button works. 'No!' Her chin comes thrusting out at me.

Here we go. 'Did you take a bucketload of steroids this morning?'

'No!' she says, not visibly referring to what I'm asking, she's just loving the word. Such an important word for our safety — no. The hardest word when you're a child. The most impossible word, in fact, when you're as powerless as a child. Whereas these days — these days yes must be the hardest for me to say. My adulthood this overcompensation for my childhood.

'Look. Sorry about earlier. I'm an awful son. I am. Come out the shed, there's sharp things in here. And you're barefoot. Your foot's bleeding. You'll get yerself stung, standing in the plums.' I hold out a hand and she tightens her grip on all our pictures.

'The police,' she says.

'Gone.'

She shakes her head. 'The police, what.'

'Wow, those extra steroids are doing you the —'

'What did they want?'

We both get a jolt from that.

'You're a right little chatterbox today.' Then I swallow, I can't help it. She smiles, inching forward, standing up straighter, the blood from her heel sticking to the dusty concrete floor, that and the rotten plum fruit squished between her toes.

I look at all the old metal garden implements and tools around us, Dad's red shaving mirror hanging on the wall beside me. I wish I could see him in that mirror now, or a little more of him in me when I look in a mirror.

There's a faded cask of wine here that he must have sat and drunk, thinking back, full of regret. Once I was a bit older, he and I used to call this his Wank Den. He lived out his days here, fattening and isolated — the death of a Pollyanna. He was always so terrified of pain and conflict, skittering and skating miles on the thinnest of reasons to be cheerful. Anything but allow himself to fall through to the real murk beneath.

It's his fault then too, what happened. He's why I had to carry it all these years.

'They wanted to know about yesterday, outside Lizzy's place. The thing that happened,' I say, but she makes a face. 'You remember. I got angry with that bastard driver who scared you?'

She nods. Then something strikes her and her face saddens.

'I am sorry about earlier, Mum.' I look down at the floor, the blood purpling on her scaly foot. 'It isn't easy for me you know, you being ill.'

She comes forward, up close, a picture of the four of us facing outwards, from that morning at the photographer's. In the image, Mum is looking into the camera like she's a queen and we're her corgis. Dad's shoulder eclipsed by hers. Those subtle fights a camera shows — the way a lens magnifies self-doubt. My dad putting his ubiquitous brave face over all that fear and disappointment. Desperately hanging on to his powerful, bullying woman.

Look at her now though, contrasted so starkly with the her in that photograph, both the women looking straight at me — supposedly the same woman. I almost have to look away. How the world turns.

She's stroking my shoulder now, clumsy and uncertain, the pictures in her arm slipping. This present-day, unrecognisable version of Mum comforting me the way one gorilla comforts another.

Her kindness always disarms me. I look up into the shed roof, there's my bicycle lying across the rafters. Dad must have sat and looked at it as he sipped his consolation wine. And so I'm reminded how unlikely it is that my secret is a secret.

She puts down the pictures and comes closer, stroking me again, watching what she's doing to my innards — stepping forward further because I retreat from the intimacy.

It strikes me though that if I finally said it out loud, it wouldn't really be my mum I'd be telling, but this old lady. Look at the difference between that version of her in the picture, and what's left of her now.

Having imagined saying it aloud all these years, writhing in the back of the family car on long journeys with wanting to say it, Robert in his special chair to stop him crawling up front or back or climbing out the window — pulling up the handbrake. Robert with the body, eventually, of a nineteen-year-old. The strength of an adult, and yet the mind of a baby, and no restraint. I feared him as much as I pitied him. As much as I'd once hated him. Robert to me becoming this living symbol of my ugliness. Of how bad I must have been to deserve my mother's neglect — my mother's apparent disgust at what came out of her. If I came out of her. I used to tell people I was a foster child anyway. It was the obvious conclusion to me. That or a mix-up at the hospital.

All this time I've imagined saying my secret aloud, writing it in a letter, or speaking it as a eulogy at Robert's funeral — here I am moving towards saying it to this strange copy of my mother in my dead dad's Wank Den. After all those daydreamed scenes of redemption and absolution, is it here, in this place, now? Is *this* the scene?

It's never like the daydreams is it.

'I did it, Mum. I hurt Robert.'

Her gorilla hand stops stroking and my legs need to sit me down.

'I'd give anything to change it, but … I hurt Robert.' I hang my head but can still feel her gaze. 'I was only eight. A boy.' Deep breaths, wipe at my eyes with a sleeve, looking at the floor. 'Why wasn't I good enough for you?'

I step closer to the answers I need but they take a step back, bumping against the shelving on the rear wall, an old rusty tin of

Gro-fast falling to the floor. She looks round at it, then back at the questions she's trapped in a shed with.

I lay a hand on her shoulder, hoping there's still enough of her left. I can't tell though. She's just looking at me, her chest going up and down. I lift my hand and show her the scar on the palm, frustrated with myself for not coming home and having this out sooner, before it was too late. Because by the look of her, I am too late.

'I was wetting my bed until I was *thirteen!*' I hit the worktop, everything jumping off it into the air, dust lifting into the weak light seeping in through the dirty windows — my bottom lip going. 'I was wetting the bed and you still packed me up and sent me off to school camp! Do you know what that was like? Sleeping in a dorm full of boys and knowing what'd happen when I woke up in a wet bed every morning.'

She makes to leave but I fill up the doorway. She's crying now too, the old lady. But it's a held-in crying, the way she used to before the comet.

'*Say* something. You've got your answer. Now you've actually got a *reason*. I'm telling you I did it. I hurt Robert. Now you know. You always knew, didn't you.' Her face changes but I don't know what it means.

I follow her gaze to Dad's shaving mirror hanging on the wall, all dusty, the reflective coating pockmarked, the red frame off-red in the places where the sun must get onto it.

'You have to take your share, Mum. Saint Mary — too busy looking after *other people's* sons.' I swallow back another watery shove from my innards. '*You* hurt Robert.'

Her teeth start then, eating at her bottom lip. I step instinctively back but she comes at me, the look on her face frightening. She snatches the mirror off the wall and brings it up and thrusts it round to show me.

There I am — that face. There's what I avoid. Her hand shaking and the image oscillating with it. There's the guilt I bury under blame and anger.

'You,' she says. '*You* hurt!' her teeth gnawing at her lip and I'm eight years old again and the mirror comes in towards me and strikes my head. Not hard, but it doesn't need to hurt to hurt.

Her face reappears in front of mine, the mirror flung down and smashing daylight fragments across the floor. I stumble out, squinting my way across the overgrowing garden and collapsing onto the grass, the clouds white and peaceful, harmless. I'm looking at them, Mum limping towards me, muttering.

She makes a sound as she hunkers down to my level and I lie flatter against the lawn, feeling its support.

She sits beside me with her cracked and mucky feet pointing at the house, her hands playing with a daisy between her legs, her eyes seeming bigger with the water loitering in them — the beginnings of dreadlocks at the back of her head from where she lies there night after night, snoring in the darkness. Such a brittle division now between her and darkness proper.

I watch her slowly lay herself down beside me, her feet lifting a little as she grunts, her stomach struggling to lower her. Then she's right here, her face turning to me so that I have to look away.

She reaches out and finds my hand, the feeling of her wafer-thin skin smooth against my scarred hand. My eyes clamp shut, my fingers around hers, something tectonic slipping inside me. We hold on, both of us, lying here looking at the clouds but thinking about our hands.

And even though she may have forgotten the truth by tomorrow, leaving me alone with it again, to carry it, at least right now it's here with us. All of it.

She keeps hold of me but rolls onto her side, her front against me. I drape an arm over my eyes to hide, her other hand stroking my chest, her face nuzzled in close to my ear, that mouth of hers a babbling brook of broken syllables. Then it forms a shape, 'S'okay,' and she shooshes me. 'S'okay.'

It makes me want to open my chest and put her right inside. It makes me want to do and say so many things but the outpouring won't let me. And I can't help but wonder how many millimetres.

16

I cry a lot in bed now and I've been thinking about it and decided I cry for two reasons.

1. I don't know why we're here. Humans. Which makes me really sad. I ask Mum and Dad but they always shrug and give small answers like 'We just are.' Or 'To tidy our room.'

But not knowing drives me a little bit crazy. There has to be a reason but I can't find one anywhere and I asked Santa Claus when I sat on his knee, even though he was really just some guy.

Plus Dad told me to wait until I was on Santa's lap then shout 'Hey what's that lump in your trousers, Santa!'

I asked Santa why we're here and he got flustered and said 'To love each other.' But that's what we do ONCE we're here and doesn't explain at all why we come here in the first place.

2. The second thing I cry about much more than the why are we here thing is that one day Mum and Dad are going to die.

Mum comes home from hospital tomorrow and I can't sleep. Robert's awake too, I can hear his floorboards. Only he's awake cos of different feelings. Robert has the feelings you're supposed to have.

I've got my TV on even though I'm not supposed to after 9 cos that's when it's the news and films and people dying. Daytimes are school and singing and work and talk shows.

Alfie's here for comfort but I have to hold him to keep him on my bed. Eventually he'll get tired and it'll be like he wants to be here.

All over the world people are dying. Right now even. I try to think about good world things like how many people are sitting on the toilet or sneezing or picking their nose, but at night and with Mum coming home it just ends up being about how many people are crying or dying. As if sadness is nocturnal. Like foxes and owls and burglars.

Everyone dies and that means Mum and Dad will die and I can't stop crying about it even though crying is scarier when it happens to me when I'm on my own. And even though I'm trying not to cry so I can sleep and not be grumpy but happy and loveable tomorrow for Mum coming home, I'm still all curled up and crying and I can't call out to Dad because I don't want him to talk about it because if I talk about it to anybody it will make it happen and I don't want Mum and Dad to die and I don't want to die and I don't think anybody should have to die. Because dying means you're dead.

Alfie's trying to get away even though I'm holding and stroking him. He doesn't care that I'm sad. I hold him harder and he scratches me and it's my bad hand he gets. I push him off my bed. Then go get him, try and make friends again but he's struggling in my arms. He wants to go downstairs. He doesn't CARE.

I open my door and carry him to the stairs.

If people stopped being born maybe God would cut back on the deaths. Grown-ups should just stop making babies, like Mum and Dad have stopped. Which might mean they won't die after all.

I creep down the stairs really slowly, Alfie trying to get away even more cos he thinks I'm going to give him his flying lessons.

I think when Mum and Dad die I'll ask God if he can let me die too. Or for us all to die in bed together watching TV.

Dad is busy laughing at a comedy. He'd probably laugh at the news tonight he's so happy. I hold Alfie tight and his body is all stiff, claws out. I open up the washing machine and now he wants to stay in my arms, his claws hanging on but I put him in and shut the lid and hold it down. His meowing sounds funny from inside.

I look at the machine's dial, trying to decide. I turn it really slowly so Dad doesn't hear the clicking. *Delicates* is probably best. I turn it to *Delicates* but don't switch it on yet cos he needs some bubbles in his bath but ever since Dad's been in charge nothing is where it should be. I can't find the washing powder.

Darkness changes normal things into magic evil, like when I wake up in the middle of the night and there's a crouching monster about to pounce but in the morning it's turned back into a school bag and a football.

Darkness is why animals cry out at night and why owls have to be wise.

Alfie's crying now too, like me. Mum comes home tomorrow which should be good but I'm going to have all the feelings that happen to me when Robert and Mum are around.

Because Mum and Robert are like having darkness around.

Maybe I'm a fox. Foxes cry alone at night too. I hear them sometimes and it's the saddest sound, after seagulls.

The world's so sad even animals cry.

17

I wake to the sound of Alfie snoring even though she's awake. Her face is up close to mine, the growth bigger than her nose now and I realise her snoring's been percolating thunderstorms and bears into my dreams.

It feels late but I refuse to give up on sleep, my eyes shut, my body stilled, willing my mind to slip away again but it's thinking about how I let the cat out of the bag yesterday. And wondering whether Mum's addled brain will have ushered the cat straight back into that black bag. Which will mean maybe I've had the relief of finally saying it, without the shame of her knowing.

Or the pain of sharing it, without the freedom of not having to carry it anymore.

Mum fell asleep on me in the garden yesterday and wouldn't rouse properly so I carried her in and put her on the couch, wrapped her in blankets and took those strangers down off the walls.

The longer I lie here the more nervous I'm getting so I dislodge Alfie and get up, check on Mum's bedroom in case she made it off the couch in the night and up to bed.

Empty.

I pad quietly back, turning off the landing light I left on for her — stand here at the top of the stairs listening for signs of life.

Silence, except for Alfie's impersonation of Darth Vader.

I dress slowly, the cat gone now that my bed has cooled. I check my phone again — no Patricia. I put in my Canadian SIM card in case there's any love coming from there. Another silence.

Downstairs, I look in on Mum from the doorway and she's in a tight ball on the couch, the blankets on the floor. Alfie is with her now, breathing that incessant noise.

'Mum?' I say from the threshold, examining her all curled up, foetal and frowning, wet with sweat.

I cross the room and pick up her bedding, touch a hand to her shoulder. 'Mum.' I check for a pulse, the skin clammy but there's a beat there. I shake her and she brings a hand up to her forehead.

'You got a headache?' A slight nod. 'I'll get you your tablets.' I'm rushing out to the kitchen. 'And painkillers.'

I don't bother with the days of the week box but empty a load of steroids out of the giant pill bottle, adding a few paracetamol. I grab a glass and turn on the tap, stuff the glass under the stream and the water cascades round and out over my clothes.

I cradle her head like it's made of burnt-through matches, still she winces from the pain. It takes an age to get all the tablets in, her gagging in between — the pressure in her brain pushing her up against those white and immovable skull walls.

I start dialling emergency then hang up and try the nurse instead, bullet points sitting on the card she gave me:

- *Are you sure your question isn't answered on our website?*
- *Is your call absolutely necessary? You may be preventing another caller with a genuine emergency.*

After the phone call I put Alfie and her nasal earthquake outside with some milk then head round to the front and smoke, pacing in the garden, checking on Mum through the window — pacing again, looking up and down the road for the nurse who said she'd be here soon.

The hedges are still half cut from where I told myself I'd do the top later but left it at what I could reach from the ground.

It's a long time before the little branded car pulls up about fifteen metres down the road. I head for the gate to go and meet her but peek round instead, watching her leaning into the rear-view mirror, applying make-up, doing her hair. This takes her something like two minutes. And despite the *genuine emergency*, seeing her do this wakes up the doughboy.

She gets out and I head quickly inside and click the front door shut, wondering why I'm taking the trouble to pretend I don't know she's arrived. It's stupid. Another of those little-white-lie acts we put on. Like when you're meeting someone and you're there first, eagerly looking for them but when you see them you pretend not to have noticed — assume the pose of someone engrossed in the paper, the menu, a book. White liars, all of us.

'The nurse is here, Mum.'

I watch her through the security eyelet as she comes up the path. She looks even more volumptuous seen through that glass. Dad's word, not mine. He always noticed volumptuous women, but married the opposite.

I watch her through the peephole as she does her hair on the doorstep, looks down at her cleavage, undoes a tunic button. Does it back up, then reaches in and lifts her tits higher in her bra. Finally she rings the bell and I wait a bit, my heart going.

'Vicky, I was starting to think you weren't coming.' I step back only a little so she has to squeeze by. She goes to give me her front side but does an awkward exchange and gives me the back.

I can't wait.

'I was with another patient.'

'She's in the lounge.'

I watch her waddle off before I close the door.

'Hello, Mary. You feeling poorly, eh? Let's have a look at you then.'

Vicky perches on the edge of the couch and it's clear Mum's been sick while I've been pacing outside.

'Can you get me a bowl or a bucket.'

I head off, my heart beating with a different urgency. I bring the bowl and Mum is vomiting, Vicky having got her over on her side, Mum's head cradled gently. Green coming out. Such withering retching sounds, Vicky stroking and shooshing — no sign of disgust, only tenderness for a stranger. Vicky right up close to something I'm not sure I could face and it's my own mum. Although maybe Vicky wouldn't be so calm if it was her mum. I don't know. I just know nurses are amazing.

'I'll need a tissue too,' she says in the same tender voice she's been using on Mum. I go for the tissues, Alfie outside the window, steaming up the glass. That piece of mica rock glistening at me from the window ledge.

Michael rock, Dad called it.

Mum is reclined and panting when I return with tissues, Vicky stroking her forehead. She mops at Mum's mouth and hands me the bowl. I can't look at it, carrying it finger and thumb into the bathroom and turning away, pouring, my breath held. Perhaps a few drops joining with Grandma's blood on the U-bend. I flush the toilet and come back with a bucket.

'Can you hear me, Mary?' Vicky's voice raised as if to be heard over the sound of the wrecking ball swinging inside Mum's head. 'I'm going to give you your medication by injection, Mare. It'll make you feel better. And something for the nausea.'

She opens her bag, one of her hands never leaving Mum's. Mum holding on too.

Then there's me a few steps away from the back of the couch.

I couldn't hold Mum's hand from here.

'I gave her some painkillers and steroids just before, Vicky.'

'I noticed,' she says.

After the injection she lifts Mum's eyelids and shines a light.

'What does that tell you?'

'I can see how the pupil reacts, but also distortion to the optic nerve from the intra-cranial pressure. Pressure in the skull. Can you do me a favour? Go and get your mum some ice cubes to suck on, she's probably thirsty. And put the kettle on, eh? She's not the only one.'

When she's finished her examination she makes some notes, then sits for a moment just stroking Mum's forehead, the room so quiet, just the three of us breathing.

'*I'm going to have a chat to your son now, Mary.* You'll be alright here for a bit. Just rest. Stay on your side. There's a bucket in case you feel sick *but the medicine works very quickly.* We won't be far.'

We both creep away as if from a sleeping baby.

I've opened up the back door to let some breathing in, Vicky and me at the kitchen table, teas steaming. I take my phone out of my pocket to make room, plonk it on the table.

'She's on the maximum steroid dosage now. That mightn't necessarily stabilise her, we'll just have to see. I'm concerned though. Have you had a chance to go through the leaflet I gave you, about the hospice?'

I nod. I am intent on what she's saying. I really am. But even her South African accent is starting to seem attractive. Her cleavage soft and inviting. My desire tainted by a stab of guilt that I'm capable of thinking about this with Mum ill in the next room. But what better time for comfort than this? And what better comfort.

'So you're ok for me to go ahead and call them, put a bed on standby for her? I don't think she'll be at home much longer. It's not fair on either of you. If the system were better there'd be more support available earlier in the ...' She's got nice hands. The one not cradling her mug of tea is a little towards me on the table, no wedding ring and no tan line from where she might take it off for work '... In any case, your mum's reached the stage where she does qualify, and the Santa Christi is just lovely, I promise you. They'll make her very ...' My heart is that squishing of a kinked hose, my good hand ready, her chest a little exposed '... do you think? Someone who can give you some support too?'

It's like I'm surrounded by static electricity as I reach for her, my hand on hers, my face set to earnest, and feeling it too.

'Thank you for the way you've been with my mum. Seriously.'

She stiffens a bit from the touch, looks down at her tea, sits up a little straighter, my hand on hers, eyes burning into the top of her head, then her cleavage. My touch wandering up her arm and I can see her uniform going in and out, in and out from her breathing deep and full and I don't care, I run my hand up over her shoulder, caress her neck, and the line is crossed and way back behind me. I'm out in no man's land and there's that glorious finish line. She looks at me now, her face flushed and anguished with wanting, both of us panting. It's pathetic.

Push a lever ...

'You look even better than in your photos,' she says, breathless, shy. 'But this is totally against the ...'

My whole body standing on end, my caress nearing her chest and as I'm about to cup a breast her mouth comes at me, wide open long before her lunge has brought it to mine, her teeth clashing on my lips, hurting, her saliva plentiful and warm and then we sort it out, a rhythm, standing as we kiss, her hip bumping the table and tea spilling, hands everywhere, mouths locked, my mouth not leaving hers as I bend my knees enough to get a hand lower than the hem of her skirt, and I'm standing full height again, my phone starting up ringing, making us both issue a short giggle but she gnaws so hard on my neck my mouth's wrenched open by the pain, her hands at my belt, *Patricia* showing up on my ringing mobile-phone screen and I could almost answer it but we're locked in that flesh madness, the table banging against the wall.

18

Mum is in bed upstairs, steroids fighting the wildfires burning in her head, the hospice brochures down here on the table among all the empty beer cans. I'm pacing, beer swilling in my stomach, the TV on but down low, the carpet damp from where I had to mop up that mess.

I've got a date with Patricia but it's hours away and I shouldn't be going out at all. But I can't stay in and I can't go out, like I've got an itch in the centre of my brain. An itch all the alcohol I've had is failing to scratch.

I head upstairs and dress for the date, then go check on Mum, hoping she'll look tucked up and peaceful in bed so I'm allowed out to play.

She's in bed, that's true, but she's not quite tucked up, her face dappled with perfect beads of sweat.

I plonk myself beside her and undo my shirt button, trying to resign myself to staying home — a quiet night in with the screaming in my head.

I sigh, looking at the telephone sat silent on her bedside table.

Bingo.

I snatch up the receiver from its cradle and dial my mobile

from it. Once it's ringing I place her phone down beside her pillow and march off in the direction of my jingling mobile and answer it.

Contact! With her phone off the hook and connected to my mobile, I'm the world's most portable babysitter.

I'm almost skipping up the road, my phone warm in my breast pocket, the charger with me and a cigarette smoking in my mouth. One of the smokes you actually really enjoy, one of those rare ones that doesn't feel like injury, or servile, pointless addiction.

I take my mobile out and listen to the phone-call silence. Still, I'll hear her if she shouts out.

'I've drunk too much again, Mum.'

It's dark now, mid-evening, not long till Patricia and my half-nine dinner date. Her idea to make it late. Nice and late. I can tell what she's thinking and I like it.

In the meantime I don't know where I'm going but at least there's movement, plus more fleshy comfort to look forward to, my shirt collar buttoned up close against my neck to hide the regrettable love bite Nursey left behind. She was all panicked afterwards, worrying about her transgression.

It's so easy to disown pleasure, once you've had it.

Up ahead is another beacon of my unsightliness, the photographer's studio, the pavement outside it ablaze with light from inside. Even at this hour.

I can't resist peeking in through the window and that must be Gary or Bill or Don Vincenzo or whatever. He's in his forties. New family photos up on the walls. New window glass. He's at the desk working on a picture. I can't tell what it's of but it's a large image, no made-up faces in it. No pretence of happy. Only colour and shape. Looks like he's just finished framing it — his face calm and content as he wipes the glass down with a cloth.

He can't see me out here with those lights blazing inside. I put the phone to my ear and listen to Mum again, watching the photographer step back to admire his work, wringing his hands a little in a cloth he's holding.

'Shall I, Mum?' I say, staring at the photographer I vandalised but listening to the sound of all that distance, the call signal travelling much further probably than the actual distance involved. The sounds converted into binary information in order to fly through the air and along those lines, so that I'm standing here listening to the ones and zeroes of Mum.

I knock on the shop door, a *Closed* sign looking at me, my innards rallying. He squints to see out into the dark where we are, Mum and me. Now he's coming over. I fidget, doing up my shirt collar, undoing it.

He peers through the glass, a hand cupped to block out the light behind him. I'm wearing my best reassuring grin, trying to stop my body swaying, the phone still at my ear.

He unbolts the door then makes a show of switching the *Closed* sign over to *Open*, gives me a wide grin, the smell of marijuana coming out along with his head when he pokes it round the door. 'Can I help you?'

'You the owner?'

'I am. Everything alright?'

'Is that one of yours there you're framing?' I point in at the picture on the desk.

'Sorry?'

'That arty picture. It's not like these other ones. Is it one of your own you've taken?'

He's looking at me, his eye drawn to the phone in my unsteady hand. 'Yes I took it, it's —'

'How much d'you want for it?'

'You can barely see it from here. Why would you —'

'I saw what happened to your window. *Terrible.*' I give him a rock solid tut-tut and a shake of my head. 'Kids, I s'pose?'

I'm picturing Mum listening in from her bedroom darkness, eyes open, mesmerised. Like this is a seminal radio broadcast I'm giving. The photographer staring at me, along with those airbrushed, framed, fakey faces in his window.

'Do you mind if I pop in for a look? I'm an art dealer.' I pat my pockets. 'Don't have a business card on me just now but — I'm not interested in these happy-clappy ones in the window, you must have more as good as that one there you're framing.' I put a palm in the air to show him I come in peace, then cover the phone's mouthpiece with my finger. 'I'm interested in what you're smoking n' all.'

We're ensconced now, empty beers all over the table, I'm rolling a joint, he's putting one out. Both of us with that bodily abandon of the inebriated — seated unorthodoxly on our chairs, tilted back on two legs. Elbows draped. My phone over on a ledge by the door. I don't want her hearing this.

'Hey, I lied about being an art dealer.'

'No shit,' he says. 'You're still my first buyer though,' his face beaming at the picture, also by the door. 'For one of my own, anyway.'

'I won't be the last,' I tell him, pausing mid-lick of the rolling paper. 'Were you insured?'

'Insured?' he says, picking absentmindedly at something caught in his back teeth.

'The window.'

He nods, fingers still in his mouth, those eyes of his sneaking a look over at me from time to time. Even with all this inebriated camaraderie we've established, he keeps doing that, looking at me like I'm dodgy.

I sneak stares at him too. Watching this man I wronged but

feeling like I've righted some of that wrong with the arm and a leg I just spent on his picture.

'What work *do* you do?' he says. I glance over at my mobile – drop the unfinished joint on the table, go fetch her. 'Nothing. I lost my job.' I look at the phone screen for a reaction.

In his drunkenness the photographer laughs at me. 'What d'you do, shag the boss?'

'Ah, you wouldn't understand.' I'm regretting embarking on this with him — a little flexing waking up in my innards. I sit heavily back down in my chair, set Mum on the table.

'You did didn't you, you *dirty dog*,' he says, all lecherous and lit up. 'I bet a face like that would get you into big trouble with the ladies. Look at yer neck.'

I push my beer away, pushing away the emotions, telling myself this is the last smoke and drink if I'm going to be on form for Patricia.

'Mind if I save this for the road?' I say, gesturing with the joint, and eyeing his big bag of weed. 'I worked in the prison system as a guard. A paedophile was beaten to death, I got the blame.'

'They deserve exactly what they get.' He fidgets, leaning closer. 'Did you though, you know, bust him up?'

I put the joint behind my ear, a little claustrophobic suddenly — standing up, feeling how much more overcooked I am now, reaching for his stash and grabbing a good pinch. 'A small sweetener for all that money I just spent on your new career?'

He wafts the question quickly away. 'Sure, but what did you do to him?'

I lean on the table, supporting my weight, 'What would *you* do? Not what you like to think you'd do, what you'd actually be able to do. With these.' I show him my hands, letting him notice the scar. 'Locked up in a ten by seven, just you and a terrified old man. No repercussions.' I straighten again, looking at him.

I don't tell him (and Mum) how the prison system is what used to keep me going. How much I loved being part of that clumsy brotherhood. I loved it. As small-minded and brutal as it could be, it was all I had for a while.

I don't tell him how obvious it is that someone like me worked with the guilty.

'In fact,' I say, quieter now, pocketing some tobacco and rolling papers, 'What would you do if you were alone in a room with the person who broke your window?'

I light the joint, the flame warming my face for a second, making the room vanish, my hands shaky.

'What if it was just an eight-year-old boy who broke it? Would you punish an eight-year-old?'

I exhale the smoke, suck in another lungful, sucking back the tears – children looking at me from the walls, all of them forced into formal, scratchy clothes, hair pulled back, tied up, flattened down, squashed.

'I don't get it,' he says, a long swallow running down him, his body right back against his chair.

'I was angry, but I didn't mean to hurt him. It was an accident. Even Robert knew that. I've never meant to hurt anyone.'

Again, it's her reaction I'm after, not his. Now I'm hiding mine by heading for the door, opening it – struggling to gather the enormous picture I bought.

'See you, mate,' I say to the street, my back to him in the open doorway. 'I'm sorry about your window.'

19

Dad is singing Hey Now My Wife-friend's Back and laughing at his jokes more than usual, which is a lot. Plus cleaning like a madman and making me do a thousand jobs. Robert doesn't have to and it's not fair but Dad says I can either do the chores or he can tell Mum I tried to put Alfie through the washing machine.

Leeks or broccoli.

'Where's the washing powder, Dad?' he says then looks at me all seriously even though his good mood is shining through. 'I see you with that cat again and I'll have your guts for garters.'

I'm doing horrid jobs when I should be in my lion's den with my Transformer. Today it's the monster.

When I grow up I'm not going to have any feelings at all. I'll be a computer or a robot. And I'll know everything too like the computers on telly that can have a conversation and fly the spaceship even while solving big problems. Unlike Dad who talks slower when he's pulling out of a junction.

Robert wants to go along to get Mum from the hospital but Dad just rubs his head and smiles.

Now Robert and me are sitting at the kitchen table and listening to Dad's reversing noise which sort of sounds horrid right now, maybe cos I hear it when it's time to get up in the mornings.

Robert is having trouble sitting still. So is my tummy.

'Do you want me to make you something?' he says, pointing towards the kitchen.

I shake my head. I'm turning my Transformer from a monster to a robot, back to a monster. My hand is healing nicely but still looks a bit scarred for life.

'Which one are you and which one is me?' I say, showing him the robot, then put a finger up to make him wait. I change the robot really quick as I can, keeping my tongue in. Robert looks impressed.

I show him the monster.

He shrugs. 'Which one do you think?'

I don't know. I'm too busy staring at how happy and excited he is. I turn it back to the robot. Meanwhile it's really quiet in the house between us like we're divers in one of those pressurised tanks they have to sit in for days. Like me and Robert have got the bends.

The whole house is one of those metal pressure containers with bolts in it that could fly out any minute.

I stand up to get away from my tummy, go into the kitchen. I turn on the gas burner and light it with the special lighting thing. I like doing that when Mum's out, burning the gas.

I hover the robot high above the flame then take it away, feeling the face and how hot it is. A bit sticky too. I do it again, feeling excited, putting the robot-robert face right inside the hot blue flame and it turns it purpley green. Black smoke. The face is burning. I like that. I LIKE it.

'What's that smell?' Robot comes in.

I hide it behind my back. 'I'm off on me bike then.'

I cycle really fast up our hill as if there are enemies chasing me and I'm in a film. Or Dad is timing me.

Maybe me and Dad could go away and leave Mum and Robert. Like when sometimes I run away and take water and fruit to stay missing a really long time so they worry.

Sometimes I just hide in the washing basket, or go down the garden and climb the plum tree if it's summer and the leaves can hide me. Unless the plums are ripe cos then there are too many wasps. Bees die when they sting you.

Normally I just get too bored and come home and they don't seem to feel punished or have missed me at all. But if Dad and me went away we would be really missed and I wouldn't be bored or lonely like when I run away on my own. We'd come back weeks or maybe months later, years, and Mum would sob and hug me and Robert would shake my hand and be all 'Hey kid I missed you, you know.'

Or maybe he'd be gone already if his parents somehow realise it isn't the 60s anymore.

I cycle across Malfour Park and think about stopping to throw stones at the pigeons but I feel brave enough for the bomb crater.

The bomb crater is a double scoop left behind by a gas explosion but Dad likes to pretend it was from war. Bombers dropping their bombs.

One crater scoop is bigger than the other like ears and eyes and boobs and balls are.

I'm a bit scared of the craters and sit at the edge first. Scope it out. Three Lips Macavoy wouldn't be scared.

There's some new junk dumped down there, and the same old fridges and metal containers, as if the war bombers dropped junk bombs.

I wish I hadn't burnt my robot. I turn it to the monster but it got burnt too. Robert's fault. I cycle down into the crater even though it's quite steep and I can't breathe until I reach the bottom and go up the other side, almost to the top just from the downhill speed.

I set my monster on an old fridge to guard me, then cycle around the crater sides like a stunt rider. I even go down the steepest hill,

Everest, then Round The World which is the big arc at the bottom with a tree growing at the centre. My monster is watching me and my tummy feels like it has that junk in it too. Old rusty metal and bits of wire and fridges poking out the thin pink of my stomach.

The crater is making the back of my neck stand up. I drop my bike and stop the wheel turning. Someone could hide in a fridge and catch little boys. I kick the side of a fridge and it dents a bit. I kick it again and there's some more dent and the white coating cracks and is rusty underneath.

I'm riding home fast as I can with my monster because I think maybe Mum might be home by now and Robert grinning and being all Robert and everyone hugging then going indoors and Mum not noticed I'm gone. They'll just shut the door and the knocker will do that thing where it lifts and taps, depending on how hard you slam it.

They'll be inside together and I'll just be stuck on the outside looking in.

I cycle through Malfour Park faster than lightning, war planes diving overhead and bombs going off, fridges and metal containers landing all around me and denting the grass, soil flying and I'm swerving and leaning forward with the monster in my pocket poking my tummy. I go like the crappers past the park benches and the duck pond where there's no ducks really anymore, the metal bombs dropping and I can hear the pilots talking into their radios.

I am the special war baddie they're after, and Mum and Dad are hugging Robert while he's pointing at a book he's holding and Mum and Dad look like they're off an advert they're so happy about what Robert is telling them. I'm the only one who knows that Robert is a robot spy. But the bombs are dropping around me not Mum and Dad and Robert who are getting into bed and snuggling up and watching TV together. Dolphins on the telly.

I go through the park gate and a woman has to get out my way and says something telling off. She doesn't know about Robert and the bombs.

I stop at the junction, waiting for the traffic lights, planes flying over. Imagine if a fridge landed on the road right now, in front of a posh car. Imagine.

Come on, lights!

I'm bouncing and fidgeting like I need the toilet or the ants are in my pants, and I'm pretending I can smell bomb smoke like firework in the air.

The lights change and I'm pedalling through the war again, planes dive bombing and Mum coming home.

At the top of our hill I stop, my shoes scratching on the tarmac. Even the war has stopped cos I can see our garden down there and the stepladder glinting, a bit of sound coming from the hedge-trimmer. Me and the monster watching Robot down there trimming Dad's hedges.

Meanwhile the snake is so big it's about to split my stomach open and all the Krispies will splatter out onto the pavement.

'That's a fine job of work you've done,' Dad will tell Robert when they get home, and Mum will be impressed too about how grown up and good Robert is.

Robert is up the ladder while I'm up the hill with my mouth open like somebody just died. Like Grandma is down there bleeding to death in our bathroom with her teeth smashed out and Dad mopping and mopping.

'You're not allowed to, Robot,' I say.

They're Dad's hedges and he'll come home and Mum will be right there and Dad'll say that's a fine job of work. Like he says about my painting or gear changing, or making a mess. The stepladder looks shiny like this is an advert for stepladders.

'YOU'RE NOT ALLOWED!'

I let my brakes go and pedal like mad, the monster digging into me and lots of wind like I've got a hundred conch shells strapped to my ears, all the oceans in the world. I'm flying so totally lightning down the hill that my tummy goes tight and I can't breathe when it gets like that. I just go red and stiff, the speed making the tarmac blurry, the hedge-trimmer sound getting louder in my head like the wasps in the plum tree.

I leave the pavement where the kerb goes down low to the road like a monster came and stood on it in the night. All towns have flattened kerb lips where the monsters walk through in the night-time stealing bad children.

I even forget to look for cars because I'm not in my body but up in a helicopter filming myself. Like the pictures they beam from right above the stadium on the big sports days. I like that but one day I want them to drop the camera so everyone gets to fall all the way and thud into the football pitch.

I'm holding on tight flying through the gate and I'm angry with the ladder legs and shutting my eyes, the hedge-trimmer going and going and me not stopping.

Then BANG I stop dead, my front wheel buckling a bit wonky against the ladder and I'm nearly over the handlebars. The hedge-trimmer is so loud up close, teeth eating the air and Robert swimming up there, the ladder wobbling like a great big steel tree. His face.

TIIMMMMMBERRRRRRRRRR!

I don't like it.

He drops the trimmer and it hits the ground with this expensive cracking sound but its teeth keep going like a barracuda. Barracudas even have teeth on their tongue.

Robert's face is open wide. It takes forever. Then there's all this other noise as the stepladder makes its clattering hitting the ground sound and Robert makes his head hitting the ground sound.

Now there's just the hedge-trimmer noise.

I don't look at Robert but lay my bike down and go press the orange lock button on the trimmers and they stop. Dad would be proud. I've got my hands over my eyes and it's very quiet apart from my panting.

'Robert?'

I peek a look and Robert has his eyes open, looking up at the clouds. His leg looks uncomfortable bent underneath him like that. But he looks very calm. Not angry with me at all. He never really gets angry with me. He's quite nice really.

I leave him to rest while I go and pick up the ladder but it's very difficult and I'm making noises so he'll hear how hard I'm trying to be good.

'Dad is going to be very mad with you, Robert. This is his job, not yours. You shouldn't be out here playing with these things even though you are thirteen. You're only just thirteen.'

I get the ladder to stand up but one of the legs is a bit drunk from where my bike … In a minute Robert is going to stop looking at the clouds and get up and go indoors.

'Robert.'

Crying would only make everything scarier. Plus I need the toilet badly so I start to walk indoors but the hedge-trimmer has a ginormous earthquake crack running along the plastic red and white stuff around it.

This is when Robert starts breakdancing on the floor like the man in that advert warning about electricity. Dad says the advert is supposed to be scary but we always laugh a lot at it and Mum gets funny with him so he tries to wipe the smile from his face with his hand and I try and put it back there with mine and his face is all crispy from his beard growing all day.

Robert is doing the advert really well, his teeth shut and noises trapped in his neck. He's dribbling. The noises are scary, like he's being strangulated in his throat. The power cord is under him.

'Robert?'

I hold on to my doodle through my trousers to stop the toilet. He's looking at the clouds. Only his eyes and clothes have any colour in them.

'Robert?' I whisper it. 'Robert!' I cry a bit but try to stop, pacing with my hand on my doodle. 'Mum will be home soon, Robert. You won't tell? I'll stop hiding stuff in your room and let you watch my telly.'

He's really breakdancing and all this dribble foam coming like he's had his mouth washed out with soap. Plus the hedge-trimmer is cracked open broken and maybe the back of Robert's head is like a boiled egg when you dent it with your spoon before you cut the top off and scoop out all the runny stuff inside.

'I'm just putting my bike away, Robert.'

He's still making those noises! And tensing bits of his body really hard. He hasn't blinked once. I drop my bike and run in, unplug the power from the hedge-trimmer in case he cut the cord. When I come back he's still moving and vibrating like when you lie on the bouncy castle while everyone else is jumping.

I'll never hide stuff in his room again and he never even told on me. He just let them think he was a worse hoarderer than he was.

Then he stops a bit and there's the bubbly water drying on his face and he's wet himself.

Fish and chips smell.

I take out my monster and turn it so fast into the robot and put it down next to him to help. I pick up my bike. 'Back soon.' He doesn't look like Robert. I think maybe he probably hurt himself in the fall. His leg looks unhappy in that position. He should move it.

'Stop pretending, Robert. It's not nice to pretend. And you've wet yourself, look. Mum'll be home soon.' I'm holding on tight and dancing a bit from the wee in me. I push my bike down the side of the house and it's rolling a bit funny with the front wheel like that.

I put it in the shed like Mum tells me to but I normally don't bother. I put it right at the back then rush out again cos the shed scares me.

Back round the front I peek at Robert. He's still there. Mum and Dad's car isn't but it will be soon. I run over and loosen the posh shirt collar he put on for Mum specially. I loosen it like they always do on the telly.

I give him a wobble and lean over him to block his view of the clouds, wave a hand in front of his eyes and he doesn't blink. He just looks so happy and calm. His eyes are open, he isn't dead. Except one of his eyes looks funny with the black bit in it all big and open wide like you could see into his brain through it. The other one is really small. I think maybe he broke his eye when he fell.

I lay the ladder down again. It's heavy and difficult but I lay it down where it was when it fell. When Robert fell. I put it how it was when I found him. I was at the park. Then I walk to the far corner of the little garden and crouch under a bush and look at him. I'm holding my wee in just barely. He's still lying there.

Maybe Robert and me have the meningitis. That's why he fell. Maybe I'm ill. I go and get some fruit. Mum says fruit's good for you. I put a banana next to him, along with the robot standing guard, but keep a banana for me, and an apple.

'Robert, you should eat some fruit!' And I'm dancing the wee wee dance while I'm waiting for him to answer.

I run inside and slam the door, speeding up the stairs and jump inside the lion's den. I forgot my torch so I'm panting in the dark, the sound of my breathing scaring me. Like in the freezer. I cry a bit then stop. I don't feel like eating the fruit but slip some of the banana in and it makes me feel vomity. I can taste Krispies.

I hold my doodle and pray to Grandma and God that Robert didn't hurt himself in the falling over. I pray sorry for wetting the bed and looking at her bloodspot and promise to wipe it off if she helps us. I'll wipe it off and never do anything bad again.

I concentrate on lying very still cos I've been here the whole time.

Next thing a car door slams and Mum is making this enormous terrible scream noise and I can't help it, it all comes out and if I wasn't so high up above myself in a helicopter, I might cry. The fish and chip smell in here with me and turned up very loud.

I feel tiny.

Mum stops screaming and there's just my panting in here again and the smell of the wet. The front door slams open and Dad is shouting.

I hear the phone get hung up very hard and he's roaring my name.

Feet like thunder.

When he comes in the camera switches to extreme close up and I start crying like I'm letting out a lot of saved up crying. He unzips my lion's den and squashes me close. His face looks very different. He holds me out a bit so he can look at my body and check I'm in one piece. I can feel him shaking, Mum calling and calling Robert as if he has to come in. Dinner's getting cold and school tomorrow.

I wish it was just dinnertime.

Dad undresses me very fast and holds me under the shower, soaping me all over. I can't hear him or say anything. I'm up high with the camera. Then I'm out the shower and my body is wobbling with the towel rubbing me really quickly, then drying my hair and it goes all dark and I wish I could just stay in here.

When the drying stops I can hear the sirens coming.

'Where's Robert, Dad?'

'He fell off the ladder. He's had a nasty bang to the head and we're going to take him to hospital so he can get better.'

I nod. Robert will get better.

'Can you tell me what happened, do you think?' Dad says.

I shake my head. 'I was at the park.'

The sirens are really, really close and they stop and doors slam and there are voices and Mum is sort of shouty crying. Plus I can hear more sirens in the distance, like we're all going to need an ambulance.

'Get dressed,' Dad says and I can see his face is the shape it makes when he's going to cry.

Mum comes in with my robot in her hand and she's right up close with her finger almost in my nose and her face like a boxer that lost. 'What did you *DO?*'

Dad grabs her. 'GET OUT!' Tree roots sticking up from his neck. 'GET OUT!' He's really crying now and Mum is walking away sounding like the sirens.

That's when the Krispies come out.

20

Patricia is late. I like to get to a date first though. Arriving first might give the other person the grand entrance and the sense they've made you wait, which they think is good. But it actually means they're entering my territory.

I usually like to arrive first because however keen that may make me seem, I get to choose the seat that gives me a view of the rest of the bar/restaurant. So all my date will have to look at is me and the wall. I'm the one who summons the waiter, I'm the one in charge. It's so simple when you think about it, and yet I so often see men in the wrong seat.

Here I am then in the date driving seat and Patricia is the late type, that's obvious. How can you be on time when you're too scared to disappoint people. How can you get away? Meaning she probably ends up doing the one thing she's desperate to avoid.

My body is still ringing slightly from the photographer. My brain reeling from the drink and the smokes. Mum still on the phone with me.

I shouldn't even be here, that enormous stupid picture I bought leaning on the wall beside me. I should be with Mum but I promise I'll spend the whole day at home tomorrow and then on Monday an ambulance will come without siren or lights to take her to that last bed.

I've already had the menu brought, decided what I want, sent the menu back. Patricia will be late and flustered and have to work out what she wants to eat *and* try to settle, but I'll have done both those things already. I'll still take a menu though — make it look as if I'm up against what she's up against, but doing better.

I put my mobile on the table and fish the charger out of my pocket. There's a socket behind me. I plug the phone in so Mum stays charged.

I should be at home but I'm sitting here in my best effortless-looking outfit. Except my outfit doesn't quite look effortless because I've had to wear a shirt done almost all the way up to hide the raspberry stain on my neck from Nursey trying to suck my blood.

My second double vodka is sweating too.

It's a half-nice restaurant Patricia chose, not too posh, not too shabby. Polished floorboards, linen on the table, not fully covering but linen place mats, proper cutlery.

The taste of vodka in my mouth brings me back to the glass, sipping again and again. Putting it down. Moving it away a little, a small sweaty patch on my place setting. I swap my linen with hers. Move the drink away. Wipe my hands off on my trousers again, adjust my collar again.

Sit still! Hands in your lap. Feet on the ground. *Elbows off the table. And we don't want to see what you're chewing, thank you.*

I upend my drink and the ice bumps my lips, my head still, the drink airborne, a few more vodka drops oozing round the ice and into my mouth.

I put the glass down harder than planned and eyes turn my way. I signal the waiter that I want a refill — staring down the other people having hushed conversations, drizzled sauce on their plates, knives and forks down while they chew.

The other drink arrives and waiter-man takes the empty and gives me a look then waddles off again in his penguin outfit – takes up residence with the waitress hanging out at the barista machine, looking for a plate or a glass to empty like pickpockets scoping a crowd.

I take a swig and think about the hospice. Despite the glossy pamphlet and its well-chosen adjectives, hospices are like those dirty plates of half-eaten food I can see back there waiting for the dishwasher. Hospices are where the unwanted leftovers sit congealing, until something picks them up and slides them into the bin.

My mouth has gone a bit numb and my third drink is half empty. Or half full, depending. It's all Patricia's fault I'm sitting here thinking about these things.

The name, Patricia. So *nice*. The 'a' at the end, rounding her off with this snobbish sounding 'ah'. Partrishiaah. It's sick is what it is. Why not Trish, Tricia? Anything that softens all that nicey-niceness out of it. But no, she introduced herself as Patrishaah. I bet she hates the shortenings.

I order another drink and am beginning to wonder if there might be a slim chance I'm being stood up. I rearrange myself in my seat, getting my bits out from where they've slid under me — a nosy chick catching me rearranging but what can you do.

The drink arrives and I make the waiter wait while I keep the empty glass held up to my mouth and have the ice bump against my lips again, those few drops of meltwater and vodka slipping into me.

Vodka tastes like hairspray, let's face it.

I reluctantly give up the empty for my new fresh drink and watch as he saunters smoothly away, a snail on ice skates.

I gulp some of my new drink then put it down on the other side of the table, far away. On a date with a drink.

She's LATE. Meanwhile therefore ipso facto I have to sit here thinking I should be at home with what's left of my nemesis. Plus Trishy-poo's retardiness is making me drunker so that I'll be overdone when she finally deigns to arrive. Which means maybe she's trying to get the upper hand.

Sneaky wench.

Right now I'm probably still just about al dente, alcoholically speaking, but I'm heading for overcooked.

Al drunké.

The more I think about it the more I realise she really probably is doing this on purpose. And I drink faster when I'm angry. Which makes me drunker. Which makes me angrier. Plus I'm getting a touch of hunger anger.

I'm hangry.

I put my drink down under my seat, smack my lips to wake them up a bit, swill some posh bubble water round my mouth instead. Straighten my clothing out again, my hair. Checking my collar covers the blemish.

I go to get the drink from under my chair but stop myself.

She should be here by now trying to choose her food and settle in while I babble urbane stuff at her so she has to nod and be gracious while not holding me up by taking her time deciding.

It takes people a few minutes to actually arrive in a place so she'll be saying things like, do you know what you want? Which is this code to make me stop talking/distracting/challenging her, and shut up and choose my food. But I'll have already closed the menu having looked for only a few seconds. That'll panic her more and she'll be hurrying, seeing words but not being able to take them in: *sole, wilted, seared, raspberry coulis, filet, blanched* ...

You can judge a place by its adjectives.

And yet she isn't here, is she. And she should be. And *I* shouldn't — my mum on her last legs at home.

But I am, aren't I. Here I am in search of comfort and approval.

A prize dickhead sat here on his own with nothing but an enormous framed picture and a mobile phone for company. Everyone looking at me like I'm a ticking attaché case in an airport.

Even my drink is staring at me from under my chair.

Bugger-it. I reach down for the glass. When in Rome.

You *can* judge a place by its adjectives. Open the menu and you know what you're in for. If it's one of those littered-with-adjectives menus where they can't say simple words, they have to say feathered or tickled. Well, not either of those. The ones where it's all, you know, stroked aromatic stuffed flowerettes, or whatever.

That's my drink finished again and I could cry, like I accidentally swallowed a long-lost friend. I miss my long-lost drink already.

I put the phone to my ear and people are looking over at me on my own with an empty guess-who's-been-stood-up seat in front of me.

Menu adjectives are actually just a cover-up for a big kick in the balls when the bill comes. Let's face it, adjectives replace good food.

Or when you get your hair cut and they sit you down in one of those stupid straitjacket gowns — then it's Can I offer you a free drink, sir?

Free. Don't make me laugh. So you sit there in your hairdresser straitjacket-garment thing and the drink-offering moment comes and I always just think, great. Whoo-fucking-pee — a shafting.

One day I'm gonna say No I don't want a drink thankyouverymuch and you can take it off the price, and while you're at it you can stop looking at my *arse.*

The door opens and in walks a couple.

I try to click my fingers at the waiter. I give them a lick then do manage a click and waiter penguin-man looks at me but continues sashaying antarcticly over to suckle up to the new customers.

I go to sip my friend but he's still dead.

My napkin is wedged between my legs in this tight sort of

balled-up napkin rock. I always do this. Some people have their napkin flat and smooth when the meal's over but mine is always like an old man's ball sack.

I try not to do that to my napkin because I know it's this blatant metaphor for my psyche. I've tried to iron the habit out of myself but obviously I've failed.

Today this is Trisha's fault. I put my half-ironed-out scrunched-up napkin on her seat and steal the one from her side of the half-empty or half-full table — lay it elegantly in my soon to be shagged lap.

The vodka taste makes me go for my drink again and the barista bunch see that and talk to each other with the sides of their mouths. Seems I am the main event tonight. The spectacle.

I click my fingers at them again and wave them over. Waiter-man forgot me after he sat the couple down. Plus the man side of the couple is sitting there with his jumper draped over his shoulders. I hate that. *Hate* it. Put your jumper on or take it off. You're not Batman.

I wave at the penguins but they're purposely not looking over here now. I wipe my lips with the back of my hand, bang a fist on the table and the cutlery jumps. Penguin looks at barista girl and she shrugs then launches off for an empty plate like a dog after a ball. Woof!

My head feels like a Friday-night fairground.

The waiter has his hair slicked back and a moustache — a caricature of himself. He oozes his way over towards my table and I imagine this trail of glisten left on the floor behind him, snail eyes poking up out of his hair.

Here he is, a hand behind his slimy back, the other collecting my empty glass of hairspray. 'Are you sure you wouldn't prefer to wait for your guest before ordering another, sir?' He's wearing the type of smile that leaves his eyes unchanged. 'Or perhaps you're hungry.

I could arrange some bread and olive oil, or garlic bread. Something to tide you over?'

'Perhaps you could arrange me a garlic fucking drink.'

'Excuse me?'

I waft my comment away like a fart. 'Doesn't matter' — *hands in your lap, and sit up straighter.* 'Do I look like I couldn't handle another drink?'

'It's not that, sir. I just thought you might be hungry, you've been waiting a long time.' He gives me a knowing face as he says that.

'I'm not being stood up, you know. I'm not! I *am* a little peckisshsh. But I'm more thirsty than hungry. A drink, waiter-man, if you please.'

'Leave it to me, sir,' and he takes his slimy beetroots away.

I handled that pretty bloody well.

Just then the door opens and in comes the woman of the hour late. I go to stand, keeping my (her) nice ironed-flat napkin in my soon to be shagged lap, bumping the table a bit and a knife or fork or spoon clangs noisily on the floor for about an hour and a half.

I sit again, not wanting to burst my bubble of slickness. Keep it cool. I pick up the knife. I've got about two hours to get her back to my place, check on Mum then, bingo.

She's looking a bit racy is Patrish. Hair done and a nice blouse thing on, a skirt, tights. Effortless effort. Little handheld handbag, big enough for a lipstick, which she's not wearing, only lip gloss that makes her look like she's been eating greasy chips on the way here.

She leans down and I let her kiss my cheek. 'I'm sorry I'm late,' she says, her perfume stroking me. And suddenly it's fine that she's late. It's fine.

She goes to sit down but picks up the balled-up napkin from her chair, holding it up between finger and thumb. I put my hand up close to my mouth to stage whisper, 'They don't run a very tight ship here. Shabby, very shabby.'

Oozy the Penguin comes over and offers to take Pashrish's coat but she declines, hands him the old man sack and he takes it from her like it's a warm nappy.

He gives me a particular look, then swaps my dropped knife for a clean one.

'Trish, what you drinking? I've just ordered one.'

The penguin gives me another, slightly different particular look while Patsy, still standing, tries to work out what she's having.

'What are *you* having?' she says — that habit indecisive people have.

'Hairspray.'

'Er, I'll pass on the hairspray I think. White wine — sauvignon blanc?'

The penguin nods and backs away with the warm nappy. Meanwhile Trish sits her bits and pieces down and looks me over. I pull my collar in close against my vampired neck while she's turned to the photographer's big picture leant up against the wall by our table, then to me, her eyebrows raised.

'Just pur-chased that, Tri — Patrishia. It's art, apparently.'

'I wouldn't go that far.' She taps a manicured nail on my drink. 'You've given yourself quite a head start.'

'Tough day at the office.'

'Oh, your mum. How is she?'

While I tell her the bare minimum, Patricia is hanging her coat over the back of the seat and getting comfy. Like I said, people take a while to arrive.

The drinks and menus come and we Cheers! then open them up to choose. I have a peek before snapping the menu closed and putting it down. I sit on my hands to refrain from drinking but my sore knuckles hurt and I need a hand free to keep checking my collar is hiding the love bite on my neck. Why do people do that? *Hate* it. Ugly.

I give the other diners a smug look for thinking I was being stood up. Pah!

My mobile phone has *Home* sitting on the screen and the call-duration clock ticking up and up inside the darkened face. I put it on top of my thigh, imagining the phone's radiation filling my body — Mum burning yet another hole in my heart.

'What you laughing at?' Patrish says.

'Myself,' I say, pulling myself together. 'I'm laughing at myself,' and wondering what other self-indulgent thoughts I don't notice.

I lift the phone so she can see it, charger lead and all. 'In case Mum calls.' I put it down on the table.

I'm getting a bit of a sweat on, Pat talking about her day, me picking up the salient details of what she's saying while trying not to get caught picking out the salient details of her. She looks good — saying something about the last few weeks of a course she has to do before she starts this new plush job. Neurophysysomething. Looking at brains.

'... People who've had what your mum has, actually,' she says, like we're talking about the flu. The menu is open in front of her, my finger blocking the phone's mouthpiece for a sec. She's quite insensitive is Trish.

'I see,' I say and take a slug of drink and they've not given me a double but a single. Plus Batman over there still has his knitted cape on.

'D'you already know what you want?' she says, looking at me sat back trying not to down my drink. Then she's mumbling to herself, looking at the menu — not reading it, just scanning the adjectives, freaking out.

This cheers me up.

Except my brain has started doing lazy forward rolls in my head, the room getting just a touch spinny. I check my collar, sit more firmly back in my seat, trying to inform my body I'm not spinning. I wish I was in her seat facing the wall instead of this whirlpool room. Plus waiter-man has got all five of his eyes on me. So has Patricia now.

'You ok?' she says from half a mile away.

'Yeah. I'm good.'

'What happened to your neck?'

'Toilet,' I say, stumbling to something approximating standing. 'It's a birthmark, Patrish. One of the ones that comes and goes. If the penguin comes can you order me ...' I look at my closed menu. 'Order me ... *Shit.*'

'What?'

'Forgotten ... I'll just have what you're having?'

'The *caesar salad*?'

But I'm stood here looking at the second balled-up napkin I'm holding.

I chuck it onto the table and lurch off in search of the toilet, my brain doing forward roll after forward roll in my skull.

When you're looking for the toilet in an unfamiliar establishment it's genetically prohibited to stop and look round for it. You have to make an urgent, desperate stab, don't you — keep walking at all costs. You say to yourself, that way looks the most toilety. Then you take a deep breath and hope for the best.

I pass Batman and can't resist tugging his jumper from his shoulders. 'You dropped your cape, mate. Here, let me put it on the back of the chair for you.' It takes a while to tuck it in between his back and the chair — waiter-man oozing closer, ready to pick up the pieces.

I walk on. Don't stop. Keep walking, keep walking.

There's the toilet door. Praise the Lord! And I'm through it and — outside the restaurant.

Outside toilet?

I head round the corner, up a cobbled little dead end and lean back against the wall.

'Had too much,' I say to the clouds, but I like the numbness.

I should be at home. Plus Mum's phone call and Patricia are sat in there at the table together. Bit early for her to be meeting the parents.

I keep changing my posture to try and keep my head in the right spot. I put it against the brick and bang it a few times.

Now my hand is rubbing at the back of my head, my stomach starting its squeezing. I swallow it all down. Taking deep breaths, thinking about Mum dying.

And I'm thinking about grief. How frightening grief is because you don't know how big it's going to be. How swallowed whole it's going to render you. I'm so scared of feelings.

Leaning forward now, breathing, trying not to throw up. The nausea coming at me the way feelings come at you.

And I'm thinking how much I love that there's always suicide. Like a fire blanket on a kitchen wall, you never want to use it but it's so important to me that suicide is there. Just in case. Something between me and being overwhelmed.

The waiter shows up. Aren't they supposed to *wait*.

He hands me my mobile phone and charger. 'I think it's best you don't come back in, sir, don't you?'

I breathe back the nausea. 'No I happen not to think it's best. I happen to be on a date with that Patrisha in there. I happen to think I have every right to come back in.'

He shuffles on the spot. 'I'd rather you didn't though, sir.'

'Stop calling me *sir*. And what's it got to do with you whether I come in or not?'

He scoffs. 'Well, it's my restaurant. I think I can decide.'

'Bullshit it's *your* restaurant.'

'Well, I don't own it but —'

'No, you don't own it.'

He makes this tired face but something in him is heating up. You learn that working with criminals — with the dangerous. How to locate the little thread to pull, to unravel it all. But mostly it's about knowing what to avoid.

'You're not allowed back in and that's fucking final, *sir*.'

Our bodies square to one another, our relative heights becoming apparent but Trish struggles up to us with the picture.

I look at the waiter-penguin, then down at my phone lit up with # 9 on the screen from his clumsy bloody fins.

'Whatever, Happy Feet. Whatever.'

'What's so bad about a bit of drunkenness?' Patrish says as we're meander-wandering down the street. 'Did you tell him your mum was ill?'

I shake my head. The lampposts are ruining the night with their orange, the street full of parked cars and expired meters. The photographer's picture ungainly enough for a sober man, let alone al drunké here — Mum still hanging on the other end of the line despite the waiter's clumsiness.

'I bet he'd have a skin-full too if his mum was ill.'

'I would've drunk less if you'd been on time,' I say, giving her a smile, getting a gentle shoulder barge in reply that knocks me way off balance, my side steadying me against a wall. She emits a snort which she catches in her hand.

'Still,' she says eventually, 'a few drinks isn't criminal, is it.'

I like her sticking up for me but I wonder if she would if she knew.

'What about your dad? He still around?'

I shake my head and look upwards. 'How about you?'

'Both my folks are still around. Still together. Sorry about your dad.'

'Brothers and sisters?'

'Only child.'

'Same here, sort of.'

'People think you get spoilt as an only child, don't they,' she says, becoming animated. 'Rather than caught between your parents. What d'you mean *sort of*?'

I sigh and she offers to help with the picture so I give her one end, the glass facing uppermost and catching the lamppost light between us.

'Sort of?' she asks again, meeker now.

'It's such a long story.'

There's a silence after that and I feel bad for holding back. We walk a bit, me wanting to tell her I was fostered, that I don't know who my real parents are. Wanting to tell her all about my prison-service career. How great life is in Canada.

My usual stock standard bullshit.

'Hey, let's go in,' she says pointing to Malfour Park. I smile for her, trying to look enthused when I just want to get her home and grab some healing before I have to face my last day with Mum in the house.

We both catch the giggles at the park gate, struggling to get the enormous picture through.

We take up residence on the swings, both of us swinging, Patricia's shoes kicked off and her hair flying back at the top of her arc. She's going much higher than me, my stomach still uncertain and half my mind focused on getting home to Mum. The other half though is happy to be here, grinning occasionally at this woman.

I scuff my shoes on the rubberised concrete, stopping the swing, my chin coming to rest on my hand where it's holding the swing's chains — watching her going backwards and forwards.

She stops trying to swing, letting the momentum drop a bit. 'You've gone quiet.'

'Sorry.'

'It's ok. Tell me about your job. Prison, huh? That must be full-on.'

She's all offhand, breathless, perhaps happy to be back on a swing again — some sort of childhood nostalgia. Her happiness making me feel the aching separateness between all humans. Making this seem pointless, Patrish and I. Making me think that so much of loneliness is simply due to the habit feelings have of happening out of synch. Affection, contentment, sadness. Love. We're so often alone with our particular mood, as if Patricia and I are communicating by letter. That delay between me feeling my emotions, and her corresponding with them.

'I don't work in the prison service. I don't know why I said I did. I lost my job three months ago.'

'You're having a really good year, aren't you.'

I give a weak little laugh at that, trying to meet her at her mood. Halfway at least.

'How'd you lose it?' she says.

'Ah.' I sigh, the alcohol having pulled up the handbrake in me. I look at the phone in my breast pocket. 'Some of the officers were planning to lynch a frail old guy. He'd tried to abuse a kid, problem was it was a kid one of the prison guards knew. He must have been the world's unluckiest paedophile. He got caught and the cops wangled it so that he was to be held on remand with us before trial. I'd had a gutful of being forced to turn a blind eye to what they did to prisoners, so I tipped off the authorities. That's how.'

'That's awful but *good on you.*' And her voice shows the strain of leaning back to push more momentum into the swing. 'Sticking up for fairness, I mean.'

I'm getting dizzy watching her going backwards and forwards, a perfumed breeze blowing on me each time. A little more of that ache hitting me — she thinks my story's no big deal.

'It didn't make any difference, he was held on remand with us anyway. Officially he committed suicide but I know what he'd have gone through. Hours of one-on-one time with prison guards.' My eyes are threatening to fill now from a sudden sense of what it cost me, my need to be in that brotherhood. The things I had to turn a blind eye to in order to feel part of that all those years. The few things I did when I first got there, when I was too young and isolated or needy to know better. 'They did worse probably than he'd have ever done to the girl, then they let him hang all night before they raised the alarm. I'd phoned in sick but they made out I'd been the suicide watch.'

She's stopped working the swing now, her arc slowing. 'That's a *disgrace*. But why would you lose your job for trying to protect an untried paedophile.'

'I've done worse.'

'I didn't *mean* it was a bad thing.'

'Well.'

'You think you did the wrong thing?'

I'm slowly sinking lower into myself. 'Just that, sometimes it doesn't seem to matter what you do either way.'

She's still now, sitting on her swing beside me, her hand coming out and resting on my arm. I have to turn away though because she's looking at me like I'm odd. Like she doesn't know why I'm telling her this.

But I can picture Mum curled up listening in the darkness, a proud tear running down her face.

21

I don't want to be a weatherman when I grow up anymore, I want to be a rubbish collector. The bins are collected from outside our house on Fridays and even though it might be a stinky early bird job at least I'd only have to work on Fridays. All those other six days off. Easy! Which is heaps better than school, and school's supposed to be easier than work.

Whenever I don't want to go to school Dad says 'Let's swap. You do what I do till seven in the evening and I'll go put my feet up and listen to some sexy teacher.' Which is annoying and not the point because I'm not choosing between work and school, I'm trying to choose between home and school, which is like between chocolate and leeks. But he's making it like broccoli or leeks. Not chocolate at all.

Only it's dark chocolate because Robert isn't getting better.

When she isn't at hospital with Robert, Mum takes me to church. Meanwhile Dad has to stay home and find a job. He winks at me while Mum's upstairs rattling her tablets. He says the kitchen is his office now.

He always eats while he cooks and says he's only taste testing. Then when he sits down he usually says he's full of taste, but shrugs and eats all his dinner anyway. He's quite big now, my dad.

I like going up to him when he's watching TV and pulling up his t-shirt and pulling up mine so I can rub stomachs with him. Skin is in love with skin. That's why it feels so good when we rub bellies.

Mum comes down with some tablets and asks him for a glass of water and he brings it but says 'Why not take a rest on those just for today?' She looks at us, then hands them over to Dad and goes upstairs again.

Dad's got some food spilt down his top already but that's cos it sticks out so far. Sometimes I think his belly's going to catch fire on the gas flame and he'll lose weight just like that. His whole fat lump will burn away and he'll be healthy again.

People stare at Mum and me in church. Simon told me everyone calls her Saint Mary behind her back. I told Mum that to cheer her up but she said it wasn't a nice thing they were saying. That calling her Saint Mary was a sarcastic thing and she's not trying to save the world, despite what everyone says about her.

I think grown-ups are confused. That's why good things can suddenly be bad and bad things good.

She shuts her eyes very hard and her lips move fast even when she's supposed to be listening to the priest at the front. He says we're all born sinners. Which must mean only bad people go to church. Mum says it's the opposite, but she was never that bothered until Robert got ill.

I hide comics down the front of my shirt when we go to church cos the comics have lots of pictures in them which makes it harder for God to see inside me.

God is scary, you can tell by his house. All those statue eyes and violent stained glass with thorns on and Jesus bleeding from our sins. I like the feeling of the comics although I get sweaty and have pictures on my skin afterwards like I've got stained glass skin.

The comics are itching me and the priest is going on about sin

sin sin and having the devil in you. I can feel him in my stomach and I don't like it.

I know he's in my tummy cos of the time Adam and Eve were in Eden and the devil was there and he was a snake. That's how I know where the devil is inside me. He's the snake and I don't know how to get him out.

I grab Mum's hand and she comes out of her dream and winces, moves her rings round on her fingers from where I hurt her squeezing, lets go of my hand.

She has a ring for every birth and marriage and will you marry me and proper anniversary and I wonder if Dad'll give her a ring if Robert dies. Except he probably can't afford a ring now his office is the kitchen.

Mum pats me on the leg and gives my head a kiss, looks round at the people staring at us. Even the priest is eating us with his eyes, all the stained glass windows staring. I pray the comics work but prayers probably can't get through comics either. Then I pray that Mum and Dad don't lose the investigation or go to jail.

They're investigating us since Robert got hurt. I wonder what Three Lips would do. He'd put the moves on them.

I roll up my sleeve and carry on with colouring my arm in with biro. I like that. I'm going to colour the whole thing and maybe my entire body and I'm already black from my wrist to my elbow. Turning myself black and blue makes me feel better and by next week I'm going to be an entirely new colour.

Mum slaps the pen off my arm and mega frowns at me.

Now the priest is talking about a man who tended his neighbours' crops so much that something happened to his own crops and his family starved. The priest is saying it and eating Mum with his eyes and as soon as he's finished and the hymn starts she leans over and says 'We're going.'

'But the singing's the only good bit!'

The clouds look angry too so we wait at the bus stop.

When the bus comes it does that hiss I like, as if it's pissed off with carrying people and is pausing for breath. Like horses do when they flutter their lips and it sounds like 'Bugger me, I'm tired' in Horse.

Buses are the modern horses and Mum and me get on and it sighs again then clip clops off down the road and I love how the windows vibrate the outdoors when the bus is trying hard, then stop vibrating when it takes a break to change gear. Maybe the bus driver would let me change gear for him. There looks like there are a lot.

Mandy the social worker came over yesterday and brought the police with her. I knew there was trouble because of the police, plus when they came in the door all three of them had put their lips away.

I spied from the top step between the banisters. There was a lot of crying and shouting from Mum. Dad kept going out to boil the kettle and then not make tea. Then go back in. Then go out again, like he needed the loo or something. Meanwhile the social worker's voice didn't move left or right or up or down at all. It could only go straight ahead like it was high up on a dangerous mountain path.

Mandy has eyes like the statues in church do. She can probably see through comics.

Then my name started coming up a lot so I went and got in my lion's den and prayed to Grandma. I have to have a plastic cover on my bed again now and it makes scrunchy walking on snow noises when I fidget.

'Two steps forward, three steps back,' Dad said.

I pray to Grandma a lot, asking her to stop the nightmares. Dad tries to stay calm about my wetting the bed. He used to be really calm all the time but now he always has spiky hair from sleeping in front of the TV. And he quite often shouts at me then cries when I cry.

I don't ask them about the investigation into Robert's accident but he might get taken away. Mandy even asked me about Robert's accident but I don't know anything cos I was at the park.

Besides I'll just run away if they try and take me to a new house. Or if Mum and Dad go to prison I'll just go with them and we'll sleep in bunk beds and it could be fun.

Dad says prison makes it hard for you to sit down.

Mum is asleep on the couch instead of being at the hospital with Robert. I go into the kitchen and make her a cup of tea. White with one.

Even though I'm tall for my height I have to use a chair to reach the tea things. I put the milk in after the teabag and water so I can get the shade just right. Mum likes it the colour they make it on the telly, in the ads. I get it perfect and wipe up everything and even put it in Dad's mug with Boss on it.

I creep over to her and she has the newspaper next to her on the floor and her new reading glasses on her forehead even though she's asleep. I put the tea down on the table beside her and it's all steamy.

There's some grey in her hair and I wonder if it was there all the time and I never noticed or if it might be new, like when people see a ghost on Scooby Doo.

She could break her glasses sleeping in them like that. I reach out and take a hold of them. I'm not breathing at all in case I wake her up or if my breathing might jog my hand.

I'm a spy and these glasses have microfilm in them. I pull a bit but they're behind her ears and make them curl a bit with the pulling.

She sniffs and I stop. I take some breaths to the side. I can smell her hot tea.

I use my other hand to prop up my elbow and then reach in again and hold on to her glasses, not getting anything on the lenses like the way she tells me to when she sends me upstairs for them.

I pull and the hook bit comes off one ear. I stop. Nearly set off an alarm. If I'm killed in action there'll be a state funeral without my body and Mum will be there and really, really crying so much that they'll have to carry her out and take her home and give her tablets, like the ones she takes since Robert had his accident. Ones that make her glide like an ice-skater.

Sometimes I can cry just from thinking about Mum being sad at my funeral. She's SO upset.

I take a hold of the glasses again and her forehead starts needing ironing. I pull a bit and her ear moves and she flicks awake, her arm coming out and the tea spilt on the carpet and her eyes all blurry and red and scary and looking at me for a second and then 'What the EFF are you doing, I'm trying to sleep!'

I take two steps back. 'I made you tea.'

'Do I LOOK like I need tea! DO I? I need sleep!' She makes a loud sighing noise that uses her voice. 'And what were you doing with my glasses!'

'You might have crushed them.'

She stands up and huffs off. I follow her. She gets the cloth and runs it under the tap, squeezes it out and grabs the kitchen towel. She starts to come back but sees me and stops. Her hair is sticking up and it makes her look even scarier.

'What?' she says. 'What are you looking at!'

I shake my head at the floor, her little toe's nail looks like a tiny scab. Like the very last bit to come off when you've hurt your knee.

She walks past me. 'Why don't you go play with the traffic or something!'

Mission failed, repeat, mission failed.

I go upstairs really slowly.

This is the first time I've been in Robert's room since he hurt himself. I sit on his bed, looking at everything. He got hurt because I'm wetting the bed again. And cos I burnt my hand. Cos I'm bad.

And now Mum and Dad are going to prison and I'm going to be sent away.

One day I'll get the hang of people the way Robert has. Maybe when I'm his age. Maybe then.

22

Patricia gives me a look as she opens her front door. 'It's not very tidy.'

While she makes herself busy with drinks and nibbles I set to work building the perfect joint, loading it pretty full to relax her but not so full I'll overcook her. Meanwhile our bodies are probably firing up certain systems in readiness. Our minds on our inner feelings, sifting the excitement and fear and reticence and guilt — whatever cocktail of complications we're overlaying on what is a simple, animal need. Pushing this lever.

'It's rude to poke your tongue out,' she says, depositing the wine on the coffee table in front of me.

'I can't concentrate without my three lips,' I say, forcing a smile then going back to building the joint.

When she's gone again I reach for my phone and it's hot to the touch from the long call but hung up somehow by my pocket. The screen blank.

I get up and do a circuit of the room, anxiety filling my innards.

Patricia shuffles into the room holding a lighted candle, her other hand masking it from the walking breeze. 'Don't judge me,' she says in jest, nodding at the bookshelves I'm pretending to inspect.

She goes away again and I sit down, give my hair a good rummage, resigning myself to just one more hour or so before getting back to Mum — a hamster running a wheel in my chest.

I lick the joint, lighting it from one of the candles and letting my shoes slip off onto the floor — bring a foot quickly up near my face to check for smell.

'Nice,' she says from the doorway.

'Just checking your carpet's clean.' My turn to blush, hers to laugh. She sits down beside me and nuzzles into my neck, more out of shyness probably. I put an arm round her and just smoke, trying to keep my breathing under control. She can probably feel my heart too.

She smells faintly of alcohol, perhaps from swigging in the kitchen. Lubricating the inevitable machinery.

'I don't get it,' I say, handing her my smoking creation then inching a little away and bringing my feet up onto the couch, wrapping myself round my legs — a weather system breaking over her face from my pulling back. She takes a drag then admires the joint, looking it up and down.

'You don't get what?'

'Why you want me here. You must have a thing for car crashes.'

'Oh, shoosh,' she says. 'We're all car crashes. Anyway, I didn't know what was going on in your life when I first met you. I found you attractive then, before I knew.'

'Knew what?'

'Why you being like this all of a sudden?'

I hold my fingers out for the joint and she obliges. I take a drag. 'Like what?'

'Belligerent.'

I shrug. 'I wouldn't want me here if I were you, that's all.'

'Well, you're not me. Besides I invited you in for a drink not a marriage.'

I exhale, blowing smoke rings.

'I'm not stupid, you know,' she says. 'You don't fool me with your sexy loner act. I know more about you than you might think. We know someone in common, you and I.'

I pause midway through passing her the joint, waiting.

'Don't you hate small towns,' she says, excited by the information she has that I don't. 'My mum taught you! When you were at Wilson's. Remember Mrs Stevens?' She takes in my facial expression, reassured now of her facts, and beaming at the small worldness of this moment.

I nod at the carpet. 'I wasn't there long. Not even a school year.'

'But you told me a different first name, or did you change it?' She sits forward but I lean away. 'She didn't tell me much. Just about the fostering and an accident. It sounds tragic. Your mum seems like she was amazing.'

'*Is* amazing.'

'Yes, sorry. Mum was sad to hear she was ill. She sends her best.'

'Right.'

My eyes are stuck to that patch of carpet, even as Patricia risks coming in close again, wrapping herself around me, my body stiff but her hands lifting each of my arms and arranging them on her in the shape of a hug.

'Come on,' she says. 'I come in peace, *sexy*.'

I get off the couch, away from her disgusting sympathy.

'Oh, for fuck's sake,' she says, knees right up now, her chin planted on top.

'What!' But I know what and I don't want it happening either. Yet here I am doing it — a car sliding on ice, all its brakes on but skidding slowly, inevitably …

'Don't plead ignorance,' she says.

'Why don't you tell me since you already know everything about me.'

'Forget it.' She's firing up now, flush-faced and hurt. 'Fob someone else off with your fake name and your depressing anecdotes about a job you don't even have anymore.'

I go to take a petulant drag but the joint's gone out and her anger breaks into laughter, me too but only for a moment, my heart pumping the levity away.

'Come on,' she says, softening. 'Or can you only stand it when it's straight sex — *me Tarzan, you Jane*. Then you can cope alright.' She tries to infect me with a laugh but gets left out in the open with it because I'm staring at that face of hers and imagining telling someone like her about someone like me.

I pick up my phone and jacket. 'You're right, Trish. Forget it. I take it all back, ok. *All* of it.'

She stands up, sensing an opening. 'What? *What* do you want to take back?'

But I've realised this is hunting season for *her*. She's the one in charge. I'm the wild horse in the paddock, she's holding the head collar.

And I'm bolting, her voice calling after me but I'm out into the night, her front door slamming behind me and pretty soon I'm fifty metres from her house with wet socks, cold feet and a gone-out joint. Panting in the middle of this pathetic little park, watching her door. Feeling four foot six. Afraid she'll come, terrified she won't — the same worldwide conflict between the unbearable heat of intimacy and the cold of isolation. As if there's nothing in my solar system but a choice between Mercury or Pluto.

Leeks or broccoli.

I walk towards a bench at the park's edge, near a path — the night quiet. My chest going up and down, my arms wrapped around myself, giving myself the hug I should have given her.

Out in the cold again, an idiot with goosebumps.

I take a seat on the park bench, listening to the distant interruption of sirens. I'm not the only one with an emergency then.

Down the way an old man is wandering along the path, through the puddles of light at the feet of the lampposts, his dog just ahead of him, its claws making little clicking sounds on the pavement, pausing at each post to sniff and maybe pee.

When the old man nears I ask him for a match and he pats his pockets, his eyes rheumy in the orange streetlight, a sad look to him but also that fearlessness old men can have. Like they're too old for violence to find them now.

'Just taking Rocket here for our constitutional,' he says, still patting pockets. His border collie looks back and wags its tail, wanting to go on but having reached that unwritten distance he likes to be from his master — trotting about with his tail in the air and his bum looking at me. Quite a happy sight really, I decide.

'Rocket,' I say, trying on the name.

'Yep, he's a one,' the man says, love coming off him. 'If I don't take him out his wet nose gets me up in the middle of the night. Little bugger.'

He finds his pouch of tobacco, opens it and digs out the lighter, hands it over and I light the joint, thank him, hold his lighter back out to him. He doesn't take it, doesn't notice, so I stand here with it in my hand, blowing my smoke away from him. He has his pouch under his armpit while he gathers a cigarette together in expert fashion, then spits a little tobacco from his tongue after he's licked the gum and rolled it, just like that.

'You'll catch yer death out here,' he says, nodding at my socks. His work done, he gathers up his accoutrements and puts them in his pocket.

'Argument with the missus,' I say, rolling my eyes, inviting him into a gentle conspiracy against women.

'Ah, the fairer sex.'

He's patting his pockets again, frowning, a hand coming out with his pouch of tobacco. He looks inside it, puts it away, patting again, eyes upwards to help his hands feel.

I hand him the lighter and he chuckles to himself, lights his rollie and returns the lighter.

'Thank you,' he says.

'It's yours.'

'Oh, I couldn't. Very kind and all that but I have my own. Somewhere.' He pats at his pockets again.

'No seriously, it's *yours*.'

'Oh, yes!' He laughs louder than old people usually do, he really laughs. 'The slippery slope. You know, ageing. Taking my chances buying green bananas nowadays.'

I laugh along for him. 'You're not that old.' I glance at Patricia's front door, take a drag of joint, bouncing a little on my legs, trying to warm myself.

He stands up straight, as if for a photo. '*How* old?'

'I'm not playing that game.'

'Go on, I can take it. How old?'

Rocket barks at us and the man shooshes him.

'You guess my age first, then. That's fair.'

'Oh,' he says.

'Exactly. It's an awful game.' I take another pull of smoke and so does he, looking at me, something else in him shining out suddenly.

'No, bugger you,' he says. 'I'll guess your age. Just hold on, let me get my bearings. Gets harder to tell as you age. People are having sex at about twelve these days, looks like.' He steps back, straightening out his big, thick coat. 'You gonna give me a spell on that wacky baccy then or what?'

I look at the smile on his face, at the wolf sitting in there beneath those folds of skin — that disguise. The young soul still in there underneath all that old age. I grin at him. 'You sure you can handle it, old man? I don't want to be holding your hair while you throw up.'

'What hair.'

'Fair point.' I hand him the joint and he gives me his rollie to guard, the end all brown from soaked-in saliva. He takes a puff and looks at the workmanship, appreciating the difference. Then his eyes are on me and I try to meet his gaze, my attention flicking repeatedly to that front door.

'You're about twenty-five I'd say, pretty boy. Though you've still got a lot of growing up to do for a man. I'd been married three years by then. You married?'

I shake my head.

'How did I fare?' he says and takes another pull of smoke.

'Close. I'm twenty-eight. What makes you say I've got growing up to do?'

'You're not married.'

'Not everyone has to do that. It's old hat.'

'Well, you're not living your life are you then, unless you give it away. Everything's a lot easier once you stop focusing on your own stuff. It's never-ending you know, that stuff.' He hands me the joint, takes back his cigarette. 'Thanks for that. ROCKET!'

I look round as the dog comes bounding from a garden, tongue out. He jumps up at his owner then turns and does the same to me. I stroke him behind the ears, feeling the man watching.

Maybe if I got a dog. Dogs are good company.

'He likes you,' he says. 'Animals can spot souls, you know. Like children can. I always say to myself — Reg, I say, if he's alright with Rocket then he's alright with me.'

Reg.

I bend and let Rocket's tongue lick my neck and then it's wet and warm and right inside my ear, my mouth opening, eyes squinting shut. I straighten again, wiping off the wet. 'It's impossible to think about anything while a dog's licking your ear. Someone should patent a machine.'

'True,' he says. 'You married to that reefer?'

I take a drag then hand it over again, our interaction seeming imminently at an end and yet we're both still standing here, waiting for something — hoping for some truth.

'I look like a good soul then, to you?' I say, my gaze alighting on him briefly.

He breathes out the smoke, inspecting the remnants of joint, rearranging it between his fingers for better purchase. 'You do,' he says, resolutely — takes another puff, exhales. 'So, how old am I? Go on.' And again, he pumps himself up for a team photo.

'Doesn't it all become much of a muchness after seventy?'

'Bugger off. Who says I'm a day over sixty!'

He erupts into a gale of laughter which threatens at all times to descend into rampant asthma — the phlegm rattling in him.

Once he recovers he stands up again, waiting, drops the joint on the grass and scuffs it out. I'm circling, giving him the once-over.

I subtract a few years, for safety. 'Sixty-eight.' He absorbs it, smiles in a way that isn't readable as satisfaction or disappointment. 'I guess when you get up to those numbers a few years under is no great compliment, is it,' I say, giving him a grin.

'Pretty close,' he says. 'Pre-tty close. You got any more of that wacky stuff?' His eyes are even more bloodshot now, shining in the streetlight.

'I have.'

'Shall we?' he says, looking over at the bench — a little somewhere for sleep-starved mums to bring their prams in the early morning. Or for teenagers to fumble at love in the twilight. Men to smoke behind their wife's back at night. Or phone their mistresses.

I'm rolling us a joint and feeling the beginnings of a smile. We're sitting here without expectation, just strangers striking up a moment with some weed. I could hug *him.*

'So what you and your lady argue about, if you don't mind my asking?'

'Long story.'

Rocket grumbles as he lies down at Reg's feet, his head alert and perky, his ears picking up things we can't.

'Well, if that's code for mind your own business, that's fine. Otherwise' — he looks at me — 'I've got time.'

I busy myself with the joint. A door slams across the park and I glance up but there's no sign of her.

'Hear about the old chemical plant?' he says.

'No?'

'Caught fire. It's burning now. Just awful. National TV.'

And at that, a sharp bubble rises up through my middle and out. 'My mum's dying.'

He straightens. I'm not looking at him but I turn away while he's gazing into the middle distance.

'I'm sorry to hear that,' he says, really soft and steady. 'What of? If you don't mind.'

'Cancer.'

'Oh, that bastard. I'm sorry to hear it, son.'

'Well, you know.' I lick the joint.

'How old is she?'

And I have to think about it, working back based on landmarks in my life. 'Sixty-two.' I hand him the joint so he can have the honour of going first.

He looks at me, doesn't take the joint, turns away and stares at nothing in the middle distance. 'After you, son. After you.'

Son.

'What's your mum's name?'

'Mary.'

'Reg,' he says, and shakes my hand.

'Michael.' The same lie I told Patricia, not that it worked. Reg smiles, looking away again, speaking to me now from the middle distance. 'Where does she have the cancer? Or is it too painful? We can chat about the weather. I can talk about nothing till the cows come home. You learn that at my age, once there's enough you can't talk about. There's too much that happens to you once you get to seventy-four to not get good at skirting round.'

'Seventy-four? Wouldn't have guessed it, Reg,' and I give him a smile but he's waiting for my answer. 'Brain cancer. Knocked out her speech. She has the most aggressive cancer there is, apparently. Lucky us.'

He sucks air in over false teeth then tut-tuts them. 'And is your father still with us?'

'Heart attack.'

And at that Reg sags a bit. 'How old was *he*?'

Old people always ask that, I realise. Anything happens, they want to know how old the person was, as if to ameliorate their own fears that it could be them. Everyone always makes it about themselves.

'He'd be approaching your age now if he'd lived. Sixty-four. Died seven years ago. He was sat there one morning before work and he said to my mum, you look nice. She went upstairs for the dirty washing, came back a minute or two later, and he was dead. He was a comfort eater — fat as a small house by then. I left for Canada after he died. I'd had enough. Not bad for last words though are they — you look nice.'

'Sixty-*four*.' He breathes out some smoke, a hint of a cough tickling him but he holds it in.

'Bet you're glad you bumped into me, eh, Reg.'

He smiles a wan smile. 'Only the good die young.'

'I should live forever then.'

We share a quiet, clouds drifting over.

'So why are you and your lady arguing? You've been through a lot.'

'You can't really call it an argument. I dunno. I've not known her long.' I stay staring off towards her door, my hand coming up with the joint for him to take.

'You got brothers or sisters?'

'No. Just me now. I had a brother that died a few years back. Robert. But I'm a foster child, so it kind of doesn't matter. I mean …' I sigh. 'I mean Robert was a foster child. I was —' Rocket takes up barking and Reg is gazing at me, his eyes full of salty water, although that could be his age.

He's staring into me and it's like looking at Time — all folds of skin and age and sun spots — two glinting blue specks shining out. All that experience but he's just as confused as me. The eyes have it. Seventy-four years. All those moments, and he's sitting here near the end of his run but still as dumbfounded by it all as I am.

In fact he's more hopeful than me that everything's going to be alright. And it isn't. It isn't going to be alright. It's all wrong. He's going to die. Alone perhaps. He's alone *now* probably. Nothing left but these walks and some nice smokes, he won't enjoy them all, or even all of one of them. He just has a few of those fettered little moments to look forward to where life flaps its wings for a second and things feel alright. Those moments when you get that blink of ok-ness.

Like that hug from Mum yesterday. Like Reg here, taking an interest — showing kindness. Like walking across this park in a minute and knocking on Patricia's door until she lets me in, in every way. Then going home and reaching out to Mum.

'You got some help, son? Who's looking after your mum?'

This is all life is then, these small ok moments. And maybe a life can be measured by how many there are. So that if we fall to suicide or alcohol or violence or bitterness, it's because we fell into one of those gaps in between the ok moments.

Which must be where that eight-year-old me fell.

For some reason, seeing this seventy-four-year-old man as lost as me isn't scary. It stands me up. 'Nobody is, Reg. I should probably get back.' I hold out my hand to shake his, Rocket barking again, the sound echoing in the dark. I'm shaking Reg's hand with both of mine because the thing is, if he's seventy-four and doesn't have the answers, there aren't any. Which means my answers are as good as any. Any map is good enough when you're lost. Besides, my map is all I've got.

I walk away but he calls after me, standing there stuttering because he knows there's more he needs but he doesn't know what it is or how to go about getting it.

'Hey,' he says, that fluttering doubt in the back of his tobacco-stained throat. 'Will you let me know if you need anything. Perhaps I could help. Or, heaven forbid, pay my respects at least, when … You know.'

I turn from the warm glow of Patricia's lit window, as if going to her will be dying a happy death, or I'm an alien about to walk back up into the light of the spaceship — fly away from this earthly confusion.

'Haven't you been to enough funerals, Reg?'

But I regret saying that because it changes his face. I've caused another small stain of sadness to spread in him. I regret that stain and walk towards him. He stands a bit straighter at the look on my face, when he sees what's coming.

I wrap myself around him and he's all juddering and thin like a sparrow. I can feel his brittleness — seventy-four years have eaten him down to this featherweight presence. Life could blow him away. One more tragedy, one more insult. He smells of burnt cooking oil and cigarettes, and I can feel that miniscule vibration in him, like he's quartz and you could set your watch by his melancholy.

But it's Dad I'm hugging.

Then I leave him there recovering. I'm walking away shoeless across the park but stop and call out, 'It'll be St Margaret's when it happens, Reg.'

He lifts a hand to acknowledge me, Rocket skittering ahead of him, his tail up, transmitting information back to Planet Dog.

I can already feel that Patricia hug coming, but I get to her door and the picture is leant against the railings outside, one of my shoes on the top step, the other flung down here on the pavement, over on its side.

I knock anyway, not my bravest of knocks.

After a long silence I nod at the closed door, put one shoe on, then head down the steps and put on the other, leaving the picture behind, in case.

A last look at her house then I'm running home, the burning chemical plant showing up orange in the distance. The quiet wail of sirens.

23

Robert can come out of hospital today. Plus the police are here again with the Mandy social worker.

Dad doesn't join in. 'Lots to do round the house.'

He's making everything Robert proof. There's a folddownable seat thing in the shower now just for Robert but I like to stand on it cos it makes the shower sprayer come almost right onto my head, the water really noisy in my brain like I'm inside a shaken up can of Coke. Plus I can't really think about anything with the water noisy and hitting my head.

There's a metal thing around Robert's bed now too, like in a hospital. To stop him falling out. Dad calls it a Robert proof fence.

I don't mind Robert coming home, I don't think. Except he might not if the investigation decides it's our fault he fell off the ladder.

I go into his room and there are tools and leads all over the floor and Dad's head is under Robert's bed, a bit of his bum crack showing. Normally that makes me laugh.

'Dad?'

He turns round then goes back to what he's doing. 'Hey,' he says.

'Why aren't you shaving anymore? Is it because you're sad?'

He stops for a second then carries on. Looks like he's going to put squidgy stuff on all the sharp bits on Robert's bed. Robert might fit a lot now apparently. And he won't be going to school for a while and he'll never go back to the same one and we only just got him his school uniform. I'll probably have to grow into it.

'Can't you go and play or something? Your dad's got a lot to do and Robert'll be home in a while. You done the things Mum told you to do?'

I nod.

'Have you?'

'Yes.'

'All of them?'

I nod. 'Yes.'

'Good boy.'

I'm staring at his drill. I try not to but I imagine it drilling into my hand or my head. Or I'm picturing picking it up and putting it into Dad sort of suddenly accidentally. The drill going right between one of those spine lumps in the middle of his back which are a bit like a dinosaur's. He gets them when he leans forward.

Thinking about doing that sort of thing always makes me nervous and anxious and hold my hands as if I might suddenly do it. I don't want to do it. Maybe my body does.

'Dad?'

He sighs and stops working but doesn't turn round. Most of his head is under the bed still. 'Look, I'm not shaving because I'm not being paid to shave for now. Until I find a new job.' He turns and gives me a fake sort of smile for a second. 'You don't like my beard?'

I shake my head and he shrugs, goes back to working.

'What you doing?'

His voice sounds harder then and he says 'I'm fixing this soft foam to his bed, once I get the drill plugged in, there's no fucking power sockets in this house.'

Rude word. 'But he'll get better?'

His shoulders start wobbling like I've made him laugh without trying. He stays under the bed for a bit and takes a deep breath. Then he comes out and wipes his face, which turns into a big hair rummaging session.

'Shall I make you a cup of tea, Dad? How about I make you a cup of tea!'

He shakes his head at the floor.

I get scared when there's crying. Everyone's crying all the time now and I wonder how many millimetres.

I jump when he starts the drill, the wood bits landing all over Robert's bed sheets. Dad stops, says a bad word, then rips the sheets back and they've put a plastic cover on Robert's bed too.

He starts drilling again. Then he stops, half looking round at me.

'I will have that cup of tea.'

'Ok!' Black with none, cos of his weight. I start to go.

'Better give yer dad some milk and a couple of sugars, for strength. And see if you can't sneak me a biscuit or three.'

'Ok.'

He turns away from me and leans over the place he's about to drill, the drill nose already in the right spot where he made a mark. 'Hey ...' he says.

'Yeah?'

'I fixed up your bike wheel for you yesterday, she's going like a dream now. No need to tell yer mum.'

I go to say something but he's already started up the drill.

When Robert arrives he looks like a different person even though he only banged his head. Like he's been replaced, a spy. And he's always making faces as if he's a puppet and somebody isn't pulling his strings right. Even his hair is different and there's a big scar on the back of his head with angry metal things in and it scares me. They shaved off a bit of his hair and Dad tries to crack funnies about Frankenstein but Mum gets all explosive.

Robert can't sit still and makes lots of noises and sort of seems happier than he did. He gets excited easily and has this thing happening with his mouth as if he's chewing his tongue or his cheek. Almost like Mum's angry face but cos of happy.

He does do angry too, which is new. And cries and gets upset which is also mainly new. The bang must have loosened everything in him that was stuck and couldn't come out.

He's had his sound turned up.

He takes up all Mum's attention now but I don't sort of mind so much anymore. I watch TV a lot. Mum and Dad say I have to look after myself more and be good and quiet and just that basically I've got some quick growing up to do. Which probably explains the growing pains.

Mum and Robert have the same bedtime now. I stay up later than both of them. I ask Dad if Robert is better at all and he doesn't really answer even though he's always shouting at the politicians on telly and saying 'He hasn't answered the question!' Sometimes he throws his slipper at the TV. Which means I have to go get it for him. Then he ends up throwing it again.

When he does this Robert usually squeals. Robert squeals a lot. Sometimes when he's happy, sometimes when he's angry. Sometimes when he's sad. Sometimes he's all three.

Robert's noise wakes me up in the mornings now, not Dad's reversing.

Dad's supposed to be looking for a new job since he lost his last one. Any job. He doesn't even need to do balance the books work now. Mum says he's dragging his heels. Plus his beard is quite long which must be why she won't kiss him.

My bedwetting makes everyone angry but it isn't my fault, it's God's.

'Don't you dare!' Mum said when I said that. 'Don't. You. Dare.' Then she hugged me so hard my eyes popped out.

Mostly I watch TV in my room. Normally in my lion's den holding my eyes up close to the zip so I can see, and it's like really heavy eyelashes I'm looking through, as if I'm Madonna.

I'm upstairs and Dad is in the lounge eating. Mum has headphones on in front of a little TV outside Robert's room after his bedtime. She lies on a couch in the corridor that's too big really and you sort of have to squash by. I like running over it. Sometimes Mum's still there in the morning if she isn't fighting with Robert in the bathroom. And sometimes Dad goes and whispers to her late at night when I'm half asleep, trying to convince her about something.

They don't bother to go out to the car to argue anymore.

Robert wears nappies now and Mum and Dad have to change them. They're enormous and he's always taking them off and Mum getting upset and angry with him. She does that a lot, gets upset and angry at the same time. Like she's confused. Robert takes them off and Mum has to be careful how she handles him. He headbutted her once and she had a shiner for ages.

Robert is younger than me these days, even though he's older. I'm the eldest now and I like it.

Dad says it will all get better.

Newsflash! If I go a week without wetting the bed I get any toy I want and I definitely want a remote control car like Ralph and Simon have. They've got this really cool enormous suspension and are really fast, only the batteries don't last that long.

Mum and Dad won't let me drink anything after about 5 o'clock and sometimes I get so thirsty but Dad says drinking anything after 5 is silly cos we may as well cut out the middle man and pour it straight on my bed.

Mum takes Robert back to the hospital heaps of the time. For his fits. They might have to snip his brain so that one side doesn't talk to the other anymore. Dad showed me with a cauliflower. He makes the best cheese sauce.

This week I'd made it up to three nights without wetting the bed but Robert's parents are coming today.

I'm the only 8 year old I know who can use a washing machine. I'm growing up fast and there's even a little stepladder for me to be able to hang up the sheets in the garden. I like using a chair instead.

It is not me wetting the bed it's my bladder but when I tell Dad that he says 'Well, then it won't be me spanking you but my hand.'

I'm allowed to eat dinner in my room in front of the TV these days and use the cooker to cook for myself. I make things like cheese omelette and sometimes my recipes still taste good without ketchup.

Robert's parents will be here soon and Mum looks like Frankenstein in a dress cos Robert is taking everything out of us. I sleep with tissue paper in my ears to stop Robert's nightmares and screaming. Everything in the house is very loud or very quiet nowadays. Robert won't be helping me with my homework anymore.

Plus Mum isn't letting me fix my own wet bed sheets today but shouting at me to pull myself together and that I'm 8 years old and when she was 8 she wasn't wetting the effing bed. Only she doesn't say effing, she says the word, then she comes and gives me a hug, Dad running in with a Robert nappy brown all over his hands and Mum just lets me go and slumps down right in front of the washing machine and she's holding my wet bed sheets and is going to cry.

'Don't cry, Mum.' But I'm crying too.

Now I can hear them shouting at each other downstairs, even from inside my lion's den.

I can hold my breath under water for forty seconds. I have to block my ears if it's in a swimming pool though in case my skull fills up with water and I sink. My head is already the heaviest bit of me. Except maybe my legs. Heads weigh a lot.

It's nearly time for Robert's parents and I'm on the toilet when Mum barges in and takes some of her gliding ice-skating tablets then dashes out.

I spy from the stairs when they come. There's the big Mandy social worker woman with them who kind of runs the show and I giggle a little cos when she's gone I know Dad will say the thing about 'boobs like zeppelins'.

Zeppelin was a famous woman during the war.

Behind the zeppelin woman is Robert's parents. I remember them from intensive care. They're skinny people who are all pale and shifty like baddies in films. They see me which is strange because nobody normally notices me up in this spying spot when they come in the house. But they do and I want to run away but I don't. They're the ones that caused it all and I'm worried about them knowing where we live in case they come and steal Robert back. Or me even.

The mum looks quite a lot like Robert but the man doesn't, even though he's a man and Robert's a boy. It's the mum Robert looks like. Dad was the one who answered the door, Mum is in the garden with Robert.

After they go under me where I am on the landing I run to my bedroom and stand on the bed with my shoes on and there are no sheets just the slippery plastic cover and Mum outside struggling to keep Robert still and a pack of his biscuits there and him all slippery like he's covered in plastic too.

I'm scared Mum will cry but I also want her to because then Dad will beat up Robert's parents and Dad looks like he could take Robert's dad unless he has a knife which he looks the type to have.

I run downstairs to warn Dad but stop to get a knife for him so it's a fair fight. Usually the knife holder sits on the surface next to the sink but I get there and it's been moved. I look for it and think maybe they hid it so the parents couldn't pull a fast one.

Now I can see the knives up high out of reach. Dad says I'm tall for my height. He always says that cos he tried to say I was tall for my age once but it came out wrong and now he always says it the wrong way. I like being tall for my height though.

I get a chair and put it in the right spot and climb up and hear shouting outside already and Dad doesn't have a knife. Mum says 'It's not about the money. How DARE you say that to me! This is about ROBERT!'

The chair isn't quite high enough for me to reach the knives up on the cupboard. I stand on tippy toes and in one second the chair wobbles over and I feel this sharpness and a noise in my head, a purple flash and I'm on the ground. I jump straight up and hop around squeezing my doodle, holding on to my bladder, bouncing on tiptoes until the white light pain stops but it won't stop. My leg is really hurting inside my thigh, just below my important bits and I think I caught it on the hot tap cos the tap is running a bit.

My leg is damp.

I quickly write on a piece of paper HE MIGHT HAVE A KNIFE. Three Lips Macavoy knows these things. I fold the paper and run out and the women are up close to each other and pointing and the dads are quite a way away talking and watching, Robert eating biscuits and looking up at the clouds, on his back in the grass with this happiest look on his face and I jump over him holding my doodle through my pants. I run over to Dad and Robert is all squealy about me jumping over him. I hand Dad the note like they do on the news sometimes, handing it to the newsreader. I tell him to read it. I jump over Robert again and he squeals so I jump

over him again and again until I'm all puffed out and his mum is
shouting so loud she isn't even making sense anymore and Mum is
laughing in her face and Dad is between them and he hasn't read
my note. He's got his chequebook out.

My leg hurts and is wet but I don't look.

Then the zeppelin social worker comes out of the house and the
toilet is flushing and she gets between everyone and telling them in
a big, boomy teacher's voice to 'Sit down and air your feelings like
ADULTS.'

She has this voice and so everyone sort of looks like they might
sit but they don't sit. The mum goes to pick up Robert but he cries
and holds out his arms to my mum.

This is like a moment off the TV that Mum always covers her
mouth for.

Mandy picks him up instead and I can tell he's heavy for her
cos she looks like she's going to tear something. She hands him
to the dad.

'Go inside!' Dad tells me and I sprint indoors and bounce
around holding my bladder shut and scared of the pain in my leg.
I look down and it's a little bit red on my trousers. I run upstairs
and stand on my bed and watch their mouths moving and there's
lots of crying.

How

many

millimetres?

My window is breathing up fast and it seems like Mandy and
Robert are the only ones not crying. My thermometer says 21 and
the bad mum gets up and walks away and Dad says something to
her and she turns halfway round and is shouting. She looks ugly.

Then her face changes and she holds out her hand to the bad
dad and he digs in his pockets and gives her something. She gazes at
Robert like Dad looks at Mum, then goes into our house.

I run top speed through to the front, open the curtains and the window is open and Robert's mum comes out there and stands on the spot that … and she's smoking.

Cigarettes are death sticks, Mum says. I stick my head right out and some of the smoke reaches me but it smells of different smoke than I've ever smelt before. I hold my breath cos I don't want to die.

Robert's mum is crying like it's the end of the world. And she's pacing a bit and smoking really fast. Adults look funny when they cry cos they're out of practice.

I can see right down her top from here. She looks up and I bang my head on the window and have to rub it really fast which is all you can do when you bang your head. And frown.

'What's your name?' she says, wiping her eyes with her hands and one of them has the cigarette thing in it and I think she's going to set her hair on fire.

'Do you love Robert?'

She starts flooding again and nods at me, her face a funny shape. Then her mouth makes words but the sound doesn't come. I can tell she's trying to say 'very much'. Her lips are this shape.

'Why aren't you his mummy then if you love him?' Which makes her look like a tree that's just had the last cut made out of it and it's the tiny moment before it has started falling. I like doing that to her face.

'I am,' she says, her voice all higher like she's in the choir or holding her balls.

'It's your fault he's ill.'

TIIMMMMMBERRRRRRRRRR!

Some people look really ugly when they cry. She looks older than my mum. Dad always says that people who look older than they should had a really tough paper round as a kid. That's why.

Her face looks like lemon tastes.

She wipes her eyes again and her stomach does that judder thing.

'I can't be his everyday mum right now that's all.' She says it in a crying voice.

'Why not?'

She thinks for a long time, her arms round her body to stop it shaking. Her cigarette thing might set fire to her clothes now. I might like that. Then she looks up at me. 'Some people find life a bit harder than other people do. Not everyone's got what your parents have. Silver spoon. Some of us have a lot on their plate.'

'My mum says everyone has a lot on their plate but some people just have small appetites.'

She looks at me and sniffs, smiles this sort of smile.

'And no table manners,' I say, remembering the rest of the saying.

'I think you'll find Robert's ill because he was left home alone, you jumped up little shit.' She wipes her eyes.

'That's a rude word,' I tell her. I'm braver up here. 'Do you still think it's the 60s?'

'What?'

'Dad says you and Robert's dad still think it's —'

Zeppelin Mandy appears down there looking up at what bad mum is looking at and I bang my head again and go inside and am rubbing at it really hard. My jeans are wetter and sticky.

I go to my room but there's a lot of shouting so I race back to the front to see the bad dad stumble into the front garden and Dad is out there after him with his sleeves rolled up and Mandy shouting something and keeping them apart. The bad mum takes a cheque out the dad's hand and chucks it towards my parents but it only seesaws slowly down to the grass, the bad dad looking silly running around trying to catch it but he can't till it lands and I'm bouncing up and down and joining in with my fists and helping Mum and Dad fight back!

I dash down to help and I can see Robert through the window, still lying on the grass in the back, smiling up at the sky. Mum shutting the front door and Dad marching in straight past me shouting about 'the gall and the nerve' and he has a really red face and these marks on his neck and Mum is all crumpled.

They start laughing and I don't think they're going to stop until Mum changes to crying and Dad finally gets to comfort her.

I wrap myself round their legs and hold on tight in case all the water washes us away. Grown-ups aren't supposed to cry.

24

I'm walking Hawke Street Hill with my head down, out of breath from trying to run myself sober. That orange burning on the horizon is just a glow now.

I stop and sniff the air, standing right about where I paused on my bicycle and watched Robert on the ladder.

I long for that day the way you're supposed to long for a lost lover. Wishing I could live it again. I've rewritten it so many times in my head and I can't help but wonder where I'd be standing now if I could.

I take off my shoes and damp socks, my feet feeling good on the cool concrete, the quiet suburban night wrapped in close around me — people sleeping in beds behind all those identical windows. Curtains blinked shut.

I light a cigarette and try to reconnect with the exact brain state that was once in this spot, that little eight-year-old mind. I kneel down so my head is where his would have been. As if the space–time continuum could be disrupted and I could affect the thoughts that were there. Here.

I can see the hedges. Malfour Park sleepy behind me, the cirrus cloud a little reddened from the chemical plant burning. People probably out in their dressing-gowns standing looking at it, faces creased with sleep.

I go in through our gate and the poorly cut hedges snag on me as I slide by. I ignore our front door and head down the side of the house, rummage in the darkness of the shed, finding what's left of a seat to sit on.

I ran home to her but now I'm here I've stopped at the perimeter of her.

I light a candle to build a joint by, rolling myself some oblivion — smoke it rocking back and forward out on the lawn.

Then with the joint still glowing in my mouth, I'm clattering over everything in the shed, the bike overhead. I dig out the extension lead and hedge-trimmer, the ladder — staggering back and forth and setting it all up in the front garden.

I put out the joint and exhale the smoke, watch it disperse and rise in the night air. The clouds have changed again, gliding silently over the house. Dawn can't be a million miles away.

I used to sit and watch Robert looking up at that sky, trying to see what he saw, trying to savour it the way he did.

I unroll the full length of lead and find a chunky repair in it — black gaffer tape wrapped round and round the thin orange cord.

All his talk of idiot-proof orange. I'm looking at the gaffer-tape repair like it's a piece of Dad. His fingerprints might be fixed somehow under all that sticky tape. I look up at the sky again, my thumb stroking the repair.

You never lose anyone completely. They embed themselves in you, motifs of them everywhere.

I can't help but think about the way he must have felt sad or lonely. That maybe his life looked tragic to him. My dad who lived out his life in the ice age after the comet struck. Me, I'm the comet.

I hold on to his repair and want to cry for all the times I must have planted a sadness in the centre of him. Every moment I snubbed him in some way. Every time I had a tantrum. Every time I ran to Mum instead of him. For every moment in which he didn't feel like he was enough. For every moment *I* didn't think he was enough.

And for that moment when I wasn't enough — that eight-year-old.

But what eight-year-old is enough? I'm twenty-eight and I'm not enough.

Now Dad's in the ground and I'd give anything to have him stretch out those arms. I'd never reject him again. Part of me wanting to unravel this gaffer tape, put it under UV light and show up the grease of his fingerprints stuck in among the adhesive. Get just a little bit of him back.

Maybe some UV light could shine there where Robert fell too and you'd see something, some black mark from where his head hit the ground.

I get my key out, open the front door, pull the lead in by its plug, the house making my body stand on end. It's dark inside and I'm stoned, nervous. I search for somewhere to plug in the hedge-trimmer but a noise stops me — a sound like a creaking door, but sharper, hoarser. It's coming from the kitchen. That gagging and retching. It brings my hand up to my mouth, still holding the electrical plug.

She's throwing up in there, the tumour pressure in her brain too much for her body and all it can do is empty her. I put my fingers in my ears, shut my eyes, locking myself into the darkness, the sound of my own life pumping harder inside me now.

Robert used to make that retching sound. After the accident his stomach was like this weakling. We had to feed him simple foods like pureed carrot and sweet potato — the blender going all the time and Robert still making that noise. The blender jug always sat there in the sink, full of water and claggy bits of vegetable, fruit. The house revolving around the chaos inside his split head.

Then, maybe an hour or so after food, if we couldn't keep him quiet, that sound would come and I'd turn up my TV. Shut my door. A deep, back-of-the-throat noise Mum always used to be so terrified of. Her and her vomit phobia.

Now she's making the same Robert noise and I'm crouching down, my breath held, the cord still snaked around my hand. My fingers in my ears. Each gag almost overlapping with the next so that she's gasping for air in the seconds between them — struggling to stay afloat in high seas. Engulfed as another wave comes over her, tumbling her under. She comes up behind it for air but another comes, another. The oxygen deficit filling her.

She surfaces again, spitting bits of the seabed out. Her own body buckling under, forcing her into being as much a gasping witness as I am. Those flywheels spinning inside me, harsh and electric — my panic turbines firing up. Because there's no 'It's just something I ate' for her. There's no 'You'll be fine tomorrow.'

Cancer is not something you flow around.

That black walnut has its back against her skull wall, hobnail boots pushing on her brain, shoving her off her stem, down and out of her own head.

I plug in the lead just so I don't have to hold it anymore, glancing at the gaffer-tape repair to see if it'll light up electric and show me Dad's fingerprints in the dark — an impression of his hand to hold.

She cries out and I'm running, the smell hitting me when I reach the kitchen. The lights off, darkness, I slip on the wet, babbling at this Mum-sized shape in the dark near the sink. I can't see her face, not properly, just a sparkling where her eyes would be. The outline of her abject helplessness.

I can't believe I've punished this unravelled woman.

I get down on my knees with her, my own stomach threatening. 'Where's your steroids, Mum? You probably just forgot your steroids.'

She takes my hand and all her rings are on again even though she's too swollen for them. All the memories the nurse made her take off, wedged halfway back onto her fingers, just beyond the first knuckle. Probably the ring Dad bought her when I was born. And that one from the night he proposed to her at the race track.

The plain gold band he put on her on that day I've seen in the pictures. Carefree pictures, but that enormous truck in there somewhere, in the background, invisible. The truck that's hidden in every happy photograph, thundering closer with its shipment of reality. Here it is now. Here's the truck, in the kitchen with Mum and me. There goes that hiss of air as it puts the handbrake on.

'No Mum, not yet!'

I grab at her hands, one of the rings falling away and even with her body's convulsing, she's groping the floor for it. I help her, my fingers finding the ring, wiping it off, putting it back on the end of her finger. The wedding finger. The ring she wore even after their entire marriage had emptied out through the crack in Robert's head.

I stand from her, go over and switch the TV on, something for sound and comfort — just a little light. The screen tingles to life and somewhere there's a cricket match happening, commentators babbling into microphones. Somewhere it's a sunny day.

She screams then, reaching out to me from her hands and knees on the floor, her head staying down, focusing on keeping some control over what's happening inside. Trying to keep an even keel on the deck of a struggling boat.

'D'you want me to call an ambulance, Mum!' Partly because I need a phone-call-sized moment away from this. 'Do you, Mum? Shall I call an ambulance!' But I kneel down with her. 'Please don't. I'm just *SO sorry*.' Those words are an axe thunked into my breastbone.

She grips my hand but she's flailing about like a caught fish on this boat deck we're on. Me holding on to her as her mouth gasps for life. My body trying to breathe for her. Both of us far out in the dark centre of a capricious ocean. There's nobody out here with us. Nobody coming to the rescue. We're alone with that basic, lonely fact of life. Alone with that truck. With how alone we all are. Alonely. The way I can't help Mum with this even though I'm right beside her. Cricket on the TV. The players dressed in the cleanest white. The commentators with their polished, calm voices commentating on my mum's dying.

She crawls spluttering into my lap and I'm rocking her back and forth in an awkward semi-embrace. She's stopped flapping, just her great blue fish eyes looking up at me, the TV sunshine caught in them. The crowd applauding and the cricketers run, one of them jumping into the air midway across the wicket, his bat aloft. This bloated and tired fish in my arms, gazing at the screen. The boat windows hinting at the red of dawn.

The commentators laugh. The batsman adjusts his groin with a big glove — spits.

She's looking at me now, something clearing or clicking back over. She makes a noise, struggling with a movement or change inside her. Some final reconfiguration perhaps. She's making noises about it but her face is calm, her throat shaping the sounds, her mouth shut. The sea becalmed around our fragile little boat and Mum this beautiful shining thing. A pulse bumping out at her temple, rings all over her fingers, the kitchen walls green suddenly from a close-up of the cricket ball running across the pitch to the boundary. Applause. Her face nothing but this regret. Her expression speaking so clearly, How is it that I'm leaving you?

I burrow right into the same neck I cried on so many times as a child. In where I used to be when she carried me over-tired and emotional up to bed. In the nape of where so many things have been healed. And so many scooped out and scarred.

Her shoulder flexes and her arm comes swinging slowly round

like a crane or a boom, lands straight and simple on my back. Both of us wrapped in a clumsy embrace and this hammering of our hearts. The cricket crowd cheering something somewhere far away, on dry land.

Her arm falls away and I rush to the phone, dialling the number so fast I dial too many and have to end the call. I punch in the numbers again but there's just silence. I tap frantically at the button to end the call, listen again. Silence.

I rush out the room, thunder upstairs, the phone still off the hook on her bed. I start to dial emergency from here but hang up and race back, the distant sound of applause on the TV.

'Hang on, Mum.'

A clinical voice answers and I say '*Ambulance,*' the word like jelly and the crowd erupting again as the batsman hits a shot, the ball airborne, the cricketer waving while he wanders out to meet his team mate halfway, the ball landing in the stands.

Immediately the replay is going at a tenth of the speed, the batsman leaning back, his lips gone, pulling the ball into the air, his eyes shutting at the moment of impact, the ball followed, the camera operator a genius for tracking it against the sky — all that air and just a little red ball, the kitchen walls and windows turning sky blue for a second.

And in this moment, everything is in the air.

I look back to Mum and her chest has sunk, her eyes gone and the ball lost into a load of outstretched hands.

'Ambulance service. Go ahead, caller.' All those hollowed-out emergency callers' voices he hears on the line. This just another night at work for him, a cup of tea steaming on his worktop, a picture of his wife. How does he hear these things night after night without running home and never letting her go.

'My mum's dying. She's got cancer.' This image of a little tape recorder going round, pulling this phone call onto it.

'Is she breathing?'

I watch her chest in the TV half-light, the camera focused on low black cloud slung over the city, just beyond the cricket match, the commentators' voices dropping a little, talking about my mum's motionless chest.

How many of us see a chest doing that, just sitting there. Still. She's sunk under the water.

'Mum?'

The clinical voice says 'Sir?' from above the surface, the TV showing an image of a man in the crowd holding up the ball he caught. He looks like Dad. There he is smiling at me.

The kitchen changes colour again because we see the sudden glare and vibrancy of the adverts.

'Mum!' I hang up the phone and go over to her, hesitant, then leaning in. I touch her face, stab the mute button on the remote control and the ads are silenced and we're in a sudden quiet, the walls of the room changing colour with the high-speed editing of the selling. Her body motionless but that expression of soft and loving regret still on her face.

I sit on the floor and lift her head into my lap, the phone starting up hammering its sound into the silence — ringing and ringing.

Then stopping.

After a while the tears come. Slow, vacant tears I'm not quite connected to. I just sit here stroking her forehead even though she's already asleep.

25

Auntie Deadly says there's a special place for bad children in hell and the devil visits every day after work to burn them. Plus parents can't visit.

When we get to Deadly's house Dad helps unload my things and gives me a bad hug. Auntie D is standing in her doorway, filling it up. I don't like the hug Dad gave me even though he's getting very cuddlier. It was like the ones he used to give me when he'd had a bad day at work. You could tell his bad days cos his hair was spikier.

These days his hair is normally always spiky even though he hasn't got a job at all.

Plus he's going to leave me alone with Auntie Deadly which is like being dropped off at a giant lobster's house. She looks like a lobster does Auntie Deadly. One with hairy armpits and a moustache. All big and pink and googoo eyes and claws for hands and a tough shell and she'd probably make you sick if you ate her. Like Dad and the lobster he had when we were on holiday and he was pigging out.

Tahir from school has a Muslim God instead of our God. Tahir isn't allowed to pig out. He muttons out.

I don't get that and nor does Tahir. He's just using his dad's jokes like they're his. It's stupid.

On the way to Auntie Debbie's Dad said we're going to try to adopt Robert if we win the investigation. 'Just letting you know,' he said, 'so it can start cooking in that big, hairy magic box of yours.' Then he messed up my hair.

I did my hair again.

I thought I'd feel something when he said that about adopting but when I stuck my feelings dipstick into my tummy it came up empty.

'The hearing's the day after tomorrow so it's only a few days with Auntie. Don't look like that, your mum and me just need a little bit of time. You know what fostering means to her. She needs some smooth sailing for a bit, no rocked boats. Social Services have got their beady eye on us, and if the worst happens at the hearing ...'

Auntie Deadly shows me my room which smells of pot puree and has a pink towel on the bed with flower patterns all over it and a window up high in the wall like in a prison. Only without bars. I swallow a lot when I first get to her house and she whispers with Dad before he leaves.

I watch his car go and have this tummy feeling that I'm never going to see him again.

'I do NOT want your grubby little paws touching my net curtains, thankyouverymuch!'

I want to cry. The longer I stay here the more Mum and Dad will fall out of love with me.

'Can I go home please, Auntie Debbie?'

'Not a chance. Just be patient and behave yourself.' She lights a cigarette and sits in her chair, filling it up. 'You'll do well to pull your horns in while you're here, my boy. You got that? *Sensitive* my behind.'

Dad packed me my Transformer even though I don't play with it anymore. It just stays half changed between a burnt robot and a burnt monster.

It's dinnertime and I have to sit at the table until I've finished my LEEK and potato soup. It's taking me ages and the soup's already cold and I'm only halfway through. Meanwhile Auntie D is finished and watching TV in between spying on me, and all I've got to look at is soup plus some pictures on the wall of Auntie Deadly in smaller dresses before she had a moustache.

Sometimes Dad does the 'What's the difference between a walrus and Auntie Deadly?' joke. I always get the giggles and Mum looks skywards. 'One of them has a moustache and stinks of fish, and the other one's a walrus!'

We always say the punchline together, even Robert used to.

I put my spoon in the bowl to rest and Auntie D looks round and shouts at me to EAT UP and I jump and the spoon catches under my wrist and flicks soup over me.

While she's wiping my face and t-shirt with the same sponge she probably uses to clean meaty dishes and disgusting stuff, she's saying 'And you better not go wetting the bed here like you have been. You better pull yourself together and toughen up, my boy.'

I'm not hers. I'll never be hers.

She throws the cloth at the sink and it lands on the floor and she says a French word then takes a tea towel and wipes my face, my bottom lip rolling down and my nose squashed flat. Through the tea towel I can hear her saying that every time I mess up, my bedtime will get earlier by half an hour and my wakey-wakey time later by half an hour, until I'm trapped in my room the whole time if that's what it takes to pull me together.

I'm not staying. No way. The longer I stay the more likely I'll get stuck here forever. Like if you pull a funny face for too long you can get stuck like that too.

If I stay here with Deadly I'll definitely go mad and talk to myself and think there's rats in bed with me eating into my skin until they reach the white of bone like when Jimmy McGee broke his arm in the playground and you could see how perfectly white the bone was next to the blood. Like the bone was white cos of how it had never ever seen the light of day. Which is what Dad says about Auntie Deadly's purse.

It's night and once I hear her snoring I uncover myself from the blankets and TADAAA! I already have my clothes on. She came in to say goodnight and didn't notice!

I rule.

I spy on her and she's fast asleep in front of the TV which is turned down quiet. I sneak to the front door and open it, peeking out at the street. It's all silent and scary and I'm scared to walk home but scared to stay. I want to be with Mum and Dad, not sent away like a bad person.

I look up and down at the dark street then at Auntie D's car right under a lamppost like it's had an idea.

I go back inside and there's her keys with a car one on them. I don't shut the front door, I'm just running away from monster hands that are about to grab me from behind.

Auntie D's car doesn't smell so good, ashtray and gone off yoghurt. But I like it in here cos I can lock the doors. Plus it's a different type of quiet.

Only problem is when I can reach the pedals I can't see much of the road. I look for a first aid kit or something but there's only empty cigarette packets and chocolate wrappers.

I push the driving seat back so I can sort of perch on the edge and look through the gap in the steering wheel. Lucky I'm tall for my height though cos my feet can reach the …

There's only TWO! I look at the gearstick and it's an automatic one. Trust Auntie D.

I'll just see if it starts. That's all. Just to see.

I get the squeals then with the engine running and me out here in the night. I check Deadly's door and the dark street. Three Lips

Macavoy would be lighting a match on his stubble, smoking a fat cigar.

The gearstick says P then R then N then D then 2 then 1. I set the mirror so I can see myself, like Mum does. I'll just take the handbrake off. That's all. I don't know what the letters mean so I set it to 1 and the car starts moving by itself and I'm not even pushing the pedal!

I turn the wheel fast and hardly really touched the parked car in front much and I'M DRIVING ALL BY MYSELF.

I put it in 2 and it goes faster without me revving.

I can do everything on my own now. Mum says nobody likes you if you're needy, independent is the safest way.

A car goes past me and hoots. I give it the sign.

I'm really scared and really happy and really sad and really excited. All at once like Robert.

Right up until I see the big roundabout at the end of Deadly's street. I try to work out what Three Lips Macavoy would do but he'd be doing 90 and driving with his knees.

I stop at the roundabout. I can't do roundabouts and I can't get out and walk because I have to keep pushing the brake or the car moves by itself, plus drivers are angry at me. Meanwhile Mum and Dad are playing happy families with Robert and nobody loves me anymore.

Cars are queuing and hooting and revving round me and I'm crying and shouting at them and pushing the brake, my leg hurting from holding the car with a mind of its own.

I remember the keys and turn off the engine, pull up the handbrake very hard, climb into the back, my stomach gone and all the doors locked again but no Robert and no Mum and no rain, only angry cars and darkness.

Three Lips would know what to do about the police lights. He waves them round but they won't go. Three Lips definitely isn't speeding but they just sit behind him with the flashing lights going round inside the car like it's a disco. If they're in a hurry they should just squeeze by. He gives them the sign, then goes back up the business end in case he needs to make a quick getaway.

Three Lips turns the headlights on. He didn't forget them, he's been in stealth mode until he was far enough away from the evil lobster.

Now an enormous cop is walking up to Three Lips' sports car and trying to see in through the window. Meanwhile Three Lips is just puffing on his cigar, casual as. He's on a tough enough case as it is without the law on his tail too. Maybe the law are involved.

The cop taps on the glass. He probably wants a bribe. Three Lips Macavoy can't be bribed. He winds down his window and the officer seems surprised. Three Lips takes a puff on his cigar, casual as.

'Beat it, cop. I'm on a case.'

26

All the hedges are out, nothing between me and the street but little stumps poking up. I'm slouched on the lawn in the bright, early morning, torn-out hedge all around me as if I'm nesting in our front garden. My front garden. The ladder is over on its side, the orange power cord scribbled across the grass.

I stand and take my torn-up hands into the house, bits of green flecked in with the scratches and bleeding on my palms. Indoors everything is thick and cloying, some peculiar gravity emanating from her body on the kitchen floor.

I sit at the family table sipping vodka from the bottle and watching my scarred hand shaking. My wrist resting on the table edge, my hand shaking. I watch it. There's a part of me making that happen, a part of me I can't reach.

Who do you phone when someone has died. What's the official procedure.

I go over to her body. To her. The vodka tagging along in the hand at my side, a fist wobbling up in front of my mouth, my palm hurting with all the hedge cuts in it.

Her body is still but I notice the chest going up and down and even my hand stops trembling. I watch for another sign of movement.

'Mum?'

I remember being told about this now. Just one item on the talking-shit agenda during the night shift at work. One of the other guards, Frank, who was once a hospital orderly, telling me how a dead body can look like it's breathing. Your brain is so used to seeing chests going up and down it puts it there. That fictional step we live away from the world.

Just like when I think back to childhood I don't know what's real anymore, the neglect or the jealousy. Which really happened? Was there just my jealousy or was there neglect too?

I picture an ambulance coming and men in gloves taking her from me. No sirens. No lights.

She looks like an apple left too long in the fruit bowl.

I've known that face forever but this is the beginning of another part of my life. The part without her. For the first time this is the beginning of life after Mum. One day I'll have lived longer without her than with her. And Dad. One day I'll have been alone more than I've been a part of something. Even if it was something painful.

I imagine the men coming and taking her away all messed up like that. Me sitting at her unattended funeral and staring at the coffin, knowing she's in it looking that way.

I put my hands in my pockets to stop them shaking, the scratches hurting me. There isn't much in my head and I rummage around for a feeling. There should be lots of them but there's emptiness, the odd thought bubbling up out of the numb. Mainly of them burying her in that mucky outfit. Her rotting like that. One slipper on, one slipper off.

I meander down the side of the house and start rolling a cigarette in the shed, the birds chirruping, the bicycle overhead.

I can smoke in the house now so I walk in, the cigarette smoking into one closed eye. I stand looking at her shape. She's mine now, finally. I can get as close to her as I like. I can *touch* her all I want. Yet I can also feel the same forcefield around her.

I take swig after swig of drink, chuck the cigarette in the sink, put the bottle down — standing here breathing through the anxiety and the chemical sharpness of the vodka.

I hold her under the armpits and lift, her head lolling back, her mouth open — her eyes. I set her down again, her feet parting outwards. With an uncertain hand I close her eyes, then take her in my arms, not looking at her face, my head turned. Looking away and yet greedy for the looking. Having to turn side-on to fit us through doorways.

At the bottom of the stairs I'm tempted to carry her out into the street and roar at everyone to wake up and see what's happened. My mum's dead and they're sleeping.

I place her at the foot of the stairs and sit panting, staring, my eyes unfocused, such a final silence gathered around us. The vodka clogging my head.

I scoop her up in my arms and strain to a standing position again, her head lolling and mine brimming with bursting at the strain.

I take the fourth step, the fifth, each footfall an uncertain thud as I carry her up, my innards held taut against this proximity. The early morning light changing quickly now, colour filling the house, altering the atmosphere. The sound of birdsong such a gentle unkindness.

I stagger across the landing but can't hold her anymore, putting her as carefully as possible onto the floor.

In the bathroom I turn on the bath taps and sit on the edge, letting the cold water run down over my wrists and hands, a little of my blood colouring the water.

The temperature starts to warm and I adjust the taps to get it just right for my dead mother. I leave it running and go out and kneel in front of her on the landing, her chest seeming to move for a second again. My brain playing with me. The taps thundering into the bath.

'Let's get you cleaned up, Mum.' I lift her, struggling to stand, pivoting her on her legs, both of us teetering towards toppling down the staircase but my shoulder braces against the wall and I lurch us into the bathroom, setting her down again beside the bath, the windows fogged over. My own chest going up and down.

I turn off the taps and there's that silence again, louder somehow because I'm sharing it with this absent presence. I wipe my eyes, wiping away tears I'm still not attached to. I'm dreading the ones I'll be attached to.

Sitting on the bath edge, leaning over her again, my arms hooking her armpits. I haul her up onto my knees and then have to slide out from under, holding her torso on the side of the bath, her shoulder blades catching on the edge and keeping her there, my hand pushing into her stomach to hold her. Her body not yet cooled. I hurry around to lift her legs, cradling the head as she slips in, her foot clattering across the taps and turning one to a trickle — my face and chest covered with water as it seesaws back and forth in the bath, licking right up the walls on one side, then thumping onto me and the lino on the other. The spillage spreading silently across the floor and darkening the hallway carpet.

I hold her head above the water, her clothes wanting to float up away, her eyes open again. I close them then pull my other hand from behind her head and stand.

She stays there, her head squashed a little awkwardly against the end of the bath, perpendicular to her body so that her chin is on her chest, staring at her belly. Checking for meningitis. And I can't help but mimic it, taking me back to the day when she was that butter colour in hospital. Robert sitting on her bed looking like he was loving her so hard, when actually he was just trying so hard to be loved.

I traipse downstairs for the vodka, wincing at the taste but savouring something clean. Me and the bottle heading back up a heavy step at a time, her engagement ring left behind on the carpet halfway up.

Back in the bathroom I get a jolt when I see her. A swig from the bottle tries to wash it away. I turn the dripping tap, hating the quiet that comes after.

With finger and thumb I take the one slipper off her and help that foot slide off the side of the bath and into the water. Her ankle such a raw rainbow of bruising. My hands shaking again.

I go to her bedroom and start rifling through her wardrobe for an outfit she might think elegant. I pull out clothes and throw them onto the carpet. Take a dress and hold it up against me for size — toss it aside, open a bottom drawer but there's just a large dress box, clothes behind it. I go to bring the box closer and it's heavier than it should be so I lift its lid enough for a peek, then take the whole thing out.

Inside is my childhood. Every picture, every school report, even the bad ones, a baby book with its sections filled in — records of my growth rate and first solids and first crawling, a lock of baby hair. Pictures of me in the crib. It looks like me. A picture of that big rock in the cemetery too, just like that black chunk of it we still have downstairs. Here's some milk teeth.

She's caught every drop of my childhood. My Alonely poem, the creases still in it from where she screwed it up. Ribbons from sports day. I move more paintings and scribbles and homespun birthday cards aside and there's a travel book on Canada that opens naturally to my town. Even a brochure about a career in the prison service here.

I can't help but let out a sound at the thought of her trying to understand my life. And the idea of her living over here alone, sad. Me over there, alone and sad. And sulking.

There's the beginning of a letter to me too — many stalled beginnings, words crossed out and written over. I can read as far as the first sentence before the paper blurs and I have to replace the lid for now. Her half-written letter slipping into my wet pocket.

I go to return the box but at the back of the drawer is that video of Robert. I sit and look at it, the spools of tape showing through the plastic window, then I stand and carry it with me, putting it at the top of the stairs.

Back in the bathroom I get a stronger jolt, her face under the water, eyes open and staring again, a few bubbles trickling out of her nose. I get on my knees in the wet, pierce the water with my arms and lift her back above the surface — brush her hair aside, some water running from her mouth.

Tugging the bathroom curtains shut to hide the morning light, I swig from the bottle then begin to undress her.

By the time I've finished the water is cold and discoloured and I've put a big dent in the contents of the vodka bottle. I reach between her feet to pull up the plug and then can't help but watch as the water slips away, the plughole slurping desperately, her body crumpling slowly in on itself. Deflating. One of her fists clenched tight.

I lay a towel over her then go downstairs with the vodka and the video, switch on the radio for company, run the hot tap into a bucket in the sink. I turn off the radio again, wake up the old video player and slip the tape in.

I mop the kitchen floor, going to the TV occasionally and watching the footage of Robert sat there on the edge of all that sky, his hair fluttering madly in the rush of air.

'1'

Such unbridled happiness for such a tragic life.

'2'

Me having to mop round Mum's single slipper left here, before finally giving in and taking it out, chucking it onto the back lawn, the sound of Robert's recorded squeals coming at me from inside the house. As if it's back in the days when he was still alive. When we all were.

I add bleach to a final bucket, starting to feel a kindling of warmth inside me — some illusion of regained control, that I'm finally doing right by her, even if it feels too late.

I stop in the twilight of the kitchen and the smell of bleach, my chin on the top of the mop handle, the video ended, just static on the screen, my eyes staring out the windows. Slow tears running like somebody else's tears.

I take a cloth, dipping a corner of it in bleach and go through to the bathroom and the faded ochre stain on the wall-side of the U-bend. Grandma's stain.

My dad got down on his knees in this tight space and cleaned up all her blood rather than let Mum face the reality. Or to save him facing hers. I kneel where he knelt in this small, tight space and finish the job for him, the old blood stain resisting for a while then lifting in granular stages.

I wash my hands for about the thirtieth time today, my skin creased as if from a long, luxurious bath.

Upstairs again I stand in the bathroom doorway, expecting to see goosebumps on her skin but there's no such life on it, only that slowly dimming colour. The house clogged full of silence.

Getting her out the bath is harder. Especially now she's heavier, the sound of water sloshing inside her every time I pause for breath. Reminding me of when I was a boy, filling up on water so I could hear it slop about inside me when I wriggled my belly.

By the time she's dressed and in bed I'm drenched, Mum's outfit not sitting on her right. She looks worse now somehow, like waxwork.

And although she's in bed, she doesn't look like she's in bed. She's there and the bed's there too, that's all.

I perch on the edge for a second, then rush downstairs, hit the eject button on the video player but it gets the tape caught in its throat. I bang the top over and over, pushing the eject button, the old motors whining. Out it comes and I hold it against me, walking back to the stairs but catch sight of the mica rock sat there on the windowsill. I collect that too and go up to her, lay the rock and the video on the bed — tease that fist of hers out into a hand.

It feels good seeing her with these important artefacts of her life. I smooth the care out of her forehead and lie down beside her.

Her body smells clean and smooth. My head in near her shoulder but frightened to burrow right into that neck — the sounds of activity beginning outside. Me lying here, never closer to her even though she's never been further away. The room still and quiet and restful, the pictures of family on the walls — sunlit sunshine days shining out from the frames, full of airborne confetti and smiles and teeth. The captured moments we put up to make life look comprehensible. Palatable. Celebrated.

I lie here with her in this certain type of silence, an unfamiliar quiet inside me now too. Only the occasional car and voice outside puncturing the sense that the world has stopped.

Eventually I go downstairs and out into the back garden, dropping her soiled clothes on the grass. I come back from the front dragging hedge debris with me, dumping it in a heap next to her wet clothes, then going back for more hedge.

When I've finished there's a trail of leaves from the front garden to the back. I pile it all up then get an old, empty cardboard box of fertiliser from the shed and tear it into strips still greasy from the chemicals. Chemicals which glow blue-green when I light them.

The hedge won't go up though, it just pops and smokes so I'm back in the shed kicking around until I find a faded red petrol can with a little left inside it for the lawnmower. The vodka making me stagger and stumble.

I douse the bonfire then add the best part of a bottle of olive oil from the kitchen to slow it down. A swig from the vodka then I empty that on too, disgusted at the taste and my drinking and hiding.

I take a stick from the pile and light the petrol and oil mixture covering the end of it — chuck it on and whoof! I smile at that. Start adding the stolen pictures of the families and brides and couples, their faces burning slowly away and the fake gold on the frames peeling off in a green flame. Fool's gold, like family is.

I use another stick to pick Mum's wet clothes up, putting them on the fire where they hiss and complain. Another link with her going. Her slipper smoking on top of it all.

As the fire starts to struggle I head indoors looking for more to burn. Gathering up our real family pictures — the one of Robert in those orange overalls. Everyone loves this picture, from that day he had — the one in the video. I grab the photo of me and my new bike on the front path. Me and my first day at school. Broken Robert strapped into his chair, chocolate cake all over his mouth. The other Robert, dressed in his new school uniform on his birthday, Mum's arm around him and both their heads chopped off. That picture of Dad doting on Mum while she's just looking brightly, confidently into the camera lens. And the one of us at the photographer's, that eight-year-old in his scratchiest clothes, a swirly oil backdrop behind him.

I touch a blackened finger to his face. That boy is running around inside me somewhere still, his head comically oversized for his body. He's the little fuse in our family that snapped. The most sensitive part of the circuitry, so that the whole family stopped working afterwards. He was the only one expressing that which was otherwise unexpressed in the family. So that he is our family's anger. Its brokenness. Its neglect.

What am I then?

And I don't know. Except that I'm all that's left.

I get out of my wet clothes and put them on the fire too. The morning sun feeling kind on my skin but I can only think that she can't feel it. That she'll never see another dawn. She can't smell this smoke, the way it takes me back to autumnal Sundays and sweaters and dusk. Dad sweeping leaves then using his hand along with the rake to dump them on the fire, almost choking it out. Having to stagger away from the smoke, his cheeks puffed out, eyes clamped shut. Swearing under his breath, laughing. The sound of dishes clattering in the sink and the feel of Monday morning and school already in my stomach.

I went through so much of childhood with that Sunday night stomach.

The shed windows are looking at me, a smudge in the dust from where Mum bumped her head the other day looking up at the clouds I was pointing to.

That's it now then, just the smudges the living leave behind.

I lie back on the grass, out here under our patch of sky, a wispy cloud up there, right in the top of the blue, bumping space maybe. It looks like bone seen on an x-ray. I watch it getting whittled slowly away as it heads east, and I'm trying to make something out of the shape before it's gone. The way Robert would. The way he did.

She'll never see another cloud.

27

The sunshine tells me how irrelevant my loss is. Not a cloud in the sky. I sit and smoke an acrid cigarette while spotty young undertakers prepare to take her away. Men who look like they should be loitering in snooker halls or where drugs are sold. They tell me about the fire at the chemical plant, like it'd be big news to me on a day like today.

'I know, I was up.'

They nod in understanding. Of course, their faces say.

We wait for the doctor to come and tell me what I already know. While he's inside, just another day's work for him, the men smoke cigarettes. Standing there on the pavement like beacons of death, announcing it to the street with their cheap suits and black ties, knots tied narrow and small — taken off over the head at the end of the day, never undone.

The doctor comes out the house looking like he only stopped by to pick up cigarettes and milk. He tells me how to get the proper death certificate, then tears off a form he's filled. The undertakers get a copy from him, the pink. I get the blue. The doctor keeps the white, heads off in his swish car and the death men go indoors with a trolley and a bag.

I wait out the back, poking at the fire.

'Excuse me, would you like the rock and the video tape to go with her?'

I nod and he backs away before he turns, goes inside again.

I've searched high and low for her will but she's not done me that courtesy.

In the shed I stand looking up at the bike, then lift it down, dislodging dust that gets in my eyes, floats in the sunlight. I carry the bike out and hold it ceremoniously over my head, a noise escaping me as I chuck it on the fire, sparks flying up.

I hear a car door slam, and one of the almost-flat bicycle tyres lets out a lacklustre pop.

I walk round the side of the house as one of the men is returning from the van, Mum in there on her back, in a bag, looking up at nothing.

I'm presented with a clipboard, a multilayered pad of printed paper on it, the sheet already completed in advance so I don't have to wait too long. Even these men have finessed the art of tiptoeing around grief. Their finesse needed all the more because of how unpractised their customers are. Every day these men work with people who are navigating something furthest from everyday.

We stand by the van and I feel like it's vibrating or humming slightly. An electric fence. I sign something and one of them asks me where she was when she passed. He says it like that, *passed*. Like it's a test.

'In bed.' As if it's any of their business.

He gives me the pink then puts the pad in the car and quietly shuts the door, comes back.

'It's just that she has water in her,' he says, the smell of cigarettes coming off him. Both of them eating me with their eyes.

'Is there something else you need me to sign?'

One of them breaks the silence eventually.

'No, that's everything thank you, sir.'

Sir.

'Sorry again for your loss,' the other says as the van's suspension creaks under the weight of them getting in. 'We'll be in touch regarding your funeral wishes.'

Two slams, fractionally out of time. Maybe in a year or so those will happen in unison. They'll have worked together long enough then, even their doors will be in time.

The engine starts and I jump, a black cloud coming out the exhaust, the engine clattering under the polished bonnet. I watch as she moves away, the driver's face getting bigger for a second as he leans into the side mirror to get a look at me.

I watch her go. The shrinking van climbing away up Hawke Street Hill, its indicator coming on at the top. They've probably already got the radio on. Nobody in the traffic knowing there's a dead body among them. The sun shining. My mum and all that water wobbling around in the back.

I head for the house but can only face the back garden, plonking myself down by the fire, taking off my t-shirt, letting the sun and embers warm my skin. The hedges slowly giving up their moisture and burning, a low-lying wet smoke cloaking the lawn. The bike charred but holding its shape.

My mobile phone wakes me up with its ringing in my pocket. It takes me a moment to work out where I am, having passed out last night in my old sleeping bag, in the shed. I rummage for the phone in case it's Patricia but it's someone from the undertaker's, phoning from the front door.

The fire's still smoking, the bike blackened now in the wreckage, its spokes popped off the rim, just a sticky stump left where the saddle was.

I don't invite the undertaker in but leave him outside in his sombre suit while I venture into the house and put the kettle on, rinse my face in the kitchen sink, flatten my hair and come back out the front with two chairs from the dining table, set us up in the front garden, feeling guilty for having Mum's good chairs outside. Cups of tea steaming up at us.

Without a will I have to guess. I opt for cremation, scatter her with Dad and Robert. I'm betting more women are cremated than men. One last vanity. Better to quickly burn than slowly rot.

I'm still sitting here staring into space, an empty chair in front of me and the undertaker's untouched mug of cold tea at a jaunty angle on the grass when a police car pulls up.

I finalise the joint I shouldn't be rolling, tapping its end repeatedly on my fingernail to pack down the contents. The police door opens, I slip my creation into my shirt pocket and cross my legs. Uncross them.

A guy in a suit gets out and locks the car, coming towards me with his face in this shape. He's clean-cut, in his forties, nice-looking and knows it. A plain-clothed shark.

He checks the number on our gate but comes through where the hedges used to be, stepping over the stumps and looking back at them in that exaggerated way. Calling me mister so he can pretend he's being respectful even though the power is all his.

He doesn't shake my hand, shows me his ID which I don't focus on, only gaze at it like it's an exam and I just turned the paper over.

'Is there a reason why you didn't respond to my telephone messages?'

'I've been ignoring the answering machine.'

He gives a nod of having understood more than I've said. 'Would you prefer some privacy, perhaps if we go inside?'

I shake my head.

'Mind if I sit then?' he says and sits.

'Cup of tea?' I say, pointing at the undertaker's leftovers.

The detective looks at me then bends down and picks up the mug, finger and thumb, puts it where he can't knock it over. He wouldn't want to blow his image.

'First of all,' he says. Here we go, my insides feeling like someone just stuck a vacuum cleaner up my arse and switched it on. 'I want to offer my sympathy at this difficult time.'

'Fine. What's this about?'

His suit is this rich blue. He looks very good. I don't. I adjust my posture again, stand enough to pull my trousers up. He opens his little book. Cops love props. A posh pen appears from his inside jacket pocket.

Click-click.

'Just a few questions about the circumstances of your mother's death, I'm afraid. Procedural things in most cases, but you understand we have to do it. Probably nothing to worry about.'

'What d'you mean?'

'There's just some inconsistencies we need to iron out.'

'Terminal cancer must be among your tougher cases to crack.'

He puts out a placating hand, manicured nails. 'Before you say anything I have to inform you …'

While he's doing that official, right-to-legal-representation speech, I have all these conflicts going off inside me. Part of me isn't scared — Mum's dead and who gives a stuff what the government or the police or procedure is. Nothing trumps death, it's the lowest common denominator.

Part of me is terrified.

'I'm aware your mother had cancer but am I right in saying you told the undertakers she died in bed?'

'No.'

He fidgets forward on his seat, looks at me, waiting.

'You think I killed a dead woman, officer?'

'We're not at the accusation stage. She appears to have water in her. Reason enough to ask some preliminary questions.' He pauses, gives me a look. 'Let's just get the facts down, shall we, try not to cross any unnecessary bridges? The autopsy should clear up any confusion. If there's water in the lungs then ...' I could bury him in the back garden. Take him out back and beat his head in with the shovel, bloody up his sharp blue suit. Or chuck him on the fire along with that bike.

'I haven't agreed to an autopsy, nobody said anything about an autopsy. She had brain cancer.' My body goes to stand me up but I turn it into a fidget, straighten out my trousers again — sit back, cross my legs.

He watches this then takes out a form, almost a conjurer's flourish in the gesture, his voice all monotone again. 'I'm obliged to inform you that you do not have to sign this form but if you refuse an autopsy we'll be forced to lodge a request through the courts which will almost certainly be granted but usually also necessitate a delay to the burial of your relative and result ...' I could drown him in the bath '... increased sentence in the event that a prosecution were to proceed. Subject to a conviction. The delay can also make it more difficult for the autopsy to deliver a clear picture of the cause of death, which could cloud any resultant criminal proceedings. I'm obliged to remind you that you are under caution but that you have the right ...'

I look at him, the feelings sloshing in my belly, distracting me. Meanwhile he's got the form held out to me on top of his closed book, the pen offered in his other hand.

I leave it all dangling there in the space between us, my arms folding. 'It doesn't much sound like I don't have to sign this form.'

His gaze never wavers. 'You aren't accused of anything. This is not yet a criminal investigation. But if I were in your position I'd sign it, answer some questions and I'm sure we can have everything settled. I'm not here to make this difficult time more arduous. Prosecutions are rare but we have to go through the process.'

He puts the form down on the grass beside him and plonks his ID on it to keep it there — hangs on to his little book. 'We'll leave the autopsy to one side for a second, shall we? Focus on the events around your mother's passing. Were you with her when it happened?'

No, I wasn't. I was on the phone like a coward. I left her in her final moment of need. 'Yes.'

'Pardon?'

'*Yes.*' I stuff my scratched-up hands in my pockets, the pain making me wince.

'And where was she at the time?'

'In the kitchen, with Professor Plum.'

He presses the button on his pen once to retract the nib, taps it gently on his lips. Nice lips. I take out the little joint and tamp it down on my nail again. 'Mind if I smoke?'

He shakes his head, waiting during the little opera of my lighting it. I struggle to do it smoothly, then put the photographer's lighter away and blow the smoke over my shoulder but the breeze brings it back past me and into his face. He lifts his nose a fraction, taking in the aroma. I look at him, my heart kinking in my chest — take another drag, wipe nothing from my trousers, recline back in my chair, spellbound by my own petulant stupidity.

He gazes at me for a while. 'If you could explain the events immediately leading up to your mother's death and the actual moment. Leave nothing out.'

I flick the ash, watch it fall. 'I'd been out.'

'With?'

'Do we have to involve her?'

'Your best bet is to tell me all the facts.'

'You can come back for that after the autopsy, can't you. You don't have anything until after the autopsy.'

'And if you have nothing to hide …'

'I came home, about one-ish, the chemical plant was ablaze — arson?' He shrugs in reply. 'Mum was on the kitchen floor, throwing up.' I take a drag and don't bother trying to keep the smoke from him. He uses a hand to waft it away, a vein showing up at his temple and for some reason the sight of it calms me a little. 'I called an ambulance but while I —'

He looks up from his notebook. 'You called an ambulance?'

'I rang them but she, while I was on the phone …' My body tries to stand me up again.

'Did you call from your home number or a mobile?'

'Home.'

'I've got that, haven't I.' He's rifling through his book, a bit flustered now.

'You told me you left a message.'

'Yes. Good. What time would this have been approximately, the ambulance.'

'Dunno.'

'Well, was it soon after you arrived home?'

'Sorry, I was drunk.'

'And stoned?'

I smile confidently at him but a blush rains on my parade. I stub out the joint prematurely, put it in my pocket so he can't collect it as evidence. He watches this, pleased.

'Mr Rossiter and' — he consults his book — 'Mr Marchant say they collected her body from upstairs in her bedroom. How did her body come to be upstairs if she died in the kitchen?'

It sounds funny hearing that those men are a mister and have a surname. I expect them to be Kev and Jonno or something — a squalid apartment and a pregnant, smoking wife each.

'I carried her upstairs and washed her in the bath. I didn't want her buried in a mess. I know that's illegal.' I offer him my wrists. 'You better take me away, officer.'

'It's detective.' He shuts his book and does that long blink. 'There are certain options available to me in this situation. The law empowers me to make certain judgements. You might want to remember that. I could take you into custody pending the autopsy. I'm pretty confident your mum drowned, and on that basis I could delay the ...' His lips are moving but all I can hear is the tinnitus of panic. Everything falling away inside me at the image of those bubbles coming out her mouth. The way I had to keep closing her eyes '... that this is a bad time for you, of course, I'm prepared to give you some leeway but my patience isn't endless.'

He turns back to his book and says, 'That must have been hard getting her upstairs. Were you alone, any relatives present?'

'They're all dead.'

He looks up.

'And, no, I didn't kill them.' Yes I did. It's my fault. I killed them. Three down, me to go.

'Once you got her upstairs, then what did you do?'

'Bathed her.'

'Pardon?'

'I bathed her.'

'I see. In the bath?'

I nod at him.

'And during that, was there any time at which water would have got inside her?'

'I left her for a second and when I came back she'd slipped under.'

He makes a note then flicks back a few pages in his book. 'It's not impossible for a deceased person to take on a little stomach water if submerged. But she seems to have a significant amount. Plus some bruising, not just the sprained ankle. Some carpet burns.'

He looks up. 'All this was sustained during bathing her, I suppose.'

I stare down at his shiny shoes, my hands in my hair. I can hear him flipping his notebook pages over.

'Then you dressed her and put her in bed, hence the dry clothes?'

I nod at his shiny shoes, shut my eyes.

He slaps his book shut. 'Did you check she was dead before you bathed her?'

I look up at him. His mouth wants to smile, his body fidgeting for the first time.

'What?'

He repeats it, I think.

I shake my head a little. 'Did I ...'

He *is* smiling. 'Well,' he says, brightly, 'how did you know your mother was dead before you bathed her? Did you make reasonable checks? Maybe she'd just had a stroke or something. Did you take her pulse, check for breathing?'

'She wasn't breathing.' I am. I'm breathing. Mum's chest going up and down too. Her face under the water, her eyes open.

'Well, how do you know?' He's staring, watching the fireworks going off inside me, enjoying the spectacle.

'I ... She wasn't. She was dead. She was all ...' I stand up, my chair falling over behind me. 'I know what a dead person looks like!'

But I can see her chest going up and down, then Frank's face telling me about his experiences of dead-body breathing.

The detective doesn't look away, one leg still crossed nonchalantly over the other, his face craned up towards me now I'm standing. Then slowly he says, 'I see. But you can understand how the facts can also make it look otherwise? A body with water in it, plus bruising and carpet burns. A son looking after his suffering mother alone. Already on a caution for assault.'

I pace away, come back.

'So you didn't check for a pulse?' he says.

'Please don't do this.'

'Pardon?'

'You *know* I didn't! She was DEAD. And if she wasn't, *which she was*, I didn't mean to ... She slipped away right in front of my eyes. I was on the phone to the ambulance. You keep recordings. *Listen* to the recordings! Around two or three a.m. You'd probably be able to hear the actual moment. Talk to Patricia, the woman I was with.'

'You didn't mean to what?' He says it all soft and calm, like this is one of the few, non-paperwork perks of his job.

My voice quietens too. 'She was dead.' I resurrect my chair, slump down.

'Patricia's address?'

I tell him the street, make a wild stab at her house number. Bang goes *that* romance then.

He picks up the slightly damp autopsy consent form and holds it out along with a pen. 'You should've told the undertakers you had to get her upstairs. That you bathed her.'

'And you should go and solve some real crimes you ...'

'*What?*' he says, his chin out at me, imperious. 'What am I?'

I look away.

'By the way,' he says, standing up, ready to go — pocketing my signature on his stupid form. 'What was your relationship like with your mother?'

28

People walk differently at churches. They talk quieter too so they don't wake the dead people sleeping in the graveyards. Singing doesn't wake the dead though. The singing's the best bit.

The last time I was at a funeral was when Grandma died but I wasn't allowed to see her go into the ground.

Grandad got burnt, coffin and everything and I was allowed to go to that one even though I was even younger then. I was three. But with Grandma, after the boring church bit, I had to go home with Auntie Debbie which is worse than seeing someone going into the ground.

Today I get to see the whole thing except it's not a funeral but a memorial. Plus there isn't a body because it already got cut to pieces and burnt years ago. For science.

Last month these people phoned up about Michael. Mum was crying after the call, Dad trying to get her to take a hug and Robert going nuts with a saucepan and a metal spoon. You can't get a spoon from Robert for anything. Except in exchange for ice-cream maybe, but then he needs a spoon. That's what shrugging your shoulders was invented for, stuff like that.

It was these charity people on the phone, saying they'd found where the hospital had put them all after they'd done research on them and that if we wanted we could attend a ceremony. Which is today and my clothes are tight and scratchy and I'm not allowed gel in my hair, only water.

There's not many people here in the church but most of them are women like my mum's age, some older. Most are dressed in dark colours but some make the church look like it could just be the supermarket.

We sing All Things Bright and Beautiful which is a nice song, for a church song.

Afterwards we have to relocate to the cemetery which means driving and Robert has to be in his big kid seat in the back, all buckled in. He'll never ride up front again. I feel sorry for Robert but if we don't buckle him in he likes to yank up the handbrake while we're going.

Dad is driving and Mum has her hand on her mouth and her face right up close to the window. The radio is on but down so low it might as well be off.

I'm always nervous in the car now cos it reminds Mum and Dad to be angry with me. Even though Dad says it's his fault for being such a softy and teaching me about the business end.

We had to pay for the cars I scratched. Deadly's car too. Dad said when he told Auntie what I'd done she nearly prolapsed.

That's when your front bottom flies out.

I got to ride in a police car though. I like the police. Maybe I'll be a policeman when I grow up.

When we get to the cemetery, which is all the way on the edge of town, there are lots of people parking their cars. Some of the cars are parked so they take up a bit more than one space.

I miss my TV but Dad says I'll be missing my balls too if I whinge about it again. And he sat me down and told me not to feel guilty for Social Services finding out about the car incident.

Now there's no more fostering and I know it's my fault but Dad says it isn't.

Mum took Robert to Auntie D's once she found out and they didn't come back for weeks.

We can adopt Robert though. He's our consolation prize. Probably cos he's too expensive for Social Services to look after him. Plus his real mum and dad couldn't cope when he was a good boy let alone now he's broken.

It takes ages to find a parking spot and Dad has that little lump at his jaw and even Robert is quiet, his fingers in his mouth, and Dad doesn't tell him he'll dissolve them away if he isn't careful, and Robert doesn't laugh.

There are lots of people and kids in the cemetery and the sun is out. The children are happy but the parents look sad. I've got that bad feeling in my stomach.

There's a big black boulder in the cemetery which they put in especially for today. Plus the sun is really, really shining, like the people's sadness doesn't matter.

Dad takes Robert out of the way and Mum is a hundred million miles from anywhere. She has her zombie look on and no blood in her face. Probably because she's not allowed to foster anymore.

Sometimes Dad calls me Ayrton Senna when nobody's around. I think he's secretly proud of me driving. It's just Mum who knows I'm bad.

Dad says we've got enough on our plate anyway and Robert is like twenty foster children.

Plus me makes twenty-one.

I think it's funny to mark all those dead baby babies with something like a big black jutting rock. Why not put a playground in the cemetery, all nice colours and a slide so the priest could be saying his piece and the children playing on the swings. I wouldn't because I'm too old. Swings are for kids. But maybe the children would like that.

I was two when Michael was born but he only lived for 23 hours. Mum never went to see him after he was dead. Dad did.

Michael didn't even get a birth certificate. You have to live a whole day so he was one hour away from getting his certificate, like he failed a test.

Dad was the one who saw Michael after he'd died but before they took him apart to see what broke. Then chucked him in the fire probably.

All hospitals have a chimney and the smoke that comes out is made of people.

Dad says that the world has only just worked out what to do when a tiny baby dies and that the hospital should have known better. They just took him away.

There are mini grave plaques to mark the babies too, as well as the big rock. Most of them only have one date on though. Not a from and a to date like Grandma's grave. Just one date.

And some of them didn't even live long enough to get a name. Michael did. The plaques without names say things like Baby Greene, or Baby Jones, or whatever.

Here's one called Baby Strong.

The boulder to remember the babies is sharp and has shiny bits in it that catch the sun. It's mica rock, Dad says, all out of breath already just from doing nothing.

Michael rock.

All the mums who lost a baby are here. There's a nice one standing on her own in a blue coat. She looks special. Dad is way over there now with Robert and a packet of biscuits. Mum is here but not here.

All the families are sort of far apart, not bunched in close and the priest says come in closer and we move but don't really get closer at all. Some of the younger children do, they go right up and sit in front of the rock and are all excited and the priest hushes them really gently. Today is a day to be nice to children.

One of the girls has a big red birthmark on her forehead, like a raspberry.

Dad says he wishes he'd taken at least one picture of Michael, but in my head he looks like an alien because that's how babies look in the tummy when you see them on the telly. They look like aliens that have had their fingers stood on, currants for eyes. Plus Michael's body must have had cuts all over it from when they experimented on him after, to find out why. Like he was an alien from another planet and couldn't survive on earth so they chopped him up to learn about outer space.

Sometimes I think I'm from another planet. Or sometimes I think there was a mix up at the hospital. As if somehow my zombie mum's first baby died too and they thought it was some other woman's. Which could mean my real mum is here somewhere crying about me as if I died. If my real mum is here I think it would be that nice one in the blue coat.

Even the priest is crying now. I won't cry.

The mum in the blue coat has highlights in her hair and her face is a bit wonky. She looks kind though and has these blue eyes. She's crying but only gently like she has something fragile balanced on her head. The woman beside me, my official mum, she isn't crying. Even the priest is crying. Maybe he lost a baby under that rock too.

He's saying that the dead baby children are playing in heaven now and their beauty shines on and is even in the little flecks of light in that rock. Which is totally silly because the rock is millions of years old and the babies were only hours young.

He says the babies were carried but never held, and that they'll always be cherished even if they were never cradled. He looks at

everyone and puts his lips away. 'Cherished, but never cradled.'
He sounds like a stuck record.

Then his voice changes, like he's letting us into a secret. He says
he knows there's a rock inside every mother here too. That he knows
there are rocks in their bellies now where there was once that child.
And that they're so brave carrying those rocks. That they'll always
carry a rock in them for the child they lost.

When he says that the women cry even more. All these mums
standing apart together with rocks in their bellies.

I think the priest must be new to priesting because he isn't
cheering them up much is he.

Then he says God will help them with those rocks, but I don't
see why God didn't just help the babies. Then I look up and say
sorry, just in case.

I should have worn my comics.

The nice mum with the blue coat is crying and has her arms
round herself. She looks lonely. Meanwhile my zombie mum is
standing next to me and I survived and got my certificate but she is
all in love with a dead kid that she never even went and hugged and
who never even lived a whole day.

I dig my nails into my palms to put the brakes on, my eyes are
getting wet. Robert's crying too but not about the babies, biscuit
goo all over his face. Dad's hair is all spiky and he's following Robert
across people's graves which must be making all those people in the
past shudder. Walking over graves makes them shudder in the past.

I walk through the sad people a little bit to look at the blue coat
lady. I want to tell her about the mix up. She'll wrap me up in her
coat and maybe walk me home to her house, holding hands.

I bet her hand is one of those ones that is extra warm and toasty.

I go over nearer her and the ground is all uneven under my
school shoes and I stand very statue so I don't scare her off. She's
still quietly crying about losing me. Look how much she loves me.

She gazes over and her eyes are all blue and my heart stops. My breathing. Everything.

Mum.

She looks a little bit blurred, maybe cos of the tears in my eyes. I wipe them away like a big boy and go and stand right next to her even though I'm scared to get close.

She smiles and I smile back so hard my ears move.

I'm looking at her hand and the priest is saying something out of the Bible, he knows it off by heart but has it there in case. I can see Dad behind a gravestone and Robert must be down there on top of a dead person's grave while Dad's trying to stay calm and hold on to him but I can see he wants to be rough, Robert making all his embarrassing noise and people frowning at him like always.

You can't shoosh a retard.

Dad holds out a biscuit and Robert's hand appears from the gravestone and snatches it.

The blue coat lady has her hand just there at the end of her blue sleeve and there's a ring on it and she's crying about how much she misses me.

I reach out and take her hand.

It IS really warm and toasty plus she's letting me. I don't look at her but I can feel her eyes on me. She'll recognise me any minute now, my body fizzing and standing on end like I'm a hedgehog or a porcupine or a stegosaurus.

Stego sore arse, Dad says.

I've got my eyes half shut, my hand holding on, the priest having to speak louder over Robert's shouting. People shifting from foot to foot and wiping their eyes but I'm not moving or breathing or anything. I can feel my new real mum looking at me but I'm watching the girl with the birthmark. And I'm thinking how that birthmark must be from lying on the sad rock in her mum's belly for nine months.

Then the priest says Let us pray, and the lady takes her hand away and smiles at me for a second, turns her back to me, this big blue back. She walks away around the boulder.

She doesn't know about the mix up.

I look down at my hand. It must still have some of her warmth in it and I close it up tight.

I shouldn't have used my scarred for life one.

Meanwhile a lady from the church is coming round with a tray, little lumps of rock on it just like that big mica boulder to remember the dead babies.

She lets each mum take their own lump to keep and they smile at her, wipe their eyes. The tray lady has put her lips away.

I don't want to be young anymore and I don't want to grow up.

If I have to grow up I'll make my life amazing and probably be a famous weatherman, but only in summer so I don't have to give bad news and everyone will love me.

Or I'll be a rubbish collector cos they only come one day a week and I'll get all those six other days to just have fun and be nice to my family.

I'm definitely going to have kids cos then I won't have to play on my own anymore. It should be against the law to have an only child, like in China. I can't play with Robert.

And when I grow up things won't live in my tummy anymore and people will put toys and treasure in the rubbish bins by mistake. That would be amazing.

I'll be a pirate garbage man with a gold tooth and a wooden scarred for life hand and I'll ride on the back of the rubbish truck like I'm standing on the deck of a big ship. Seagulls chasing after. I'll have ten gold teeth and get rich on all that wasted treasure people throw away, and me and my family will watch TV in bed together every night and my insides won't bully me anymore.

Now I'm thinking maybe that tablet I took from Mum's handbag once made me a zombie too cos I want to cry but it won't come. I'm just standing on my own and thinking that zombie over there might be my mum really. Maybe I'm growing up to be a zombie too. Like we're the Zombie family. My spiky haired dad and Robert with his damaged brain. We're all the living dead.

Then everyone but Mum says Amen.

29

I wake up in the shed and run outside to pee, last night's bad dreams still affecting my innards even if they're already hazy in my mind.

I risk a visit indoors and Alfie is sprawled on the lounge floor, her breathing sluggish and laboured, her gurgling and snoring sounding louder than ever.

I gather her up and she whimpers in pain.

I'm glad to be out of the house, low cloud covering the whole sky and the cat warming my chest. Nothing on my feet, my hair probably sticking up in angry spikes.

Alfie feels good against me but her breathing's laboured and frail, reminding me of Reg.

Suddenly the whole world seems fragile to me. People inside those moving cars, seatbelts on, windscreens reflecting grey sky, the car tyres gripping on and everyone's heart going, for now. Everything held together only by the faint beating of our hearts.

I cut across Malfour Park, talking to Alfie, my bare feet content on the cool grass. I pass the craters that are concreted over now, skaters lingering with long hair and limp postures — taking their turn on the slopes. Everest. Round The World.

Beyond the park I cross the road, the cars giving us more

space than usual in deference to Alfie's obvious sickness. A sign outside a newsagent's with the local paper's brand on it and the headline.

Chemical Plant Burns — 11 Dead.

I head into the shop and a harsh buzzer goes, an old shopkeeper staring at the state of me. Beyond the condolence cards and the wrapping paper and the glistening packets of chocolate is the stationery. I bend to grab a thick permanent marker pen, Alfie mewing out in pain.

I throw a banknote onto the counter and walk out, the door buzzer drilling again and the shopkeeper shouting after me about my change.

My knees crack as I crouch down, crossing out the *11* in the poster's headline and writing *12*.

I have to meander up the busy high street because of everybody going about their business, stopping to chat to one another about their kids, the fire, what they're spending their time and money on. People giving me *Ah cute* looks when they see Alfie in my arms.

I walk on with the pen nib under my nose, the toxic smell percolating my teenage years back into me. Memories of ducking out of school, wedging myself in behind bus stops. My graffiti all over the town like a coded distress signal.

I pass another shop and am making *11* read *12* again, people stopping to watch, one of them asking me if another person has died overnight. I stand and they stay paused and open-mouthed in front of me. Suddenly they're keen to talk to this messy man because there's something in it for them — some juicy fact. They're prepared to make me an authority if it means drama.

'My mum died.'

One of them asks her husband or boyfriend what I said. I'm standing right here and she asks him what I said, like I'm on the TV and she can't interact with me. I'm the act. And in replying, he doesn't look away from my face, just turns his mouth to her and says, 'He says his mum died in it too.'

I walk into the vet's, hard-wearing lino on the floor, the smell of disinfectant. I twist a foot but since I'm barefoot there's no lino squeak.

A nurse behind the counter sizes up the scene in an instant and gives me a sympathetic smile.

I sit and wait, Alfie's head lolling down over my thigh if I don't hold it up — her fur coming out all over my clothes. Her chest going up and down. A little dog whimpering from behind the caged door of a wicker basket, its owner reading a magazine while I sit here trying to focus on a diamond of sunshine brightening on the floor because the clouds are clearing outside. *Another* sunny day.

Zero millimetres.

I stroke her and there's that feeling I get when I stroke an animal — a softness like a hug in my chest. I stay here in that feeling, gently comforting her, my face right down close.

'The vet will see her now.' The nurse comes over to say that, rather than calling out from her desk. I follow her through to a small room with a high table and a stronger smell of disinfectant. She leaves and the vet appears. He looks like he should be on a magazine cover, all smooth skin and cheekbones.

'Hello,' he says and shakes my hand, then gives her a light stroke in my arms. 'I remember her well. Lovely girl, aren't you, *yesh*. I'm guessing it's your mum I met on the other appointments?'

'That's right.'

He takes her from me, both of us working to hand her over gently. Still she lets out a sound.

Cheekbones makes a show of examining her but in his arms, her wheezing quickening. He and I both know what's happening but he makes a pretence of thoroughness, even though the nurse might be firing up the incinerator next door. Chucking another log on.

'Look,' he says eventually, softly, 'your mum always wanted to carry on with Alfie. And back then I understood. But now we're at a stage in her illness where she's suffering more than necessary. She's in a lot of pain, there's no doubt in my mind about that. The cancer has almost certainly metastasised.'

I take her back, focus on stroking her, give a nod. She looks so beautiful in her frail state. Animals have an innocence humans could never aspire to. Who are we to take that away with our needles. Besides, I can see a glimpse of Mum's innocence in her face.

'Ok.'

Cheekbones nods. 'Would you like to call your mum first?'

'It'd be long distance.'

'Pardon?'

'No, it's ok.'

'I'll give you and Alfie a moment then,' and he pats my shoulder and slips away, part of me wanting to trip him up as he goes. He slides the door shut and there's a glimpse of the rubber boots he's wearing at the bottom of his white coat.

I look round at the posters about worming and tagging your pet, an array of animals assembled and looking at the camera.

Goodbye isn't for the dying but for the end of an evening or the start of a week apart. It's See you soon. Goodbye isn't for I'll never see you again. We need a bigger word.

I stick my face in among her fur and she smells of home — of all the good things that happened too, not just the bad. The laughs. The moments of understanding. The positive times that happened when you weren't expecting them. Not necessarily at birthdays or Christmas, but when Dad's car was in for a service so all of us had to drive him to work together on the way to school. Or when I was ill or there was a storm and I could climb in between them in bed, soaking up adult warmth in stereo.

Or driving off to visit family friends in Mum's home town and being carried out their house after dark in my sleeping bag. Tucked up and cosy in the back of a car on a night drive, the interior lights like magic, then pretending to be asleep so I could be carried up to bed still in my sleeping bag.

There's a miniature knock at the door and Cheekbones comes in carrying a kidney dish with a small towel covering it. He puts it down out of sight and we get her onto the sterile examination table.

'Do you think she knows?' I say to him, my knee up to its usual trick.

'That she's ill?'

'What we're going to do. D'you think she's ok with it?'

He leans on the table while he thinks, gives her a stroke. 'Animals are very instinctual. I think she understands why, if she does know. I think she forgives.'

Then his face is withering at what's happening to mine. I'm wiping and wiping at my eyes, subtly as I can for her. The vet making himself busy, talking sweet nothings.

'Can I hold her as she goes?'

He looks at me and nods. 'I just need to finish getting her ready first.'

I smile at him but my whole body is doing its own thing. And I'm thinking about the original Alfie with his ears down, the hot shower water, paws scrabbling at the shower screen. The way he still let me stroke him at night. Forgiving me over and over again — opening up to hurt again and again.

Like Robert. He'd finally found the love he needed in my mum and I couldn't share her with him, not even for a few months, just while he waited for his life to get back on its feet.

Robert McCloud, innocent as an animal.

The vet unveils a portion of the kidney dish, takes out a cannula, holds her leg, shooshing her as the needle slips idly under the skin. She doesn't complain. She doesn't pity herself the way I have.

'Ok, if you take her in your arms, and we'd best get you seated —
that chair.'

I gather her up, struggling to get all of her. She's so warm against
me, her mouth open, struggling for air. 'On the floor. I need us to
do it on the lino.'

'What?'

'Please.' I lower myself down between the table and the door.
'Down here, like this. *Please.*'

He looks at me then sighs a heavy sigh. I smile up at him, my
eyes underwater again.

Cheekbones has the needle full of death now. He doesn't squirt
it to get rid of air, no need. He keeps it out of sight but my eyes are
hungry for it.

'You're squeezing her too tight, just try and relax.'

He kneels, turning to the side table to bring everything else
to our level. Then he says 'Ok?' but brings the needle in anyway,
holding the cannula with his other hand and inserting the long,
thin point and we're armed and ready to go, her eyes looking up at
me, losing focus but she's still with me. So pure in her opened-up
vulnerability. Her mouth gasping for air. Struggling for purchase.

His thumb coerces the plunger along the one-inch journey
that'll take her an infinite distance away. My shaking stopping
like Robert did when he was perched on that edge, the man
strapped to him. My eyes wide to every drop of this — the moment
I missed.

Her body deflates as if the plunger isn't pushing death in but
pulling life out. Her tongue sliding out the side of her mouth, the
light in her eyes dimming. Robert with the clouds in his eyes. The
room quiet now without the sound of her clogged and difficult
breathing. Without her suffering. My body going up and down with
its own silent unravelling. Cheekbones working quickly, getting his
stethoscope and putting it against her, his eyes looking at a listening

point on the wall. My breathing stopped again, watching his face, waiting.

He takes the scope away and removes it from his ears, nods at me without making eye contact.

'Are you *sure*?'

He nods again, taking out the cannula, a cotton ball ready and pressed on to stop any intrusive details of the death that has so obviously occurred.

He puts everything in the kidney dish and says an almost inaudible sorry as he closes the door, leaving me on the floor of this little box room with sorrow in my arms.

30

I'm sat here barefoot on the bench looking across the park to Patricia's front door. Alfie's collar is with me, some of her fur still clinging to the inside of it, my head turning occasionally to see if Reg is going to come along, Rocket's tail in the air.

I've got my sleeve rolled up and the marker pen colouring my arm black, my tongue out in concentration. Progress halted occasionally by having to stand and wander over to a tree beside me and wipe the built-up skin and sweat from the pen nib — several of the leaves with black, chemical lines defacing their green purity.

The picture's gone from Patricia's front doorstep and a part of me wants to go and peek in through her window to see if it's on her wall.

I called her last night, left a message, apologised for a visit from the police, if she had one. Telling her about the funeral, if it happens. Asking her to call, if she wants to.

I had the same nightmare again last night — Mum laid out in the old pirate-chest freezer she put me in. A strip light above the freezer blinking on and off, making that sound they do like the fluttering of glass eyelashes. Mum all hollowed out and blue behind make-up applied the way a twelve-year-old girl would, or a transvestite.

In death she looked like she would if I'd just met her. The way Robert would have first seen her. The way she probably looked to the checkout girl at the supermarket or the surgeon operating on her brain. The way a face looks before you love it. Before all those feelings and history and familiarity are laid over it. So that even after years of loving them you can still sometimes conjure what their face first looked like, when they were a stranger.

That's the uniqueness of your parents though, isn't it, that you're never haunted by that other face from before they were yours. Your parents are supposed to have always been yours.

In the dream I reached out an uncertain hand and unbuttoned her blouse, the mark from an autopsy running thick and raw up the centre of her, ragged and unnecessary. Her body dressed in some standard-issue garment rather than the clothes I chose for her.

I took one of her eyelids between shaky finger and thumb, lifting it up, her eye shocking me — the pupil unmoved. Dilated.

I dragged her into the kitchen to measure the size of her pupils in the light of the TV, a cricket match being played.

Then I was on the stairs with her again, both of us screaming as I tugged her up one step at a time and put her back in the bath, green peas and chicken kievs in there with us.

And I tried to measure her pupils in that light too, so I could know where she was when her eyes stopped reacting to the light. So I could know where she was when she died.

So I could know if I'm still bad.

Sat here now on this park bench, my heart beating away at the memory of the dream, I can't get the back of my arm coloured in so I start on the other, a little nausea building in me and I hope it's the chemicals in the pen. The nib turning my arm black and my head imagining that Reg *does* show up — invites me back to his and it turns out he's lost a son like I've lost a dad. Our particular wounds matching up.

I've read Mum's attempted letter countless times already. It's not so much a letter, more a series of false starts and segments.

You are a wanderer now and I blame myself. You blame me too and I accept that. Having children means accepting responsibility.

Being a mother feels like this permanent act of repentance for unforgivable sins. For those things I did to you in simple human moments. Except those little moments shape lives. If anything is unfair it is that. How we're supposed to endure parenting with such precariousness is hard to believe.

Michael is the little moment that shaped lives. That and my front wheel on a ladder. And Robert's inability to land on his feet. His mother's pain. *Her* mother's pain. And hers before her. It's hurt people that hurt people.

Sometimes the pain in you threatens to stop my heart.

I lift up my top and start colouring in my chest. The light is dimming, the streetlights coming on but Patricia's windows still in darkness.

This loneliness in me isn't just about being alone. It's about what I'm alone with when I'm alone. And I don't know how to be alone with all the things I'm alone with.

I always asked myself if a child is born good and I know you were. I believe in the goodness in you now. I will never stop believing. I am just sorry I wasn't always enough to keep it feeling alive in you.

There's the vibrating of my phone, my eyes darting to Patricia's house — my hair standing up and adrenalin firing like it has every time any phone has rung these last few days.

I answer the call, my body ceasing all movement at the sound of the police detective on the other end of the line. He doesn't make me wait.

'You're in the clear.'

'What?'

'The coroner gave it the red light. No prosecution. You're ok.'

I tilt my head back and look at the tree canopies above me. 'Does this mean you can't prove it or that she didn't drown? What about the autopsy?'

There's a pause, silence, the phone heating up my ear.

'If we're satisfied I think you can be,' he says.

Just like that. As if all my ugliness can empty out at the stroke of a coroner's pen. Abracadabra.

'But I need to know.'

There's a sigh down the phone. 'I told you these things rarely go all the way. No need to dig into it further. We're saying you're ok.'

I fold forward and lower myself onto the grass and it's still warm from the sunny afternoon, the phone pressed to my ear while the detective apologises in the softest of voices for the inconvenience, and for the other day — tells me he'll fax *and* call the undertakers so we can still hit our original funeral slot. He says he'll do it the moment he hangs up. Then he can't resist mentioning procedure again, that he hopes I understand. But I'm hating him for opening up a new wound. My face gazing up at the sky and the drifting cloud shapes looking back at me.

The Loch Ness monster came by once.

It's not long until the light starts to change. I can't wait for them anymore. I walk out onto the path that Reg and Rocket take each day. I get down and try to write on the tarmac in marker pen but the nib can't cope. I look around, finding a piece of rock which does leave a white scratch on the path.

Over near a lamppost so my message will be lit up, I get down on my knees and scratch and scratch at the path — giant letters.

Then I cross the little park, shoeless, like last time, and get down on my knees with the rock in front of Patricia's place.

31

The spire pokes up in the distance and I park the car close to a hedge to hide the broken window and damaged door, still a ten-minute walk away from St Margaret's. Buttoning up my dad's oversized suit, I sit here for a second in the safe cocoon of a parked car, the quiet suburban streets around me, my eyes trying to discern shapes out of Robert's biro scribbles on the roof interior.

Perhaps today's the last moment in which I have to hold myself together, my mind calculating how many witnesses I'll have to show my sadness to.

Auntie D's been ringing the whole world, I know that from the condolence cards that have been arriving.

I slam the door harder than intended and wander down the road, focusing on the trees moving over me as I walk, the shapes they cut out of the sky, my shoes sounding on the tarmac, mud at the verge, small birds hopping and twitching in the trees. My senses alive to everything.

The church spire grows larger through the trees. I kick a stone and a bird flees, tweeting warnings.

There's the dried-up old pond sitting at the crossroads, and the common with the tree on it, a small bench underneath. The pathetic war memorial standing there as a cold, stone thank-you to the dead and buried — a littering of cigarette butts and bottles left around it from where teenagers must congregate, already disenchanted with life and so turning to the blunt tools of inebriation and sex. My tools.

Robert's funeral was in that same church six years after he fell. He didn't just lose his mental configuration in the fall, he lost his immunity. Pneumonia took him in the end, then an ambulance. No lights, no siren, no rush. Dad watching it go, his hand coming out and touching the back of it as it pulled away, Mum inside the house somewhere.

Just like it was with Michael — the way Dad was big enough then and Mum distant. The way Dad hugged Michael's body and Mum didn't.

I suppose you only know who you are in the extreme moments because that's when you can't help but be how you really feel.

I remember Robert's parents at his funeral, sat on one side of the church, my parents on the other. Everyone who'd come to support us sitting on Mum and Dad's side, so that it was just Robert's parents with a whole half of the church to themselves. Me at the back feeling like I should have been with them. The bad parents, and me the bad son.

A lot of people came out to see the burial. People who had vanished from our lives since the accident. They came to gape at us. Mum leaning on Dad, both of them putting on a united front for the day. Mum touching him for the first time in so long. I remember being jealous of that touch. And I'd dared hope she'd touch me again too. Or look at me. Even with the valium blur behind her eyes.

I step over the low, dilapidated fence and meander through the graveyard beside the church, walking to their grave — my father and my adopted brother's names carved into the stone. Only it says *Robert McCloud*. A little cloud carved there too.

At Dad's funeral I had to sit up the front with Mum. Then once everyone had wandered away from his lowered coffin, those handfuls of soil on its lid — slamming car doors, starting engines — I loitered on the church green drinking beer, avoiding the wake. Hating them all for showing up after Dad's death but failing him in his life. Resenting the mourners for being alive and my dad gone.

When I stumbled in late that night, Mum was waiting up in her dressing-gown and pressed a cheque into my palm. I was on a plane as soon as the cheque had cleared.

I step back over the fence and head across the common, some dewy grass sticking to the shine on my shoes. The suit uncomfortable around me, the trouser waistband pinned at the back where I adjusted it to fit my size relative to Dad. He would have worn this to Robert's funeral.

I take my place on the little bench under the tree, pulling out the rolling tobacco and building myself a cigarette. What's left of the marijuana is in the packet too and I'm wondering if I should.

I sit here, my mind panning up out of my head and hovering high above the church and looking down at me dwarfed by this oak tree in the middle of this bit of green — a man on a bench in a suit under a tree in front of a church. That's the reality but there's so much meaning we heap on top of that.

I pack the cigarette tobacco tighter by tapping it on the bench, teenage names scratched into it. Pronouncements of invincible forever love, now coated in mildew and time.

Maybe all this will be like that one day, carved into me but softened by the elements of time.

The clouds are out, one of them looks like a dragonfly. Or a biplane. I light the ciggie and there's a head between my legs making me jump.

'Rocket! *Hello boy.*' His tail is flashing a swatch of white as it wags his behind. 'Rocket,' my hand lost in the hair on his back then twirling his ears.

I reach down and gather him up. He issues a grumpy noise but lets me, settling on my lap, his bony elbows digging in. I lean over him and take in the contact, smothering him, my eyes closed, my face in his fur.

A man on a bench under a tree in front of a church, hugging a dog.

'Good boy. *Where's* the old man.'

Then I see him smart and upright in his suit, smoke trailing behind like an old steamer.

Rocket leaps from me, a foot in my groin and he's flat out across the common, ears forward.

I can't help but stand and come out from under the tree and Reg notices me. I wave and he lifts an uncertain hand and heads self-consciously over.

I go back to the bench, fidgeting during the time it takes him to get to me. Rocket coming back, barking, shuttle-running between us.

'What are you doing here, Reg?' I say when he's in hairy earshot. He stops in his tracks.

'It was you who wrote on the path. Surely.'

I grin at him and he resumes his approach, grinning back.

'I felt I should like to come. Pay my respects,' he says.

He takes a puff of his rollie but it's gone out. I hand him a lighter instead of the hug he looked like giving.

'Clever of you to leave that message,' he says. 'These still work alright,' and he's pointing at his eyes, pleased with himself. 'I kept checking *The Church News* anyway. You did say Mary was your mum's name?'

I nod.

He relights his cigarette then puts my lighter in his pocket, making me smile. He looks dapper in his suit, his hair wetted down, mostly. His face seeming even realer in the daylight — careworn.

I slide over and he wipes at the bench and sits, plonks one bony leg over the other.

'Reminds me of Ghana, that weed we smoked. Merchant Navy. Eighteen years. Africa, now that's where *women* come from. Girls everywhere else in the world. Did you kiss and make up with yours?' He looks at me for the first time really. 'How you keeping, son?'

My turn to look away.

'Tough times, eh. Tough times,' he says and we both fall into staring.

I take out my bits and bobs and start rolling another cigarette.

'Thanks for coming, Reg.'

'Not at all. Try and keep me away.'

A car pulls up outside the church and Reg calls Rocket closer.

'You expecting many?' he says and I give my head a shake. 'Oh I brought you something,' his posture lifting a notch, then he's going through his pockets. Another car pulling up at the church, causing that familiar stirring inside my guts — Reg still rifling, taking out his tobacco pouch and my lighter, swapping them from hand to hand in order to pat his pockets.

He comes up with a neatly folded white hankie and hands it to me. 'In case of emergency,' he says, happy with himself.

'Thanks, Reg.'

'That's been with me eleven years.'

'You've washed it once or twice, I hope.'

'It was given to me at my wife's funeral,' he says, rejecting my attempts at dilution, 'by my brother-in-law. A shy man, so the gesture meant all the more. Kept it ever since. That white flag's been waved many a time. Not much call for weddings at my age — the funeral years. Anyway, it's yours now. Just in time by the look of you,' and he turns his face away from me for a moment, Rocket's wet nose appearing in my lap. Doors slamming, people heading into the church.

Another car arrives. I wipe my eyes, check the time, my stomach making its presence felt. There can't be a service before Mum's. My heart ups its ante. You aren't vulnerable unless there are witnesses. Without witnesses it's just sadness.

'Don't forget the healing's already started, son. That's it. You cry a river if you like,' Reg says, looking stoically into the distance. 'Oh you bugger, you've gone and started me off.'

Two men on a bench under a tree, crying.

There's the hearse. There she is. Reg standing in the middle of the green now, not knowing whether to come over to me, stay where he is, or head into the church. He does his hair though because he has no hat to remove, his hands slipping behind his back.

The people congregated outside catch sight of her funereal approach and make for the church, away from the body coming in the back of a car.

I cross the common and put a hand on Reg's shoulder. 'Will you help me carry her?'

He's confused for a second then looks over at the hearse cruising with false solemnity up to the front access to the church. 'I'd be glad to.' He tries to say it brightly.

The men get slowly out, their suits befitting a courtroom as much as a funeral. Whereas the dignity of pallbearers is so beautiful. A part of me wishing I could just watch her carried by these men — see her honoured in that simple way. That's if I didn't need the weight of her on my shoulder, the cut of the wood.

We're standing at the back of the hearse, the tailgate open and the coffin protruding. One of the men explaining everything to Reg and me, Reg listening intently, his face emptied of colour, his tongue repeatedly licking at his dry lips.

The undertakers arrange him at the front, me in the middle behind him. Perhaps to help me hide my face.

As we carry her I focus on Reg's back, my feet, my hand on his shoulder, the undertaker's hand on mine. Reg trembling under the weight, his body leaning out occasionally and his footsteps stuttering.

I shut my eyes at the simple weight of a stranger's hand on my shoulder, my cheek wanting to rest down on it. Nobody out here watching us carry her, except Rocket, tied to the fence. And yet we still go one slow step at a time, shiny shoes on the gravel path, the gravestones sitting up like an audience.

Soon we're swallowed by the dank stone of the church interior. Thirty or so people in here waiting, spread over both sides. The pallbearers giving Reg and me subtle, instructive encouragement as we turn to enter the aisle.

Everyone stands for her now, everything rising on my body too, goosebumped and proud. The feel of her on one shoulder, a stranger's solidarity on the other, Reg's trembling, everyone standing for my mum, people having come out to honour her — pride filling my chest until it's as expansive as this church. The darkness inside me lit up with stained-glass sunshine. I can feel it all, all the solemnity, all the respect. All for Mum.

She's so heavy though, despite the moment. Both of us are. Heavy enough that I think the floor tiles will crack under each of my footsteps, all the way up the aisle.

The priest waits at the front, the congregation trying not to look at the coffin but staring. A child calls out and her mum hushes her. Reg's ribs going in and out. Hang on, Reg, *hang on*.

We reach the front and again the undertakers are whispering tips as we lower her down onto the stand.

I regret thinking ill of these men because I couldn't do this without them. I couldn't stand up here in front of everyone, with this coffin — such a blunt motif about the reality of life. I don't care anymore who these men are or where they're from or what their house is like, how good they are at spelling, they're helping me. They're the people who do these simple things in your most enormous moments.

She's on the stainless-steel stand and everyone has peeled away. Reg walking back down the aisle, wiping at his forehead, the undertakers retreating towards the sides of the church and me stranded up here so that I feel I should say something but the priest arrives beside me, a hand at my back to show me the way.

The front pews are empty on both sides of the church. I want to go and take my place at the back again but allow myself to be led to where I sat with Mum on my dad's last day.

Today I've got the pew to myself, sitting on the hard wood, eyes down, waiting for the priest to start but he leans in towards me, arms holding back his robes, telling me that he tried to call but didn't hear back so he's gone ahead and chosen some hymns, and someone has asked to speak about my mum and do I want to?

I nod without meaning yes or no. He touches my shoulder then walks away beginning the ceremony as he goes.

I take out Reg's hankie and almost fill it in one blow, wipe at my eyes, looking down at an undone button on my shirt and the colourful front page of an old comic showing through, the feel of it reassuring against my skin.

Rocket barks from outside and I feel this strange urge to laugh but stifle it with a glance at her coffin.

Everyone stands and the organ starts.

I get uncertainly to my feet and reach down for a book, finding the page, the organist leading us awkwardly into the hymn.

All Things Bright and Beautiful.

And I *sing* it. Sometimes turning to the congregation with a confused pride — glad they're here but wondering who. Eventually finding Auntie Deadly's sly face looking back at me from the strangers. Then Marcus. Mandy. And from them I can guess who these people are.

After the hymn we all sit down and the priest introduces Mandy, saying that she was the social worker who liaised with Mary for many years.

I don't look around, just sit stiff and staring while she makes her way to the front.

She ignores the steps up to the lectern, takes her position in front of it, everything about her held in and controlled. She pauses for a second, a few papers in her hands, a lilac dress on and some sort of elaborate brooch on her lapel that looks like a chewy sweet that melted in the sun.

The congregation is stilled, Mandy holding everyone's attention the way she always did. Something in her commands it. She puts on her glasses and looks up at us all for the first time.

'Today is a sad day, saying goodbye to someone like Mary. But it's also a chance to celebrate her life. Mary wasn't just a mother, a niece, a wife — as amazing as all those things are — things which nothing can change or come between. Mary was also a foster carer.'

She puts her lips away, takes off her glasses and looks at us, some particular emotion seeming to pass through her.

Her glasses back on, she consults the papers fluttering just slightly in her hands, looks up and takes her specs off again. 'Our legacy is all that's left of us once we're gone. That and memories, of course. And love. So when I heard Mary had lost her battle with cancer I didn't have to think about what I'd want to say.' She turns to me. 'And I appreciate the opportunity to do so.' She smiles, my hair floating up on end from all the blood in my head.

'Are we all here?' she says, peering at the congregation and blushing slightly now that her attention is directed at, as yet, unseen individuals. 'Marcus?'

All the pews creak as people turn this way and that looking for Marcus who half stands, adjusting his shirt and tie, his face reddening too.

'Toby?'

And I recognise the man who waves, the same freckles and grey eyes. The one who set fire to the back of the shed.

Mandy squints at the papers again, her glasses forgotten in her hand. 'Oh, would you *all* stand up. All of Mary's foster boys, if you're here,' she says, smiling. 'Come on.'

There's a lifting of noise now as people turn to look at the men appearing from the congregation. All of them standing there with varying reactions to the scrutiny.

'Mary fostered nine boys in total,' Mandy says, just a fraction of wobble in her voice. 'Which adds up to about three years of twenty-four-hour care. Not to mention the *seven years* she gave Robert. Difficult years.' The spectacles go on again. 'What were once neglected children, taken in and given crucial care and support by Mary and her family. *Now* look at them. *Strapping men.*'

Reg starts to clap at the back but finds himself alone and stops. Others laugh.

'Foster carers are scarcer than angels,' she says. 'I missed Mary dearly after Robert. Our department let her down then — another of the great tragedies of a system that doesn't just repeatedly fail the children who most need it, but the people it most needs. Even still, Mary carried on with Robert. She didn't let many things come between her and what she saw as her role in life.'

Mandy takes her glasses off and smiles. 'Mary's left us now, but those nine stand like milestones beside a great life. Mary's life.'

Small sniffs and sighs of emotion are coming from different parts of the assembled now. Mandy looks at me, gesturing for me to stand up but I shake my head at her.

'Please,' she says, giving me a soft look.

Somehow my legs stand me up. She comes over and I can't help but lean away until the back of the pew traps me. She drops her voice, her eyes shining but she's bolt upright. 'Your family made sacrifices so that these lives could thrive. Even go on to have their own families, look. Your mum did amazing things. But your family did amazing things too. *You* did amazing things. Look around you.'

She puts a hand on my shoulder then turns it into a hug and I cling on because if she pulls away everyone will see me like this. Then she does pull away so I have to sit and lean on the unforgiving wood of the pew, somebody patting me on the shoulder from behind. People blowing their noses, Auntie Debbie falling into some old lady next to her.

I'm looking at all those faces.

'That's *some* legacy,' Mandy says and folds the papers she's holding, puts them away. 'Mary's legacy.'

I'm looking at the congregation but it's Mum's life gazing back at me with its eyes shining. Children with thumbs shrivelling in their mouths. That's my mum there. These people are what my childhood was for.

32

I'm at the wheel, Reg beside me with Rocket on his lap — head out the broken car window, ears flapping in the wind. The hearse up ahead.

'Well, it was a touching tribute to a good woman if you ask me, son.'

I turn my head enough for him to see me nod, then loosen Dad's tie and collar.

'Who was that hot young thing you introduced me to outside the church?' Reg says.

'*Auntie D?*'

'Bugger off! Cheeky bastard. I'm talking about the *other* hot young thing. Leticia, was it?'

'Patricia. She's the one I'd argued with that night. She only showed up to be nice.'

I keep my face held, Reg looking at me.

'Well, you wouldn't catch me arguing with her. She could have her way with me.' He sucks air in over his false teeth. 'Not that she'd want anything from yours truly. But back in the day …'

'I'll put a word in for you, Reg. How's that.'

'You can stop dismissing life's goodness, son. How's that.'

There's a small crunch of a gear change then, Mum's coffin looking at me from the hearse.

'Sorry,' he says. 'But I just can't work it out.'

'What?' Here we go.

'What's eating you. I mean, pardon me for speaking out. You've certainly got your hands full, nobody's taking that away from you. But there's something else. Can't put my finger on it.'

'I'd rather tell you another day, Reg.'

More silence, such as it is with the passenger window gone, Reg picking at a little square of tempered glass still wedged in the door frame. Me fidgeting in my seat at the thought of telling him. Wincing at the fact that he even knows there's something to tell.

'Are those scratches on your hands from the car accident?' he says, gesturing to the missing window.

'Gardening.'

His face lights up. 'I've got a jungle of a garden I could use some help with. I'd pay you.' He pats Rocket but gets a face full of tongue that he pushes away. 'How much per hour for gardening my jungle then, Tarzan?'

I spy the crematorium chimney before I see the crematorium. No smoke coming out of it and I wonder if they burn them at night in one batch. Otherwise you'd be turning up for a service with smoke rising out from the last. Like a surgeon coming to see you with blood all over him.

We park in the car park, the hearse going round the back. Deadman's entrance.

'What do you want me to do?' Reg says, the engine stopped and everything silent suddenly.

I stare ahead at the brick crematorium chapel — boring, square, functional. Built in the 60s or 70s when architects were too busy wearing tight trousers and taking drugs to care about aesthetics.

'I think I'll go in alone.'

'You don't have to do it on your own, you know,' he says.

There's a man to greet me inside the building. Frankenstein in a suit — cordial and creepy.

'Are you a relative of the deceased?'

'Her son,' I say, feeling like it.

'Are you expecting others?'

'No.'

I wonder how many loners he's burnt. The forgotten old people from nursing homes. Or those found at home only once their decay disturbs the neighbours. One of the many signs the world's outgrown itself.

'I'm licensed to give a short service, if you'd like?'

'No, thank you. I'd just like some time with her, then …'

He nods.

One of the undertakers appears beside us. 'That's us then. If there's nothing else you need, we'll be off.'

'Thank you. Really.'

His hand is warm when he shakes mine. I watch him go, even though Frankenstein is eager to get me in and out again.

I follow him into the mock chapel — all leadlight windows and plywood ceiling. Religion in a box.

He leads me up to the front and she's already there on the conveyor, a curtain waiting in front. He takes me right up close, her coffin hurting me.

'When you're ready, just push that button, then come out and I'll have you sign the documentation and you can come back tomorrow to collect her. I'll need you to have finished by half past so I can ready the room for the next service.'

He puts on a smile that only makes him uglier, then slips away through a side door.

You'd have to be a certain person to be attracted to a job associated with death. Just like you have to be a certain person to foster children. And to be able to love properly.

And to forgive.

I run a hand over her coffin then give the lid a tug, seeing if it'll open. Wishing I could lay her lungs out on the front pew and find out for sure whether I hurt her again.

The lid's down fast so I wander away, take a seat in the second pew from the front, the light changing in here as the sun goes behind cloud.

My cough echoes around me and I can't help but wonder who would come to my funeral. A thought which stands me up, walking back to the front, to the head of the coffin. I lean over and peek through the curtains she'll go through, this brief idea in my head that there'll be heaven and angels and Dad and Robert waiting down there but it's just a conveyor belt and a square view of another room on the other side of that wall.

Now seems as good a time as any so I push the button. Nothing happens for a moment. I wipe my eyes and push it again.

Eventually there's a whirring and with farcical solemnity her coffin moves off, stuttering into the curtains, more and more wood disappearing into the tunnel. I reach out for her one last time and my touch hits that hard coffin exterior.

The curtain drops against my hand and she's gone.

The sound of the machinery stops and I peek through at her, just down there in the other room. I let the curtain fall.

That's it then. From now on she's going to have to be the way I tend her in my mind — depending on which parts of my perspective I water, and those I allow to wither. That careful distinction between what is plant and what is weed.

I walk out of the main chapel and loiter in the foyer.

Heavy, gunmetal cloud has assembled outside, the first drops of rain. Reg stubbing out a smoke and taking shelter in the Volvo even though the window's missing. Rocket cocking his leg on the only other car in the car park but the rain picks up pace and he runs back to Reg.

The downpour's drumming on the chapel roof now, a daytime darkness having descended.

I recognise this moment I'm standing in. This is the moment before. This is that breath you take before you go on. Even if a bit of me is so tired of going on — a dejected part that's had enough of being dragged through the dirt behind this other, hell-bent, angry version of me.

Robert's funeral wasn't like today's. His wasn't a celebration of a life because he hadn't had one. There was nothing to celebrate that day, only greyness. Mum sniffling but managing a smile as she watched the video of them strapping Robert up — his face full of gangly smiles towards the video camera. His played-back face looking right at me. Someone making a comment about how great he looks in his orange outfit.

Then his hair was fluttering on the screen, a man behind him in goggles. Robert all tongue and teeth and movement, his trembling brain fidgeting him with excitement.

There is a rough edit.

His hair is blowing and he's strapped to the man in the goggles and screeching with delicious fear as they shuffle him on his bum.

From the movement of the camera you see Robert, then the aeroplane walls, Robert. Then, through the open door, the clouds. Great, billowing clouds in a vast sky. The camera panning to an altimeter on a wrist. Robert McCloud at 14,000 feet.

'1'

His tremors are still there, his eyes smiling. The man tells Robert to put his head back and his exhilaration erupts as a squeal.

'2'

He is totally still. I remember the whole room stopped too, everyone who'd come to bury him held their breath.

'*3!*'

And the cameraman, Robert and the man he's strapped to are plummeting. We see the sky the cloud the sky the cloud, then Robert, his body totally still, his face billowing and moving up towards his hair and he's plummeting. Mum, me, Dad, everyone was crying, the buffet food congealing on the trestle table and Robert falling and falling.

Suddenly the screen is completely white.

Coming through the whiteness you can make out a little bit of orange and hear a lot of Robert's delight. We're all in the clouds with him, Robert of the Clouds. He's falling through them in orange overalls and goggles, his damaged brain firing and firing with joy. Nothing but a white screen and squealing.

After a few prolonged seconds everything's blue and brilliant again, cloud moisture glowing rainbow on the camera lens, picking up rays of sun, filtering them into colour. Robert laughing and laughing despite the air rushing into him and rain moisture all over his face. Everyone in the room laughing with him now, except me. I started sobbing.

And that was when Mum gave me one of those rare hugs. Despite what she believed. Despite what we all did to each other. She held me and my tears, my face burrowed into that neck of all necks — enveloped by her, my arms wrapping round her too, her grip squeezing tighter. And through her hair and its smell of cups of tea and hot baths, I could hear Robert laughing on the screen.

Then the man pulled something and Robert was gone, floating under a brilliant white canopy.

THANK YOU

Wholehearted gratitude to Sam and all at Serpent's Tail. It's a dream to have this book published, especially by a publisher that epitomises everything I celebrate about *independent* publishing.

This book owes much to Marika, Cherry and Julie who rolled up their sleeves with me long before a publisher came along. And my gratitude and respect to Aviva, Henry and everyone at Scribe.

Juliet, Linda and all at A P Watt have truly championed my writing (and put up with a dash of eccentricity). Thank you. Sincere and warm thanks to Elena Lappin (you can find a picture of her in the dictionary under 'chutzpah').

I wonder if I'd be writing at all without my sister's early encouragement in the days when my output could only really be congratulated for its font and paper stock. She supports me still. This book is dedicated to you, Jo.

Thanks also to Jane D who read the original short story and uttered a tiny remark that led to such a big journey; Karla and family for the afternoon we had talking about something so personal; Jodie and B for keeping me on the straight and narrow regarding fostering; the Wilkinsons, just because; and so much gratitude to Glen, who helped me into my skin.

Plus a kind army of readers, writers and artists who have supported this book in some other generous way: J M Coetzee, David Malouf, MJ Hyland, Cate Kennedy, Peter Goldsworthy, Peter Straus, Andrea Goldsmith, Kate Holden, MP Gracedieu, Tom, Lisa, Gemma, Ruby, brudder Zac, Phoebe, Tash, Hazey, Michelle, Nicole,

Moo, Mal, Derek, Anne, Pierz, Stefania, Convery, Trudi, Jackson, Sahar, Jess, Dan, Helene, Mankymarkcuthbertyson, the Vampires, Margot, (deep breath), and finally, thanks to my old man.

May this novel be of sustenance for those who carry their childhoods still.

x x x

www.serpentstail.com

Visit serpentstail.com today to browse and buy our books, and to sign up for exclusive news and previews, interviews with our authors and forthcoming events.

NEWS

cut to the literary chase with all the latest news about our books and authors

EVENTS

advance information on forthcoming events, author readings, exhibitions and book festivals

EXTRACTS

read first chapters, short stories, bite-sized extracts

EXCLUSIVES

pre-publication offers, discounted books, competitions

BROWSE & BUY

browse our full catalogue and shop securely

* FREE POSTAGE AND PACKING ON ALL ORDERS WORLDWIDE *

follow us on twitter • find us on facebook